Shelby's second mistake.

In the fading light, she stared into his smoldering green eyes and lost herself all over again. She leaned up on her toes and pressed her lips to his.

He cupped the back of her head and sealed the kiss with one of his own, his mouth consuming her.

When at last he lifted his head, he dragged in a deep breath and stepped through the door. "Get your things," he said, his voice stern. "We're going back to Raleigh."

She'd been ready to do just that, but having him come back at her like what they'd shared hadn't happened was a slap in the face.

"What just happened here?" she demanded.

His gaze met hers briefly and he looked away. "Nothing."

"Are you telling me that kiss meant nothing?"

He faced her, and for a long moment he stared down at her, a muscle ticking in his jaw. "Really, Miss O'Hara, I'm just doing my job."

Dear Reader,

I always find it a wonderful challenge to work with a great group of authors and editors to bring a series of books to life. I feel honored that I was asked to be a part of this series and to be tasked with wrapping it up. And what better setting than that of North Carolina? It's full of history, beauty and charming people.

As a young lieutenant and captain in the U.S. Army Reserves, I had the pleasure of visiting North Carolina a couple times to train at Fort Bragg. We always managed to make a trip out to the coast on the weekend to enjoy the beach and sunshine. North Carolina has a variety of terrain, all of it lush, green and beautiful. I've rafted in the mountain rivers, played in the surf and sand, and enjoyed the scenery along the way.

Part of my research led me to Greensboro, North Carolina, and the Writers' Police Academy, where a fantastic cadre of men and women gave us a brief glimpse into the lives and work of our police officers, FBI agents, forensic scientists, firemen, bomb squads and first responders. We are truly blessed to have them, with their skills, knowledge and courage, working for us to keep us safe.

Please take the time to thank our heroes for all they do.

Happy reading!

Elle James

SECRET SERVICE RESCUE

—

Elle James

HARLEQUIN® ROMANTIC SUSPENSE

Special thanks and acknowledgment are given to Elle James for her contribution to The Adair Legacy miniseries.

Recycling programs
for this product may
not exist in your area.

ISBN-13: 978-0-373-27878-7

SECRET SERVICE RESCUE

www.Harlequin.com

Printed in U.S.A.

ELLE JAMES

A Golden Heart Award winner for Best Paranormal Romance in 2004, Elle James started writing when her sister issued a Y2K challenge to write a romance novel. She has managed a full-time job and raised three wonderful children, and she and her husband even tried their hands at ranching exotic birds (ostriches, emus and rheas) in the Texas Hill Country. Ask her, and she'll tell you what it's like to go toe-to-toe with an angry 350-pound bird! After leaving her successful career in information technology management, Elle is now pursuing her writing full-time. Elle loves to hear from fans. You can contact her at ellejames@earthlink.net, or visit her website, at www.ellejames.com.

This book is dedicated to my husband, who made the trip out to the Outer Banks and captured the essence of the area for me to include in this story, while I attended Writers' Police Academy. Gotta love a man who sacrifices his time to visit the beach for my research!

Chapter 1

Daniel Henderson stood with his hand on the butt of the HK40 pistol resting in the shoulder holster beneath his suit jacket, his gaze locked on the man standing in the middle of the room.

"I repeat, your granddaughter has been missing for two weeks," Patrick O'Hara insisted, worry lines etched deep into his weathered face. "I've pursued all other options. I've filed a missing persons report, but the police have no leads. I'm at my wit's end. That's why I came to you."

"What do you mean, I have a granddaughter?" Former vice president Kate Winston stood straight, her shoulders squared, her lips tight. The only indication that the man in front of her had disturbed her normal calm was how pale her face had become. She glanced around the room at her three sons, Trey, Thaddeus and Samuel. "Is there something you three haven't told me?"

The three men shook their heads as one.

O'Hara, who'd made the shocking statement, shook his head. "Not the child of one of your sons, the child of your daughter. *Our* daughter."

"What the hell are you talking about?" Trey, the oldest son, demanded.

Patrick O'Hara's eyes narrowed. "Maybe you should ask your mother."

Kate closed her eyes and pressed a hand to her chest.

"You're upsetting her." Thad slipped an arm around Kate's shoulders. "Perhaps you should leave, before we have you escorted out."

"No." O'Hara stood firm, his gaze locked on Kate. "I need help finding my granddaughter and you are my last hope. Unless you're going to throw her away like you did our daughter."

Samuel lunged forward. "Get the hell out."

Kate's arm shot out. "No, wait. Let him speak."

Patrick glanced from Trey to Samuel and back to Kate. "Shelby was at the university library Tuesday night two weeks ago, working on some research paper for her graduate program. She said she'd be home by midnight. At two in the morning, I closed the bar and went home. She wasn't there. Her car wasn't parked out front. I got worried and drove all the way into Beth City, to the university. I found her car in the library parking lot, but not Shelby." He scrubbed a hand down his haggard face. "I don't know what else to do."

Daniel's heartstrings were tugged by the desperation in the man's tone and eyes. Two weeks might as well be forever. A woman missing for that long had little chance of being alive.

"How old is she?" Kate pressed her fingers to the bridge of her nose.

"Twenty-three. She's never late for anything." Patrick stepped forward.

Daniel walked between Patrick and Kate, holding his gun out. "That's far enough."

Patrick's glance shifted to Daniel. "I just wanted to show her the picture of Shelby." He looked back at Kate. "She looks just like her mother. And Carrie looked just like you. Brown hair, bright blue eyes." He smiled, then the smile quickly faded. "We have to find her. She's all I have."

Daniel took the photo from the man's hands and held it out to Kate.

Trey intercepted it. "The man is crazy. You're not really going to help him, are you? He's preying on your weakness—" Trey shot a glance at the picture, his eyes widening. "Damn."

Kate held out her hand. "Give me the photo."

Trey handed it across. "It has to be a forgery. You can do almost anything with computer graphics these days."

Patrick's lips turned up. "She's her mother's daughter."

Kate stared at the picture for a long time, tears welling in her eyes. "This could be me as a young woman." She stared across at him. "I don't understand."

"What's to understand? You gave up your daughter. I raised Carrie, and she had a daughter, Shelby. Whom I also raised." He jabbed a finger at the photo. "Shelby Raye O'Hara. A beautiful, smart young lady with a full life ahead of her. *If* I can find her before something awful happens to her." He swallowed hard. "If it hasn't already."

If she had been missing for two weeks, Daniel predicted bad things had, indeed, happened to the girl. And nothing anyone could do would bring her back.

"I didn't give up my daughter. She died," Kate whispered, a single tear slipping down her cheek. She lifted her head, her chin trembling.

"Is that what you told yourself?" Patrick laughed, the sound completely without humor. He stepped closer. "I don't care if lying to yourself helped you throw away your own flesh and blood. I can't believe I ever loved you. You're selfish, heartless and deserved the man you married."

Daniel laid a hand on the man's chest. "Back off."

Patrick stared at Daniel as if it was the first time he'd seen him and his gun. "Kate, I don't give a damn about you or your high-society family. What I do care about is getting my granddaughter back. Alive. If you have any sense of decency, you'll help. She's your family, too."

"Mother," Sam said. "Say the word and I'll throw him out."

Daniel braced himself for a fight with Patrick O'Hara. He didn't want to use his gun; it would leave a big mess in the Winstons' house. And as far as he could tell, O'Hara wasn't armed.

"No." Kate shook her head. "If someone thinks Shelby O'Hara is related to me in any way, she's in danger."

"I've never told anyone about her bloodline. Shelby doesn't even know her mother was your daughter."

being relegated to the sidelines, gimping along until he could return to investigations.

By the time they'd arrived at the Wake County Jail, Daniel had contacted the director of the Secret Service and relayed the information about Shelby O'Hara's disappearance. Director Kincannon agreed to meet them there.

"What's going on, Mother?" Thad asked on the drive across town. "Why did O'Hara say you had a granddaughter?"

"It's a long story." Kate looked straight ahead. "I'd rather not talk about it just yet. The most important thing to focus on is finding the girl."

Daniel suspected that, like most high-powered politicians, even Kate Winston had a few skeletons in her closet. Skeletons not even her sons knew about.

Once inside the building, Kate insisted Daniel go with Thad to interrogate the prisoner. "If Robert D'Angelis has any information concerning the missing girl, the sooner we get it out of him, the better for Shelby." A sheriff's deputy led her to small room where she could watch the interview through a two-way mirror.

As promised, Director Kincannon met them outside the interrogation room. "Agent Henderson, Detective Winston." He nodded to each of them. "They've moved the suspect into the interrogation room. Do you want me to question him?"

Daniel paused outside the interview room his hand on the doorknob. "I've had more recent experience interrogating suspects."

Director Kincannon nodded. "Then, by all means, question him."

Daniel turned to Thad.

"Go for it." Thad held up his hands. "I'll stand back and listen."

"While you two conduct the interview, I'll watch from the observation room." Director Kincannon moved back toward the room where Kate Winston waited.

Daniel gathered his thoughts and entered the interrogation room, Thad close behind him.

Former Secret Service agent Robert D'Angelis sat in a metal chair with his hands cuffed and resting on the table in front of him. His face was pale with a slightly green tint. A half-empty paper cup of water sat on the table within his reach.

The tall man was hunched over, his fit body seeming to sag with the weight of his muscles. A fine sheen of sweat covered his face, and his eyes were yellow and bloodshot.

"Why am I here?" he said. "I'm not talking to anyone without my lawyer."

"Agent D'Angelis, we have a few questions for you," Daniel said.

D'Angelis blinked and squeezed his eyes tight, then opened them, squinting. "Light is so damned bright." He shook his head and blinked again.

"Are you all right? Do you need a glass of water?" Daniel asked.

"Just had one." He lifted his cuffed hands and tugged at the collar of the bright orange jumpsuit supplied by the Wake County Jail. "So damn hot in here. Don't they have an air conditioner?" He rolled his head around on his neck and stopped to stare across the table as Daniel took the seat opposite him. "I got nothing for you." He spit in Daniel's face.

Daniel removed an old-fashioned handkerchief from his back pocket, wiped the spit from his cheek and folded the handkerchief neatly before returning it to his pocket, maintaining his silence until he was finished. Then he leaned close until his face was within inches of D'Angelis's. He didn't blink, staring straight into the suspect's eyes. In a firm, direct voice, he asked, "Where's the girl?"

D'Angelis sat back in his chair. "I don't know what you're talking about."

"Do you know what they do to police officers and Secret Service agents in jail?"

"I have more years of experience than you do, Henderson. I know exactly what they do," D'Angelis ground out, his voice raspy. He coughed into his sleeve. When he pulled his mouth away from the crook of his elbow, blood stained the orange fabric. "I don't feel well. I want a doctor."

"You'll get a doctor as soon as you tell us where the girl is."

"I don't know about a damned girl." D'Angelis coughed again, more blood staining his sleeve and dribbling from the corner of his mouth.

Daniel nodded toward the mirror. "Get a doctor," he said, then turned back to D'Angelis. "I'm getting that doctor for you. Give me something on the girl."

D'Angelis raised his hands and slammed them, cuffs and all, on the wooden table. "What's it matter, anyway? They're gonna use her to get to Kate. Then they'll kill her."

"She's still alive?" Daniel's pulse raced through his veins. "Where is she?"

"It's hot in here." The man slumped across the table. "I feel awful."

"Damn it, where is she?" Daniel grabbed D'Angelis's shoulders and forced him to look up.

The man's eyes were completely bloodshot and watery.

"Basement."

"Basement of what?" He shook D'Angelis, trying to get him to focus and tell him the rest of the address.

"House on East Cabbarus Street," the man said.

"Which house? What address?" Daniel demanded.

"Sixty-two fifty." D'Angelis's head lolled and his eyes rolled to the back of his head. His body went limp and he slid out of his chair onto the floor.

"Damn." Thad ran for the door. "Get a medic in here!"

Daniel pushed the chair away from the fallen man and squatted beside him on the floor, loosening the zipper on the orange jumpsuit.

D'Angelis's hand grabbed his wrist and he raised his head long enough to say, "Don't trust—" He choked on the phlegm in his throat and blood trickled out of the corner of his mouth, then he coughed again and passed out.

The door burst open. Two paramedics raced in and bent over D'Angelis. Daniel and Thad left the room, moving to the side of the hallway to get out of the way of the emergency staff.

They entered the room where Kate, Trey, Sam, Patrick and Jed Kincannon, the director of the Secret Service, stood watching the staff work on Robert D'Angelis's inert form.

"What happened?" Kate's hand rested on her throat. "One minute he was all cocky, the next he seemed to fail in front of us."

"I don't know," Thad said.

"I do." Daniel nodded to Thad. "We're going to Cabarrus Street to find Shelby O'Hara."

Daniel led the way out of the county jail.

Thad followed, dialing for assistance from the Raleigh Police Department dispatch.

When they got outside, Daniel remembered they'd come in Kate Winston's limousine. "We can't go in that, and Mrs. Winston can't go with us."

"Take my vehicle." Trey tossed the keys. "I'll stay with Mother to make sure nothing happens to her."

"Thanks." Daniel caught the keys and ran for Trey's car, Thad on his heels.

"Shouldn't we wait for backup?" Thad asked.

"If Shelby's captors get wind that we're on the way, they might kill her before backup arrives."

"Give me the keys." Thad held up his hand.

Daniel hesitated only a moment. As a member of the Raleigh Police Department, Thad would know the streets better than Daniel, who'd only been in Raleigh a couple months since he'd been assigned to protect Kate Winston. He hopped into the passenger seat as Thad twisted the key in the ignition.

In seconds, they'd pulled out of the parking lot and raced away from the jail. "It's only half a mile from here. We'll be there before the police can get a patrol car there."

Daniel removed his gun from his holster, checked to

ensure a bullet had been chambered and braced himself for arrival at their destination.

Shelby Raye O'Hara rubbed the plastic zip tie that bound her wrists on the ragged edge of a broken brace she'd ripped from the wooden chair she sat on. Her wrists chafed and bled where she'd scraped them across the splintered wood. For fourteen days she'd been confined in the dark room, tallied by the number of meals she'd been granted and what was provided. Mornings were stale bagels and bottled water. In the late afternoons, she was given a bologna sandwich and more water.

The men wearing masks who'd grabbed her on her way out of the Beth City University Library hadn't spoken a word to her. They hadn't explained why she'd been kidnapped and hadn't given her a chance to change their minds.

From what she could tell, she was being held in a basement, the concrete brick walls as solid as they came and no windows to let sunshine in. One light shone down on her when the men fed her or allowed her to use the facilities in a small corner bathroom. There, she'd managed to finger brush her teeth, wash her face with the single bar of soap and duck her head under the faucet to scrub her hair every other day. Spit baths were a blessing, but she'd give anything for a real soak in a hot tub.

So far, they hadn't used any violence against her, but the conditions were far from the Ritz and she was tired of being kept in the dark physically and mentally. And if she didn't see another bologna sandwich in her lifetime, it would be too soon.

What bothered her almost as much was knowing how frantic her grandfather would be by now. She'd promised to be home by midnight. Two weeks ago, she'd been researching case studies for a paper she was writing for her graduate degree in counseling.

God, she'd be so far behind on her coursework if she got back.

When she got back.

She worked the plastic tie harder, refusing to give up, her skin slippery with her own blood. By the rumbling in her belly, it was close to dinnertime. One of her guards would be down with her meal soon. If she could get loose before he came…

The zip tie snapped and her wrists flew apart, the pressure and pain lessening immediately.

Hope surged, along with adrenaline.

The lock on the door jiggled, heralding another visit from her silent jailors who would undoubtedly be bringing her the bottled water and bologna sandwich.

Shelby hid the broken brace beneath her thigh and sat in the chair, slumped over, as if she'd fallen asleep.

The door opened, and light shone down the stairs, the beam stopping short of where she waited. If she could get past one guard, she'd have a chance of getting out of the basement. The other guard would be waiting at the top of the stairs.

She'd cross that bridge when she came to it. First, she'd take care of the bologna man.

He wore his requisite mask and carried a flashlight in one hand and the sandwich and water in the other.

When he reached the bottom of the stairs, he crossed to her, shining the bright beam across her face.

Shelby feigned sleep, her head drooping low, her

hair sweeping over her cheeks, shadowing her eyes.
Her muscles tensed as she prepared to strike.

Her guard bent to place the water bottle and sandwich on the floor by her feet.

With all the force she could muster, she kicked her
feet up, caught the guard on the chin and sent him tum-
bling backward onto his backside.

The flashlight flew out of his hand toward the stairs.

Shelby leaped over the man's flailing legs, snatched
the light and raced up the stairs.

Bologna man shouted, "Get her!"

By the time the second guard reached the doorway
at the top of the stairs, Shelby was there. She swung
the heavy metal flashlight with all her might, clipping
the man in the temple. He staggered backward.

Shelby ducked past him and ran for a door. She
ripped it open and found a broom closet. Footsteps
running up the stairs and muttered curses from the
man behind her sent her scurrying to the next door.
She pulled it open and ran down a long hallway into
a kitchen.

As she reached what looked like a heavy wooden
exterior door, she was hit from behind with a flying
tackle. She crashed to the floor, her head making contact with the hardwood planks and stars danced before her eyes. She fought not to give in to the gray fog
creeping in on her peripheral vision. She couldn't stop
now. She'd come too far.

The door opened in front of her and a man in a mask
stared down at her. "Time to leave," he said, his voice
low and gruff.

The man lying across her legs scrambled to his feet,

pressing a foot into the middle of her back. "What about her?"

"Leave her. And hurry. D'Angelis sang."

Shelby's head ached, her vision blurred, but she held on, trying to grasp what they were talking about.

"Torch the place," said the man who'd given the order to leave.

Her heart pounded, sending blood rushing through her system, chasing back the fog. Shelby forced herself to lie still, pretending to be out cold.

"Good, the bitch deserves to die after what she did to me."

"And me." A hand grabbed the back of her hair, jerked her head back and slammed her forehead into the floor. "That's for kicking me in the teeth."

Pain knifed through her head, bringing with it a rush of darkness. As she fought to stay awake, her temples throbbing, she heard the man at the door say, "Come on, I hear sirens."

The door opened, and a fresh draft of air washed over her.

The scent of gasoline filtered through the open door as the other two men exited. They closed the door. Seconds later, smoke sifted in through the cracks.

Shelby knew she had to get out before she was burned alive. She pushed to her hands and knees and crawled several steps before the pain drained her strength and she fell to the floor.

Lying against the cool hardwood flooring, she prayed death would come quickly. Smoke filled the room and burned her lungs. With her eyes closed tight, she accepted her fate and welcomed oblivion.

As she drifted in and out of consciousness, she felt

a cool breeze stir across her, then strong arms curl around her, lifting her from the floor and floating her through the clouds to cool, clean night air.

Shelby's eyes fluttered open and she stared up into the face of her guardian angel, a man with dark blond hair and green eyes. "Am I in heaven?" she whispered.

A deep chuckle rumbled against her side and a voice as smooth as melted chocolate filled her ears. "Not hardly. But at least you're no longer in hell."

Chapter 2

Daniel had taken the back of the building and Thad had gone through the front. The entire house had lit up like a bonfire, thanks to the gasoline used as an accelerant. Worried they wouldn't find her in the burning structure in time to save her, Daniel had practically fallen over Shelby when he'd raced through the back door into what appeared to be a kitchen. She'd been out cold, lying facedown, smoke filling the room over her head.

Without stopping to think, he'd gathered her into his arms and run out of the inferno into the fresh air. The woman was light, petite and curvy.

Ambulances, police cars and fire trucks, all with their sirens wailing, converged at the location.

Not wanting to put her down on the damp grass, Daniel held her until a paramedic rolled a stretcher out of the back of the ambulance and urged him to lay her on the clean white sheet.

Only then did he let go. Despite her tangled and dirty hair, and a bruise the size of a goose egg rising on her forehead, her pale face was beautiful. Her dark brows arched delicately, and high cheekbones and soft, pink lips tugged at something in Daniel's heart. Something he thought long suppressed in his determined march down his chosen career path.

"We'll take care of her." The medic stepped between him and the girl to position an oxygen mask over her face.

Daniel didn't want to leave her side. "I'm staying with her." Based on the photograph Patrick O'Hara had shown Kate, this was Shelby O'Hara, granddaughter to the former vice president of the United States. He turned to a cop and told him to let Thad know he'd found Shelby.

"Anyone else in the house?" the cop asked.

"I don't know."

Firemen went inside, checking the rooms one by one until they all came out, declaring the house was clear. Whoever had kidnapped Ms. O'Hara had gone, leaving her to burn to death.

Daniel's hands clenched into fists. If this kidnapping and attempted murder were in any way related to Kate Winston, one attempt on Shelby might not be the last, given the rash of attempts over the past few months.

Thad joined him at the back of the ambulance as the paramedics loaded the stretcher with the pale woman strapped down. "She gonna be all right?"

The paramedic paused with his foot on the back step. "You a relative?"

Thad shoved a hand through his smoky hair, a half grin on his face. "I think I'm her uncle."

The paramedic frowned. "You think, or you know?"

Thad stared down at the woman. "She has dark hair like our mother's. Yeah, I'm an uncle."

The paramedic rolled his eyes and gave him the news. "She has some nasty bumps on her head and possible concussion and smoke inhalation, but she should be fine."

"Where are you taking her?" Thad asked.

"WakeMed. Now, if you'll excuse us." The paramedic climbed in and started to close the door behind him.

Daniel grabbed the door. "I'm going with you."

"Are you a relative?"

"No. I'm Secret Service, responsible for the safety of this woman." Daniel flashed his credentials.

"Guess you get a free ride to the hospital." The paramedic jerked his head toward the front. "You can ride shotgun." Then he closed the door and twisted the handle, locking it in place.

Daniel rounded to the front and climbed into the passenger seat.

"I'll notify the family and meet you there." Thad closed the door, shutting Daniel in the ambulance.

Daniel twisted in his seat, peering through the window into the back of the ambulance, watching every move made by the paramedics as they checked Shelby's vital signs.

At the hospital, she was taken to radiology for X-rays of her head and lungs. By the time she was moved to a room on the third floor, the entire Winston family had arrived, along with Patrick O'Hara.

When Patrick spotted Daniel and Thad at the nurses' station, he hurried forward. "Where is she?"

"They just moved her into a private room and are getting her settled," Thad told him.

"I want to see her." Patrick pushed past the two men.

Daniel hooked his arm. "The nurses are settling her in. They said they'd let us know when she's ready for visitors."

Patrick slumped. "Two weeks. She's been missing for two weeks. What did those bastards do to her?"

A nurse emerged from a room down the hallway and strode toward the group of Winstons. "Who is Ms. O'Hara's closest relative?"

Patrick and Kate both spoke at once. "I am."

Patrick glared at Kate and stated, "I'm her grandfather."

The nurse addressed him. "Ms. O'Hara is still unconscious, but the doctor administered a mild sedative and pain medication. He'll be by to give you her diagnosis shortly."

"Can I see her?" Patrick asked.

The nurse stared around at the others. "Just you, for now. The rest of you should stay in the waiting room and leave the hallway clear for the staff."

The relief in the man's face was palpable. The nurse led him into the room, the door closing behind them.

Daniel wanted to follow them, but remained back. Part of the job of a Secret Service agent was to maintain a low profile, only stepping forward to defend those he is assigned to protect. He moved with the rest of the group to the waiting room on the same floor.

Kate, Trey and Samuel circled Thad.

"Did you see her?" Kate asked.

Thad nodded. "I did."

"What did she look like?"

Thad shrugged. "The paramedic had already slipped the oxygen mask over her face. I couldn't tell what she looked like, but she has light brown hair."

"She looked a lot like you, Mrs. Winston," Daniel offered. "Light brown hair, slight build. When she opened her eyes briefly, I could tell they were blue."

"So it could be true." Kate stared at the door leading into the hallway. "My baby didn't die like my mother told me."

"Mom, what baby?" Trey held her hand. "Who is Patrick O'Hara? How do you know him?"

Kate's gaze shifted to the window, looking out into the night. "We were teenagers when we met on the Outer Banks. I was vacationing at the family beach house. He was the bar owner's son." She smiled. "We spent the whole summer together. Young, in love and foolish." Her smile faded. "When I returned home, I found out I was pregnant. My father was livid. He'd been grooming me to marry rich. I didn't want to. I wanted Patrick."

"What happened?" Trey asked.

"My father threatened to hit Patrick with charges of statutory rape if I didn't go away to New Hampshire to live with my aunt until the baby was born." Kate's hands covered her belly as if she was seventeen and pregnant all over again. "I wanted to keep the baby. I was going to run away with it and find Patrick. He'd said he loved me. I was certain once he saw his baby, he'd want us to be together as a family.

"When my due date arrived, I was scared. My mother was there with me, but no one prepared me for what it would be like. The delivery was difficult because the baby was breech. The doctor gave me something to knock me out. When I came to the next day, my mother was crying. She told me the baby was dead."

Daniel's chest tightened at the anguish evident in Kate Winston's face. It was a lot for a young girl to handle.

"My mother told me the baby was dead." She pressed her fist to her mouth. "I was so sad, I wanted to die."

Trey hugged his mother. "But you didn't, and we're glad you didn't." He pressed a kiss to the top of her head. "We love you."

Samuel and Thad gathered around their mother, hugging her.

Trey was the first to step back. "Actually, your story would explain some of Grandma Eunice's dementia."

"What do you mean?" Kate glanced at her oldest son.

"Last time I paid a visit in the nursing home, she was babbling on about a baby girl, and giving her to her father to care for. She was really upset. The staff nurse calmed her with a sedative. I didn't think anything of it." He looked at his mother's face. "Until now. I bet it was deep-seated guilt gnawing at her."

"Why would she do it?" Kate swayed, pressing her hand to her chest. "I had a daughter and I didn't know it. All these years…"

Trey slipped an arm around his mother's shoulders and drew her close.

"How could she?" Kate pressed her cheek into her

son's chest. "My mother loved me. Why would she give my baby away?"

"Could she have done it to protect you and the baby?" Thad asked. "Grandpa Adair was a mean old bastard."

Daniel stood back, trying not to eavesdrop on the family's business, but was nevertheless shocked at Kate's story. Was this how the rich and famous lived? Stealing babies, threatening loved ones?

If it was, then he wanted nothing to do with it. He'd grown up in an average family where they had their arguments, but they loved each other. His father was as much a part of his life as his brothers. It sounded as though Kate's childhood had been less beautiful than her family had let on to the public.

Daniel made a note to himself to call home the next quiet moment he had to himself.

"Where is she?" Jed Kincannon entered the waiting room. "Has she spoken yet?"

"She's still unconscious." Daniel pulled his boss aside and told him what he knew, which wasn't much. "The kidnappers escaped and burned any evidence they might have left behind in the house."

Jed let out a deep breath. "I want to be there when Ms. O'Hara wakes up. We need to know what she knows. The sooner she identifies her kidnappers, the better. I want them off the streets before they cause any more grief."

"You and me both."

Kate stepped up to Jed. "Do you think they'll try to take her again?"

"They took her once," he said.

"But they didn't present a ransom note or any demands," Samuel argued.

"Maybe they were waiting for proof of her lineage," Thad said. "Now that we're involved, it could mean even greater danger for her."

"We can't let anything happen to her or her father." Kate faced him. "Daniel, I want you to provide Shelby's security. I trust you the most of any agent." She smiled, laying a hand on his arm. "I know you'll do everything in your power to protect Shelby, even take a bullet for her."

"I'd say he's good for it," Samuel nodded. "He took three for you."

"Exactly." Kate's hand was warm on Daniel's arm. "Take care of my granddaughter. I want the opportunity to get to know her."

Patrick O'Hara stepped through the door, his face haggard. "They chased me out." He scrubbed a hand through his hair. "She never woke up. The doctor said it's to be expected with head trauma. They're keeping an eye on her tonight, but expect she'll wake up in the morning. The good news is that they didn't detect any brain swelling or hemorrhaging."

Lucy Sinclair, Thad's fiancée, followed Patrick into the room, crossed to Thad and slipped an arm around his waist. "I got here as quickly as I could and checked in with the nurse in charge of the floor. It's like Mr. O'Hara said, she's sleeping. Other than being a little dehydrated, her vital signs are good. She should be up and talking by morning."

Trey glanced down at his watch and across to his wife. Despite her attempt to look in control, Debra was sagging under the weight of the baby. "There's no use all of us waiting for her to wake up. We should go home and get some rest. Tomorrow will be stressful in itself."

"Trey, you need to get Debra home and off her feet." Kate turned to Patrick. "You and Shelby will be staying at the Winston Estate."

Patrick crossed his arms over his chest. "You can't order me around like you do the rest of the world. I have a business to run on the Outer Banks."

Kate nodded. "I know. But we almost lost Shelby tonight. If there's any possibility her kidnappers will try to take her again, she needs protection. Can you provide that for her at your bar?"

Patrick's lips pressed into a thin line. After a long pause, he answered, "No."

"Then I implore you to bring Shelby to the Winston Estate where she can have 24/7 protection by the most trusted man the Secret Service has to offer." She nodded toward Daniel. "I've just tasked Daniel Henderson with the duty of providing protection for Shelby."

Daniel bit down hard on his lip to keep from reminding her that he hadn't agreed to play babysitter to a twenty-three-year-old woman. He'd rather be out investigating this case, finding the men responsible for the attempts on Kate's life and kidnapping her granddaughter. But discussing that in front of the rest of the family was not professional.

He'd wait and get her alone to discuss his duties in private.

For the time being, if the former vice president wanted him to provide security for her granddaughter, he'd protect her granddaughter.

"Okay," Patrick said finally. "I'll get my assistant

manager to run the bar for the next few days. And I'm only doing this for Shelby. If I had any other choices, I wouldn't have come to you."

"Patrick." Kate stared into his eyes. "I thought my baby was dead."

"Her name was Carrie," Patrick bit out. "She was beautiful, just like you."

"Was?" Tears welled in Kate's eyes.

"She died in an auto accident when she was only twenty-four. Shelby is all I have left and I'll be damned if I lose her, too." Patrick walked out of the room, leaving a stricken Kate in his wake.

Daniel turned away, unable to watch as tears slipped silently down Kate's face.

"I never knew my own daughter." Kate's voice shook.

"We had a sister." Samuel stared after Patrick's retreating figure.

"And we'll never know her." Thad hugged Lucy close.

Daniel wanted to storm through the room and yell at all of them, "You have Shelby. Don't screw it up with her."

"Mother," Trey said. "Go home. Get some sleep. I'll stay."

"No need," Daniel said. "I'll keep watch through the night. If she wakes, I'll call."

"She should be surrounded by familiar faces when she comes to," Kate said.

Patrick stood at the doorway. "Which isn't even one of you. I'm staying."

"Fair enough." Kate hooked Trey's arm and leaned

on him as they walked out of the waiting room. As she passed Daniel, she paused. "Keep her safe."

Daniel nodded. "I will."

Then the Winstons stepped into the elevator that whisked them to the ground floor. All the tension left the floor with them and Daniel let himself take a deep breath.

Patrick stood beside him, his gaze on the closed elevator doors. "She's as beautiful today as she was when we first met. If not more so."

Daniel didn't comment. He saw a lot of Kate in her granddaughter's features. If Shelby had half the gumption of her grandmother, she'd be a formidable foe and a dedicated friend.

"I'm going to sit with Shelby. There's a chair in the room that reclines." Patrick stuck out his hand. "I understand you were the one who pulled her from the burning home. Thank you."

"You're welcome." Daniel clasped the man's hand and shook it. This was a man he could relate to. He had a firm handshake, the calloused hands of a working man and an open, friendly face. "I'll stay outside her room and make sure no unauthorized personnel enter."

"I owe you a debt I can never repay."

"No payment necessary. It's part of my job."

Patrick returned to Shelby's room, entering quietly, closing the door behind him.

Daniel's leg ached, and he was tired but still wound up by the events of the evening. He found a chair and propped it against the wall beside Shelby's room. Too preoccupied to sit, he paced, dreading the boredom of being a bodyguard at the same time as he embraced the job, knowing he was protecting a woman who'd done nothing to become a target other than being born into the wrong family.

After a while, Daniel sat to relieve the strain on his leg.

Several hours passed, the clock hands spinning around the dial to six in the morning. Patrick O'Hara emerged from Shelby's room, eyes bloodshot, clothes wrinkled and chin stubbled with a day's growth of beard. "I'm going to hit the hay and then find a cup of coffee and a meal if such exists at this hour. Can I get you anything?"

"No, thank you." Daniel stood and stretched the kinks out of his sore muscles. "You might as well take your time. I'll be here."

Patrick left, shuffling down the long hallway to the elevator.

A nurse made her rounds, checking on the patients. When she came to Shelby's door, Daniel entered behind her. She checked the position of the IV needle, the bag of fluid and the monitors and shone a light into Shelby's eyes. When she finished, she left the room and Daniel stayed.

Someone had wiped the dirt and soot from Shelby's face. Clean and free of makeup, she looked younger than her twenty-three years.

She stirred, her hand clenching and her lips twitching. Behind her eyelids, her eyes moved, but she didn't open them. Daniel wondered what she was dreaming about.

She raised a hand to her chest and moaned, the sound so sad and mournful, Daniel couldn't help himself. He lifted her hand and held it, hoping his touch would ease her nightmares and allow her to sleep.

She curled into him, tucking his hand beneath her cheek, and moaned again.

His chest tightened and he leaned over her, wrapping his arms around her, shielding her from the bad guys in her dreams.

Shelby walked to her car, carrying the satchel with all her notes, the copies of the pages she had yet to read and the half-eaten sandwich she'd set aside as she'd dug deeper into the shelves of case studies and books.

Time had slipped away before she realized she should have left the library an hour before. Now she hurried, knowing her grandfather would be checking on her to see that she got back to the house by midnight.

Her car was the only one left in the parking lot, parked near a large tree. When she'd arrived, the sun had been bright and hot, the tree providing blessed shade on an unusually sultry spring day. Now the tree loomed over her two-door economy car, casting darker shadows in the light from a million stars overhead.

A trickle of apprehension skittered across her skin, making her walk faster, keys in her hand, ready to pop the locks and jump inside. Not that there was anything to worry about. She'd left the library this late on many occasions and had no trouble.

She neared her vehicle and hit the lock button on her key fob; the locks clicked open. As she reached for the door handle, a shadow detached from the base of the tree and lunged forward.

Too shocked to scream, Shelby swung her satchel

containing her notes, laptop and wallet, hitting her attacker in the temple.

He grunted and staggered to the side, bringing a hand to his head.

Before Shelby could run, a second attacker, also wearing dark clothes and a ski mask, shot out of the shadows, grabbed her and clamped a gloved hand over her mouth.

She fought, kicking and twisting, but the man was much stronger and bigger than her five feet two inches. He lifted her off her feet.

A van drove up, her captor leaped in, still carrying her, and the man she'd hit dived in beside them.

"No," she moaned. This was not happening. She couldn't let it happen. Wasn't she smarter than this? Shelby struggled, but the arms holding her tightened, the hand over her mouth cutting off her air. The shadowed interior of the van faded. The next thing she was aware of was smoke. She lay on a floor, the smoke growing thicker around her, filling her lungs, blocking her view of the door, her only escape.

A figure materialized out of the drifting smoke, a tall, broad-shouldered man. He scooped her up into his arms and ran out of the house. She nestled against his chest, her fingers digging into the fabric of his shirt. She breathed in and out, the acrid smell of smoke still burning her nostrils. She was afraid to open her eyes, afraid that when she did she'd still be in that basement, locked in the dark. A captive.

Shelby moaned, her fingers curling around fabric. No.

"Hey, Shelby. You're having a bad dream. Wake up."

"No. I don't want to go back in the dark."

"It's okay. You're free."

The soothing sound of a man's voice lured her out of the basement and into the light. She opened her eyes and looked up at a long fluorescent light mounted on a white ceiling in a clean room.

"I'm not in the basement?"

The man chuckled. "No, you're not."

She glanced up into the green eyes of a stranger and jerked back, fighting to be free of his hold on her.

"It's okay. I'm not going to hurt you. I'm the Secret Service agent assigned to protect—"

She scrambled over the bed and would have fallen off if he hadn't grabbed her wrist and stopped her.

Shelby winced. "Ouch."

He frowned, glancing down at where his hand clasped her raw skin. "What the hell?"

"Let me go."

"I will when you promise you won't throw yourself off the bed."

She stared at him, not sure if he was friend or foe and not willing to give up her freedom again so soon. "I promise," she whispered, tensing, ready to move fast once he let go.

"I'm going to release you and step away from the bed. You don't have to be afraid of me. I'm here to protect you, not harm you."

"How do I know that? I don't even know you."

"I'm letting go to reach for my credentials." He raised his free hand. "Honest."

"Okay, let go, already."

He did and she dropped to the ground on the opposite side of the bed, dragging the tubes in her arms with her. The heart monitor wires ripped loose and the machine set off an alarm. Her knees refused to hold her, shaking so badly they buckled, and she felt herself falling, her head swimming as she went down. The IV stand tilted and crashed to the floor.

The man flung himself across the bed and caught her beneath her arms before she hit the tile.

"You've suffered a head injury," he said softly. "You really should take it easy for a couple days."

"I'm fine." She leaned into him despite her desire to be free of him. His muscles were solid beneath her fingertips and his breath warmed the side of her neck. "I can stand on my own."

"Prove it."

She fought the fog threatening to engulf her and willed her legs to straighten, all the while leaning into the man and his broad shoulders. "I've got it now." Shelby planted both hands on the side of the bed, sagging against it. "I can stand on my own."

"You're a stubborn woman."

"Stubborn is better than dead."

Slowly, he released his hold and rolled off the bed, reaching for his wallet in his back pocket.

The door opened and a nurse rushed in. "What's going on? Why is she out of bed?" She glared at the man and cast a worried look at Shelby. "Ms. O'Hara, you shouldn't be up yet. Please, let me help you back into the bed."

"I don't want to go back to bed. And who is this man?"

"Why, he's your bodyguard, Ms. O'Hara. Your grandmother left word that he was allowed to be in your room and we were to do whatever he said in order to protect you." The nurse planted a hand on her hip and pointed to the bed. "Now, are you going to get back in the bed or will I have to call an orderly to help me put you there?"

"It's not necessary to call an orderly." Her stranger was there by her side, scooping her wobbly legs out from under her. Shelby squealed and wrapped her arms around his neck to keep from falling as he set her down on the mattress, the strength of his arms and the solid wall of his chest oddly reassuring and comforting.

"You really should stay in bed until they bring you something less revealing. You can see everything through the gap in the back of your gown." He grinned and stepped away, missing the hand she swung at his face.

"You're no gentleman."

"Never said I was."

"You never said *what* you were."

The nurse tsked. "Please hold still, Ms. O'Hara, while I reconnect the IV and monitors."

"I don't want the IV. I'd rather have a steak or lobster."

"There are no restrictions on your diet. Would you like me to call the kitchen and have them prepare a sandwich?"

"No! No sandwiches. No bologna!" Shelby clapped a hand over her lips. "I'm sorry." Tears welled in her eyes, clouding her vision. "I don't know what's going on, where I am and who *he* is. And I don't have a grandmother, just my grandfather. Could someone please tell me what the hell's going on?"

Chapter 3

"I'll let your family explain all that when they get here." Daniel dialed the number for Kate Winston's secretary.

"Debra speaking." Her voice was clear and cheerful, with no indication she'd been up late the night before. She'd probably been awake since five or five-thirty, preparing Mrs. Winston's schedule for the day.

"Debra, please inform Mrs. Winston her granddaughter is conscious."

"I will. Right away. Thank you."

Daniel had no doubt she would. Debra Winston was the most efficient personal assistant a person could have. He wasn't sure how Kate could operate without the other woman's help.

Shelby jabbed at the controls on the bed, making the feet rise, then the head of the bed lower. "I don't have a grandmother and I don't need a bodyguard. Damn this thing. How do I get it to sit me up?"

Daniel fought to keep from smiling, took the controls from her hand and adjusted the settings, raising the head of the bed until Shelby sat up. "Thank you," she said, her tone reluctant. "I could have figured it out myself."

"I can't have you falling out of bed. What kind of bodyguard would I be if I let you fall twice?"

"Someone else's, I would hope. I don't need a bodyguard."

"Your grandmother and your uncles think you need one. And I agree. Now, whether or not it's me is an entirely different concern."

"I don't have a grandmother, and I don't have any uncles. It's just my grandfather, Patrick, and me. You must have the wrong woman."

"No, sweetie, he doesn't." Patrick entered the room carrying two cups of steaming coffee. He set them on the rolling table and engulfed his granddaughter in a long, heartfelt hug. "Thank God you're all right. I was so scared. I thought I'd lost you."

"Believe me, I was pretty scared, too." She hugged him again and pushed him to arm's length, tears running down her cheeks. She brushed them aside and studied her grandfather. "You look like you haven't eaten in days. Have you been taking your vitamins?"

He chuckled. "God, I've missed you."

Her brow wrinkled. "I take that as a no." The next minute she was smiling, her bright blue eyes dancing, making Daniel's heartbeat stutter then race. "That's okay. I'll have you back on track in no time," she assured him.

"That's my girl." Patrick hugged her again and perched on the edge of the bed.

Shelby rolled her eyes at Daniel. "And who is this man? I have to say, after being bound and kept in the dark for two weeks, to wake up in the arms of a stranger wasn't reassuring."

"Oh, baby, what did those animals do to you?" Patrick hugged her again.

"Thankfully not much more than keeping me tied up in the dark and feeding me the nastiest bologna sandwiches and water."

Daniel's lips twitched. That would explain why she'd gone over the edge at the nurse's mention of a sandwich.

Patrick sighed. "At least they didn't hurt you more than that." He cast a glance at Daniel. "This is Daniel Henderson, an agent with the Secret Service. He saved your life."

Daniel almost laughed at the skeptical look she threw his way.

"It's okay, you don't have to thank me," he said, his voice deceptively even, the undertones dripping with sarcasm.

"Thank you for pulling me out of there," she said and turned toward her grandfather. "But why do I need a Secret Service agent watching over me? And what's all this about a grandmother and uncles? Does the hospital staff have me in the wrong room?"

"Shelby, about that." Patrick stared down at where he patted her hands in his. "There's something I should have told you a long time ago."

Shelby's lips tightened and her face blanched, but she held her tongue.

Daniel had the sudden urge to pull her into his arms and shield her from what was coming next. She was so small and pale against the hospital sheets.

Her grandfather continued, delivering the news straight and free of any sugarcoating. "You have a grandmother and three uncles."

She breathed in and out several times, pinching the bridge of her nose.

Daniel admired her for her calm and ability to take it all in without falling apart. After two weeks of captivity in a dark basement, and waking up in a hospital with the news she had more relatives and a bodyguard, Shelby had earned the right to come apart.

She asked quietly, "Since when, and why haven't I heard of them before?"

"I didn't think it was important before," her grandfather said. "But when you went missing, I had to get help. The only person I knew who had enough clout and influence was Kate Winston."

Those bright blue eyes blinked and she laughed out loud. "Kate Winston? Former vice president of the United States?"

Patrick nodded. "She's your mother's mother."

Shelby's face lost all color, and she pressed a hand to her temple. "How?"

Her grandfather chuckled. "The usual way. It happened one summer when we were teenagers, both young and stupid. Your grandmother was on vacation on the Outer Banks when we met. By the end of that summer, we thought we were in love." He stared out the window. "Your mother was born nine months later."

"What happened? I take it you didn't make an honest woman out of her or I'd have known sooner about her."

Her grandfather flinched, his jaw hardening. "I wanted to marry Kate, but she wanted nothing to do with me."

"Why?" Shelby leaned forward and cupped her grandfather's face. "What's not to love?"

He covered her hand with his and pressed it against his cheek. "It was complicated."

"Try me."

Feeling like an outsider in a personal, family discussion, Daniel moved toward the door. "I'll just leave you two alone."

"No," Patrick said at the same time Shelby said, "Please."

A knock on the door had all three of them changing focus.

Before anyone could respond, the door slowly opened and a nurse peeked in. "Hi, I'm Lucy. Is Shelby up?" She smiled across the room. "Oh, thank goodness, you're awake." Still, she hesitated. "Are you up to receiving a few visitors? There are people out here who want to meet you."

Shelby shot a glance at Daniel, her eyes wide, her fingers gripping the sheets.

Her grandfather patted her hands. "You don't have to if you don't want to."

"No." She sat up straighter. "I want to meet the woman who wanted nothing to do with you."

"Uh, okay. I'll let them know." Lucy popped back out into the hallway, the door shutting behind her.

"Now, Shelby, be nice," Patrick warned. "What happened forty years ago is in the past."

"Yeah, but what kind of woman throws away her own child? And to think, I used to admire Kate Winston." Shelby crossed her arms over her chest, some color returning to her pale cheeks.

Daniel knew he should leave, but his protective instinct kicked in. Having four Winstons in the same small room at one time was overwhelming, even for a healthy person. Their egos and their combined charisma could be intimidating.

Lucy opened the door and stood to the side, holding the door wide as Kate and her three sons entered.

As Daniel expected, the three towering men filled the room with their broad shoulders.

Kate walked forward, tiny in comparison. She wore a light gray skirt suit and a pale pink blouse, appearing every bit the poised politician. But when her gaze fell on Shelby, her eyes filled. "Oh, my God. I could be looking at myself as a young woman." Tears slid silently down her cheeks. "All this time, I didn't know."

"If I'd had any doubts before, I don't now. She looks just like you." One of the men with dark brown hair and eyes the same color as his mother's and Shelby's pulled Kate into the crook of his arm. "Shelby, this is your grandmother, Kathleen Winston. Most people call her Kate." He walked with Kate to the other side of the bed from where Patrick stood holding Shelby's hand.

Shelby held out her hand. "Nice to meet you, Mrs. Winston."

Kate ignored the hand and engulfed Shelby in a hug. "I'm so sorry. I didn't know."

The stricken look in Shelby's eyes made Daniel move forward. "Perhaps we should give Ms. O'Hara some room to breathe. This is a lot for her to take in."

Shelby muttered a soft, "Thank you." She brushed moisture from her eyes and sniffed.

Kate straightened, tugging at the hem of her suit jacket. "This is Trey," she said, her voice shaking. "He's the oldest of my sons—your uncles." Kate laughed. "I'm sorry, this is all surreal to me." Her voice caught on a sob.

"You're telling me." Shelby held out a hand to the first of the men. "Nice to meet you."

Another one of the men stepped forward. "Hi, I'm Samuel, but you can call me Sam."

"Sam." Shelby took his hand. "You're all so tall."

"We take after our father," he said.

The next man stepped forward and held out his hand. Shelby shook it. "Name's Thad. I work with the Raleigh Police Department. I'd like to ask you some questions about the men who held you captive."

Shelby's face paled and she snatched her hand away.

"Thad," his mother touched his arm. "Can't it wait just a few minutes?"

Thad frowned. "We need to catch the men who did this. Shelby's the only witness we have." One look at his mother's face and he nodded. "Okay, just a few minutes."

Sam shook his head. "You look so much like Mother."

Her face pale, her eyes wide, Shelby chewed on her bottom lip. "I'm sorry. It's going to take some time getting used to all this."

The door opened again and the doctor entered. "Good grief, are we having a family reunion?"

"We're going." Trey nodded to his brothers. "Let's give our niece some room."

"I have questions," Thad insisted.

"They can wait until we get to the estate," Kate said softly.

The doctor stepped past the people standing around and shone a light into Shelby's eyes, then pressed his stethoscope against her chest.

"What estate?" Shelby leaned around the doctor. "I'm going home as soon as I get the okay from the doctor."

The doctor straightened and tucked the stethoscope in his pocket. "That will be as soon as we can get your discharge papers."

"She's okay?" Kate asked.

The doctor nodded and stared down at Shelby. "Drink plenty of liquids and take it easy for a few days."

"I can go?" she asked.

"Yes, ma'am."

"Good." Shelby tossed the sheet aside and swung her legs over the side of the bed. "Come on, Grand-dad, let's go home."

Patrick O'Hara shook his head.

Daniel braced himself for the coming storm.

"Honey, we're not going home yet. Not until the police find the ones responsible for kidnapping and almost murdering you."

"If we're not going home, then where are we going?" Her eyes narrowed and her arms crossed.

"You'll stay with us at the Winston Estate," Kate said, her tone brooking no argument. "You'll have round-the-clock security. Daniel Henderson will be your bodyguard."

Daniel almost laughed at the shock on Shelby's

face. He wasn't sure what she found most disturbing—staying at the Winston Estate or having him as a bodyguard.

He leaned close and whispered in her ear. "If it's any consolation, it's not my idea of a good time, either."

Shelby stood on shaky legs, wearing slim-cut, cream-colored trousers, a short-sleeved cashmere sweater, sandals and undergarments thoughtfully provided by her supposed grandmother. The clothing she'd been wearing for the past two weeks had probably been condemned and thrown away as unfit for the granddaughter of the former vice president.

Though her knees wobbled and the pain meds she'd been given hadn't quite worn off and left her feeling a little fuzzy headed, Shelby refused to show even the slightest weakness to the Winstons or the odious man who'd been assigned as her bodyguard. That he was no happier about the arrangement than she was did little to appease her. Strangely, it made her more angry and disgruntled about the entire arrangement.

"I have assignments to complete. I can't do them without going to the library in Beth City," she muttered.

Daniel Henderson stood beside her, his face impassive, wearing mirrored sunglasses that completely hid any expression in his eyes, frustrating Shelby even more.

"You can't leave the estate until we find your kidnappers."

"Like hell," she stated. "I'm not giving up one prison for another."

"Trust me, the Winston Estate is far from a prison."

"It's a prison if I'm not allowed to leave."

"Perhaps *allowed* is too strong a word. But it would certainly be *ill-advised*."

She snorted. "No difference." They stood in the lobby at the hospital's entrance, waiting for her grandfather to complete the paperwork to release her. Kate and her personal secretary waited close by.

Did he have to stand so close? Shelby shifted away from Daniel. He shifted with her. His bulk was doing funny things to her insides. She'd tried to blame it on the breakfast she'd been served by the hospital staff, but it had been pretty darned good after the bologna sandwiches and bagels she'd been given for the past two weeks. She'd eaten every last bite and wanted to lick the plate, but just managed to refrain with Daniel, Kate and her grandfather looking on.

The food had given her the strength to make it this far, and a lighter dose of pain medication didn't make her head fuzzy. She almost felt normal. Almost as if her world hadn't been upended and thrown her off-kilter.

A grandmother and three uncles. And all this time she'd thought it was just her and her grandfather against the world.

Patrick signed one last form and turned toward the exit, his gaze zeroing in on Kate. She stood looking cool, calm and confident in her gray suit, her hair short and stylish with just a hint of frost at the temples. No dyes and highlights for her. And she didn't need them. She was beautiful, even in her late fifties, the lines by her eyes adding character.

Shelby didn't want to like the woman, didn't want to believe a word she said. Not when she'd abandoned her own daughter and then claimed she hadn't known she was alive. How does a mother not know her baby was alive?

Patrick's face gave him away. He might have said he was over Kate a long time ago, but the way he looked at her at that moment said the opposite.

"Oh, dear." Her heart aching for her grandfather, Shelby pressed a hand to her chest.

"What?"

"This isn't right."

"What isn't right?" Daniel asked.

She tried to think of something to say that would make it better. "We don't belong with the Winstons. My grandfather and I should just go home. We can manage on our own."

"Don't be ridiculous." Daniel captured her arm. "You were almost killed. Those men who kidnapped you are experienced thugs. What training do you have to defend yourself against them?"

Her back stiffened. "I took a self-defense class one semester during my undergraduate degree."

Daniel snorted. "And how'd that work for you?"

Shelby opened her mouth to give him a sharp retort, but she didn't have one. The reality of the past two weeks sitting in the dark wasn't something she wanted to happen ever again. "I'll be more aware."

"When you're outnumbered, outweighed and outgunned, being aware may not be enough."

"It will have to be." She smiled at her grandfather as he closed the distance between them.

"Ready?" he asked.

"I am. But I think we should go home."

Her grandfather's brows drew together. "Shelby,

honey, after what happened, I don't think it's safe. I can't provide the kind of protection Kate can."

Staying at the Winston Estate would be as hard on him as it was on her. They didn't belong with these people. The Winstons traveled in an entirely different circle from the folks at the O'Hara Bar and Grill on the Outer Banks where she and her grandfather lived and worked.

The worried look on her grandfather's face made her reconsider for the moment. She stepped outside the hospital where two long black limousines stood waiting at the curb.

"Tell me we're not going in those," she said.

Daniel's mouth twitched into a grin, although his eyes were invisible behind his mirrored sunglasses. "Then I won't tell you."

Thad walked up behind them. "If we could move it along, the cars have been waiting for thirty minutes in a no-parking zone. The hospital security staff would like us to get going."

Her father hooked her arm and led her toward the limo. The chauffeur opened the back door for her.

The closer she got to the dark interior, the faster her heart raced. "No." She braced her hands on the roof of the car and refused to step inside.

"Is there something wrong?" Kate asked.

"I can't get in. It's too…"

"Too what, dear?" Kate laid a hand on her arm.

"Too dark," Shelby whispered.

Kate's hand gently smoothed over her arm. "It's okay. You don't have to ride in the limousine." She turned to the driver. "Take it back to the estate. Miss O'Hara will ride with Trey in his vehicle."

The driver nodded, rounded the front of the vehicle and got in.

Kate's brows rose as she directed a glance at her oldest son. "You don't mind bringing the O'Haras and Mr. Henderson, do you?"

"Not at all, Mother." Trey turned away from the hospital. "If you'll follow me to the parking lot—"

The limousine engine revved and died. The driver cranked it again and the same thing happened.

"What do you suppose is wrong with the limousine?" Debra frowned, making a note on her smartphone. "I have it serviced regularly."

"Not good." Daniel gripped Kate and Shelby's arm. "Get down!"

Trey spun Debra around, shoved her behind the open door of the Jeep and shielded her with his body.

Before Shelby could react, Daniel pushed her to the concrete. Kate dropped to her stomach beside her and Daniel threw himself on top of both of them.

Shelby struggled to get up. "What the hell—"

An explosion rocked the ground beneath her, blasting her eardrums. She fought to breathe beneath the weight of Daniel lying across her as metal shards fell on her legs and arms.

Chapter 4

His ears ringing and pain knifing through his leg, Daniel rolled off Shelby and Kate and leaped to his feet.

Smoke poured from the limousine's engine. The hood had been blown off and had landed several yards away in the middle of the driveway. The windshield was completely shattered and the driver was slumped against the door.

Daniel limped to the limousine and tried to open the driver's door to get him out. It wouldn't open, and the acrid scent of gasoline and smoke made him pull harder.

Bracing his foot on the side of the vehicle, he pulled on the door handle but it wouldn't budge.

Shelby helped Kate up on the other side of the vehicle.

"Get the hell away!" Daniel called out. "There's gas leaking out, it could go up anytime."

Shelby hooked Kate's elbow and tried to hurry her toward the building.

Kate pushed her hands away. "No, that's Carlo. We have to get him out."

Thad ran toward Daniel, carrying a tire iron. He yelled back at Sam, "Call 911!" Thad wedged the pointed end of the tire iron between the door and the frame and leaned back. The door metal bent, but the door didn't budge.

Daniel grabbed the iron below Thad's hands and put his back into it. Together they pulled. Trey rounded to the opposite side of the car and tried the door. "This side is locked, too."

Daniel glanced at the puddle of fuel pooling around their feet and the smoke still rising from the engine. "We have to get him out." He took the tire iron from Thad and smashed it against the broken glass of the window behind the driver. The first strike wasn't enough. He swung again and the safety glass caved in. He ran the bar along the edges of the long side window, breaking out enough of a hole to get inside.

By then, nurses and orderlies were running out of the hospital.

Sam stood between them and the limousine. "Stay back! It's too dangerous."

A siren wailed in the distance.

Daniel shrugged out of his suit jacket, laid it over the broken window and dived into the back of the limousine. He crawled over the back of the leather seat and shoved open the window between the back and the front. Pushing his bulky shoulders through the narrow opening, he reached through and checked the driver for a pulse. For a moment, he could feel nothing, then a faint throb bumped against his fingertips. "He's still alive!"

Shimmying through the window, Daniel dragged his body into the front seat and hit the switch to unlock the doors. Nothing happened. "Take the tire iron to the other side!" he yelled, the smoke making him cough and his eyes fill with tears.

Thad rounded the vehicle and jammed the bar between the door and frame. Sam joined him with another tire iron. With the three Winston brothers on the outside pulling, Daniel kicked as hard as he could.

A scream rent the air and Daniel glanced up long enough to see flames shoot toward the sky. If he didn't get the door open, he'd cook inside the limousine with the driver.

Flames engulfed the engine and driver's side of the vehicle. Shelby screamed and pushed forward. If her grandfather had not been beside her, she would have joined the men at the door. "Don't! You'll be hurt," he said, his arm catching her around her waist.

Her heart lodged in her throat, Shelby stood by helpless as the drama unfolded. "Where is the fire truck? Why isn't it here yet?"

"They're coming as fast as they can," her grandfather assured her.

"They're not going to get here in time. If my boys don't get out of there…" Kate started to walk forward.

Patrick snagged her arm. "The best thing you can do is stay safe and away. If they're worrying about you, they won't be concentrating on their own safety."

Kate pressed her hands to her face. "I can't stand by and do nothing."

Shelby pushed her grandfather's arm away. "I have to help." Before she could take one more step, the door to the limousine flew open. Smoke billowed up into the air as fire devoured the fuel.

Get out, get out, get out! Shelby screamed inside, but Daniel didn't appear. Her chest squeezed tight and her breath caught and held in her throat as fire consumed the vehicle.

Then a leg came out, followed by another, and Daniel backed out of the limousine, dragging the limp body of the driver.

Trey and Thad took over, dragging him the rest of the way out and as far away from the burning vehicle as they could before they laid him on the ground.

A fire engine, lights and sirens blaring, pulled up next to the hospital.

Firemen leaped to the ground and dragged hoses from the side of the truck. A rescue vehicle stopped behind it, along with four police cruisers. Soon the bystanders were herded back into the hospital.

Trey ushered Debra inside, but Shelby, Patrick and Kate refused.

"Those are my sons," Kate insisted. "I'm not going anywhere."

The firemen extinguished the blaze and the hospital's medical staff carried the injured driver into the hospital on a gurney.

Once the driver was taken care of and the flames doused, the Winston sons and Daniel joined Patrick, Shelby and Kate.

While the Winstons checked out their mother, Daniel touched Shelby's chin. "You should have that cut looked at. Are you okay?"

With his fingers warm on her face, Shelby couldn't think straight. "I think so." Shelby pressed her palms to her ears and flexed her jaw. "But you sound like you're in a tunnel."

"Concussion from the blast." Daniel's hand dropped to his side. "It'll take a while before your hearing returns to normal." He faced Shelby's grandfather. "Maybe we should get everyone back inside the hospital to be treated."

Patrick nodded. "I agree. Starting with you." He turned Daniel around. "Looks like you collected some shrapnel from the explosion.

Shelby looked at Daniel's back and gasped. "You're coming with me." She grabbed his arm and dragged him toward the door.

He pulled free of her grip. "I'm okay. I'd rather get everyone back to the Winston Estate and out of range of anyone else targeting you or Mrs. Winston."

Kate and her three sons gathered around them. "What the hell happened?" Kate looked at the destroyed limousine.

"It appears someone got to the limousine and planted a bomb in it," Daniel said.

"How? I thought the drivers were with them at all times."

Thad wrapped an arm around his mother's shoulders. "I'll have security camera footage checked. Maybe it'll shed light on whoever did this. Main thing now is to get you and Shelby home."

Kate shook her head. "I can't leave now. I have to stay and see to the well-being of my driver."

"No." Sam took his mother's hand. "You have to get home. If someone is willing to bomb a vehicle at a hospital, he's not concerned with collateral damage. By being here, you're putting others in danger."

Shelby watched as Kate's brows pulled together. "I'm so damned tired of my family being terrorized. Who is doing this?"

"We don't know, but I'd prefer to get you out of here before someone tries again." Sam nodded toward Shelby. "And Shelby could use some recuperation time after what she's been through."

Kate reached toward her. "I'm so sorry. This is all my fault."

Shelby stepped away from the woman's hands, not yet willing to accept her as anything other than the person who was going to host her and her grandfather for the next few days. "I don't understand why I'm a target, or why it's because of you. But I agree standing around here isn't going to solve our problems." And she didn't want to let on that she had a splitting headache. Not when Daniel was cut and bleeding and willing to forgo medical attention to get Kate and her to safety.

"I can take a total of five in my SUV," Trey said. "I'll bring it around."

"Sam can take the rest in mine," Thad offered. "I'm staying to help gather evidence. This is now a crime scene."

Daniel stepped in front of the women. "We need to search the vehicles before anyone gets in."

"Daniel and I will handle that," Thad said. "Patrick, could you take Mother and Shelby into the hospital and have the staff give them a once-over?"

Kate shook her head. "I'm fine."

"As am I," Shelby assured him.

Thad shrugged. "Hardheaded women."

Kate's lips quirked and Shelby couldn't help but think the men were tough and hardheaded like their mother. Not an entirely bad thing in this case.

A few minutes later, Shelby was in the backseat of an SUV with Daniel riding shotgun, her grandfather at her side and Trey Winston at the wheel. Kate rode in Thad's SUV with Sam driving and Debra sitting beside her in the backseat. They'd decided to leave the second limo behind in case it was similarly rigged to explode.

Once they were away from the hospital, Shelby noticed Daniel didn't sit all the way back in his seat.

She leaned forward. "You should have had your back seen to."

"Don't worry about me. I'll be fine until I get to the Winston Estate."

"You can barely sit in this vehicle." Shelby tapped Trey on his shoulder. "Take us back to the hospital. This man needs medical attention."

Trey shot her a glance in the rearview mirror. "Thad's fiancée is on her way. She's a nurse and can remove the shrapnel and clean the wounds."

Not completely satisfied with Trey's response, Shelby sat back in her seat, chewing on her bottom lip.

Her grandfather patted her knee. "I'm sorry I didn't tell you about your grandmother."

Shelby covered her grandfather's hand. "It's okay. I guess I understand why you didn't. A woman willing to give up her baby isn't worth knowing."

"My mother didn't give up her baby knowingly," Trey said, his jaw set in a hard line, his fingers tight on the wheel.

"I didn't know she was lied to. All I knew was I had a baby to raise by myself. What did I know about raising a kid?"

Shelby's fingers squeezed around her grandfather's. "Apparently you knew enough to raise my mother and me."

"Not enough to keep Carrie safe."

"You did the best you could. You couldn't have known she would die in a car wreck."

Patrick lifted Shelby's hand and kissed her knuckles. "Not a day goes by that I don't think of her. How can I forget when you look just like her?" He smiled, then his lips turned down at the corners. "When I thought I'd lost you as well, I had to get help."

"I'm glad you did." Memories of being abducted washed over her, and she relived the terror of being so helpless. "I'm sorry I didn't come home on time that night."

"You think I could be mad about that?" Her grandfather laughed, choking on a sob. "You couldn't have known someone would target you."

"Yeah, but if I had left when there were more people out, I might not have been captured and imprisoned in that horrible basement."

"Well, it's all over now. We have to count our blessings and make sure it doesn't happen again."

And that was where Daniel came into the picture. If he was to be her bodyguard, he'd be around all the time.

Shelby's insides quivered, her core heated and her palms grew clammy. "I don't like living in someone else's house. I'd rather go home to my own home, with my own bed to sleep in and the people I know and love around me."

Patrick nodded. "I'd like nothing better. But it's clear someone wants to get to Kate through her family. And like it or not, you're part of Kate's family."

At that moment, they pulled up to a gate. Trey pressed a remote-control button on the sun visor and the gate opened. They wound along a driveway and through parklike manicured lawns and gardens, and finally stopped in front of a huge white-painted brick mansion with black shutters and red accents.

Shelby gulped, her pulse quickening, feeling more uncomfortable by the minute. "For the record, I don't like it. I don't know the woman, other than that she's the former vice president. I don't like putting my life on hold because someone doesn't like her. I've already missed enough time at school. I have no idea how I'm going to catch up. And holy smokes, who lives in a house this big?"

"You will." Daniel climbed out of the SUV and opened Shelby's door for her, his face grim, his jaw hard. "Perhaps you need to understand a few things." He held out his hand, pulled her out of the vehicle and stood her in front of him.

"Don't get all he-man on me," she said, pushing his hands away before the feel of him made her do something truly foolish. "You're just the bodyguard."

"I might only be the hired help, but Kate Winston was a good vice president and she's an even better person. She didn't have to come to your rescue, but she did. And she doesn't have to provide you protection. But she will." He gripped her arms and glared down at her. "I suggest you be grateful you're alive, thank Kate for making that happen and stop whining about school."

Shelby opened her mouth to tell the man she wasn't whining, but he stood so close she could feel the heat from his body and the intensity in his gaze. All the words she could have shouted back at him died on her lips and she shut her mouth with a snap. It wasn't in her nature to be so angry. And, damn it, Daniel was right.

She should quit worrying about school. Free from her kidnappers, no longer confined to the darkness, she had a lot to be thankful for. And she had yet to thank this man for saving her from the burning house.

Her grandfather chuckled as he rounded the vehicle. "Shelby has a mind of her own, but I do believe she's met her match." He glanced up at the house in front of him, his smile fading. "Kate sure has done well for herself," he stated.

Shelby stepped back from Daniel, her voice caught in her throat as a surge of emotion welled up in her. She was lucky to be here, and she should accept a night's protection from the woman who'd been someone special to her grandfather forty years ago.

Slipping her arm through her grandfather's, she leaned into him. "In case I haven't told you yet, I'm glad you didn't give up on me."

He pressed her arm to his side. "Never."

Shelby stared up at the house and shook her head. "Pretty impressive, isn't it?" Shelby glanced at her grandfather.

For a man who didn't know a stranger and always had a smile on his face, he looked pretty grim. "I could never have given her all this."

A thread of anger shot up her back, stiffening her spine. "You'd have given her everything she needed."

His lips twisted. "But not this."

"Funny, I grew up in your house, and I never longed for anything."

"There were a few times I was hard-pressed to put food on the table."

"We always had plenty of love."

"Remember the time after the hurricane that almost destroyed the bar? I didn't know how I'd get back on my feet."

Shelby hugged him to her side "Everyone on the Outer Bank helped us rebuild."

"When you didn't come home…" His face blanched and his throat worked as he swallowed hard. "Hell, Shelby, I could replace a bar, but I could never replace you."

Shelby blinked to keep tears from welling in her eyes. All the time she'd been held in captivity, she'd worried about her grandfather. He didn't have anyone else in the world. And neither did she. At least, she'd thought she didn't have anyone else. Things were changing.

The other SUV pulled to a halt behind Trey's. Kate, Debra and Thad stepped out.

"I hope you weren't waiting on us." Kate hurried forward. "Please, come inside. I'll have Maddie make tea and coffee and find something for lunch. Lucy's on the way. She'll help Daniel and anyone else with injuries from the explosion." Though her knees were scuffed, her pretty gray suit was wrinkled and dirty and her hair was mussed, Kate marched up the steps like a force to be reckoned with.

Shelby and Patrick both drew in long breaths and followed her up the steps into the house. Shelby told herself it would only be for a day. Maybe two, then she was going back home. She didn't belong in this big old mansion.

Most of all, she wanted to get away from the bodyguard who had such a low opinion of her and who got her stomach all tied in knots every time she glanced his way.

Before Kate reached the top of the steps, Trey and Sam got there and threw open the doors. She smiled at them and stepped inside, then turned to welcome her guests.

Beneath the smudges, her cheeks glowed a soft pink as Patrick stepped past her. Her eyelashes dipped down and her gaze followed him like a shy teenager.

Shelby was shocked by the change. From confident former vice president to shy young woman, Kate Winston was an enigma. Which was the woman who'd abandoned her baby girl and broken her grandfather's heart?

The wide front doors opened into a spacious foyer tiled in black-and-white marble. A grand, sweeping staircase curved upward to the second floor, trimmed in glistening rich mahogany. To one side of the entryway was a large, formal living room with shining wood floors and white furniture. In sharp contrast, a black grand piano filled one corner, ready to provide an elite guest list with subtle entertainment.

An older woman, slightly plump with red hair, hurried forward, her arms opening to Kate. "Oh, Mrs. Winston, I'm so glad you're not harmed." She engulfed the former vice president in a hug and then stepped back, raising an apron to dry her eyes.

"I'm quite all right, Maddie." Kate patted the older woman's back. "Just a little shaken up by the explosion."

Maddie shook her head. "When Debra called ahead to warn me about what happened, I nearly had a heart attack." She pressed a hand to her chest and took a deep breath. "I had to see with my own eyes."

"Well, now that you know I'm fine, let me introduce my granddaughter, Shelby O'Hara." Kate swept her hand toward Shelby. "And this is her grandfather, Patrick O'Hara." Her voice dropped and her eyelashes swept down over her eyes, her cheeks flushing. "They'll be staying with us until we sort all of this out. Shelby, Patrick, this is Maddie Fitzgerald, our housekeeper, the rock in our household. If you need anything, she's the one you should ask."

Sam hugged the older woman. "She's so much more than a housekeeper. She's like a surrogate grandmother." He kissed the top of her cap of short red hair. "She's really part of the family. She takes good care of us all."

Maddie smiled and held out her hand to Patrick, her gaze going from Patrick to Kate, a slight wrinkle in her brow. "You both are welcome here." She turned to Shelby, her smile widening, her hand reaching for Shelby's. "My goodness, girl, you're the spittin' image of your grandmother."

"And my mother, so I'm told," Shelby added.

Kate stiffened beside her, her face paling. "I'd better clean up. I have a meeting with the press in an hour.

I'm sure they'll want to know all about what happened this morning." She inhaled deeply and let it out.

Debra leaned close to Kate and whispered, "You might want to tell her what to expect."

With a nod, Kate's gaze captured Shelby's. "If word gets out that I have a granddaughter, be prepared to be inundated by the press." Her lips twisted. "I apologize for that, but I can't change what is." She glanced over Shelby's shoulder to Daniel. "Daniel will help to keep them at bay, but you won't be able to go anywhere without someone snapping pictures of you."

"We should be going," Debra prompted Kate. She smiled at Patrick and Shelby. "Maddie will help you two get settled." Then she ushered Kate toward the staircase, the two women walking with quick, purposeful steps as they climbed to the second floor.

"Press?" Shelby's head spun with the thought. "Why me?"

Trey scrubbed a hand over his face and grimaced. "With so much happening, I hadn't thought about that." He stared at Shelby. "Brace yourself."

Shelby's belly tightened. So much was changing around her, she was having a hard time grasping it all.

Sam touched her arm reassuringly. "The fact our mother had an illicit love affair before marrying our father will have the tabloids screaming for all the details. You'll be a celebrity by association."

"Sam Winston, don't you have something better to do than scare this poor child?" Maddie waved her hands toward the big Winston man as if she was shooing a fly. She took Shelby's hand and tugged her toward the stairs. "Come with me. I'll show you two to your rooms."

Shelby was swept away by the woman and herded up the stairs, her grandfather following and Daniel bringing up the rear.

Everything was happening too fast. From a name-less college student to the granddaughter of the former vice president of the United States all in the span of a day. Or rather, in the span of the two weeks she'd been held prisoner.

Shelby shivered, wishing she could go back to being the faceless college student who had nothing more to worry about than the next exam or the next paper due.

Daniel followed Shelby up the stairs. The consum-mate professional, he shouldn't have been focusing on the sway of her hips as she took one step at a time. In the tailored slacks and cashmere short-sleeved sweater, she looked more like one of the Winstons than the soot-covered waif he'd found passed out on the kitchen floor of a burning house.

Even in the new clothes, she still conveyed a sense of vulnerability, no matter how fiercely she valued her independence. The kidnapping had to have taken its toll on her and made her aware of just how helpless one woman could be against two strong men. Hell, a grown man would be equally helpless in the same circum-stances. Especially if he wasn't expecting an attack.

His back stung where shards of metal and glass had impaled him, but he refused to tend to himself until he was certain Shelby was secure. After he'd taken a bul-let for Kate Winston, he knew the threats to the Win-stons were real and not only in the outside world, but behind their supposedly secure gates.

Shrugging his shoulders, he winced and continued

up the stairs, concentrating on Shelby's sweet derriere. Each of her movements took his mind off the pain in his back and his bum knee.

At the first opportunity, he'd seek out Mrs. Winston and ask her to remove him from the responsibility of watching out for Shelby. She was young, opinionated and didn't want the added aggravation of someone following her around. He couldn't blame her. He'd grown up in a large family and he valued his privacy. But there was inconvenience and there was danger. She needed to understand the difference.

Shelby had to figure out really quickly which was more important. But Daniel didn't want to be the man to play babysitter to the college coed. Let someone else be.

Still, she was pretty, slim, athletic, and when she smiled, as she had when he'd pulled her from the fire, it did funny things to his insides. Apparently, she'd gone through hell being kept in the dark for two weeks, not knowing why she'd been targeted, who was keeping her, or if they'd eventually kill her. Poor kid.

She reached up to push the hair back from her forehead, the motion emphasizing her narrow waist, the swell of her hips and the sexy way she moved. His groin tightened and he had to retract his previous thought. She wasn't a kid. At twenty-three, she was six years younger than he was. He told himself that she might as well be a baby. While he performed the role of her bodyguard, he had to get his mind and his gaze off those hips. The woman was his job, not a conquest.

Chapter 5

Maddie climbed the steps as quickly and with as much agility as a woman half her age.

Tired and still recuperating from her ordeal in the basement, Shelby wasn't going to complain about the stairs. She held on to the railing and climbed, wishing she could find a nice soft bed to fall into.

"You'll have the blue guest room," Maddie was saying. "On account of it's the most feminine of the rooms. Your grandfather will be staying in the brown room." She stopped and threw open the door to a room decorated in creams and browns. The bed was made from intricately carved burled wood. The mattress was covered with a cream duvet and pillows in various shades from cream to a rich, dark chocolate. In one corner stood a deep brown leather wing-back chair and a burled wood table with a wrought iron and stained glass reading lamp. Wide windows gave them a view out of the back of the house.

Directly below was a swimming pool, the water rippling in the breeze, sun sparkling off its surface.

Shelby blinked her eyes at the intensity of the sunlight. After days spent in complete darkness, it would take time before she got used to light again.

Beyond the pool lay an expansive garden and neatly trimmed grass. Trees shaded the edges of the lawn and made Shelby long to walk among them. She had to stop herself from exclaiming over the beauty of the room, the house and the surrounding grounds. O'Hara's Bar and Grill on the Outer Banks was nothing to compare with the elegance and luxury of the Winston Estate.

Her grandfather stood beside her, his lips pressed into a thin line, the dark circles beneath his eyes more pronounced.

Maddie chattered on, "There's a private bathroom through this door and it's fully equipped with towels and toiletries. If you should need anything that isn't provided, let me know." She faced Patrick, her smile fading. "Is something wrong?"

Patrick forced a smile. "Nothing at all. This will be fine."

Shelby could tell by the tightness of his jaw that everything was not fine. She could bet what was going through his mind. He was probably comparing their home over the bar to the Winston Estate and coming up short. She slipped her arm around him and squeezed. "Think of it as a fancy hotel. We won't be here long," she whispered.

He nodded and squared his shoulders. "The main

thing is to keep you safe. Come on, let's see your digs."
He winked and stepped out of the beautiful room.

Maddie crossed the hallway and opened another
room. "This is the blue room where you will be staying, Miss O'Hara." She led the way in and crossed to
another door. "You have your own walk-in closet and
bathroom. Mrs. Winston is having additional clothing
delivered this afternoon. If there's anything in particular you'd like her to include, just let me or Debra know
and we'll add it to the order."

Shelby raised her hand. "Wait. What's this about
clothes?" She shook her head. "I don't need clothes. I
have my own."

"Mrs. Winston wanted you to have anything you
might need brought here."

Shelby glanced around at the soft blue-gray painted
walls, the gauzy white curtains and the beautiful
driftwood-style white headboard. The room was too
beautiful. Too pristine. All light and clean. Almost
sterile. Had she traded a dark hell of a prison in a basement for a lighter, beautiful cage so foreign to everything she'd known and grown up with? "I'd rather have
my own clothing. Please thank Mrs. Winston. But as
soon as I can, I'll go get my own."

Maddie smiled and nodded. "I completely understand. I'll have someone sent out to collect whatever
you want from your home."

Shelby bit down on her tongue, wanting to tell the
woman what she thought of someone else digging
through her drawers in her tiny bedroom above the
bar. But to do so would be attacking an older woman
with an open, honest, welcoming face who was only
doing what she was ordered to do.

Shelby squeezed out a smile. "Thank you, Maddie. If you don't mind, I'd like to take a shower."

"Oh, dear. After all you've gone through, you should soak in the whirlpool bathtub." Maddie opened the door to the bathroom and stepped inside with more purpose than Shelby expected from a seventysomething-year-old woman.

Before she could say anything different, the woman had the water running into the tub, bath salts and bubbles sprinkled in the water and towels laid along the polished granite edge.

"Do you need help out of those clothes?" Maddie asked as she advanced toward Shelby.

Shelby backed away. "No, no. I'm quite capable of undressing myself."

A chuckle sounded from behind her. She turned to see where it had come from.

Her grandfather stood beside Daniel, a grin spread across his face.

Daniel's face gave no indication of what he was thinking. But was that a twitch she saw at the corner of his mouth, and were his eyes twinkling? The man's face lit, making her insides flip. He was too good-looking for her own good.

Shelby squared her shoulders. "If everyone doesn't mind, I'd like a little privacy."

"Certainly, Miss O'Hara."

Not at all used to the formality and slightly irritated by it, Shelby insisted, "Please, call me Shelby."

The older woman smiled. "Shelby." Maddie waved Patrick and Daniel toward the door. "Now, you two shoo. Give the girl some space."

Patrick hugged Shelby. "I'm going to take a shower

and then I want to speak with Kate. Don't worry about coming down. Take a nap or a long soak in the bath. After all you've been through, I'm sure it'll feel great."

When she didn't let go right away, he pushed her gently to arm's length. "Don't worry. I'm not going anywhere. I'll be downstairs should you need me for anything."

She let go of her grandfather, not wanting him out of her sight for even a second. "I missed you," she whispered.

He nodded. "I know. And I missed you, too." He turned and left, his eyes suspiciously bright.

Daniel stood inside the room. "I'm not leaving until I check out the room."

Maddie frowned. "Oh, yes. Of course. One cannot be too careful."

Shelby watched as Daniel checked the huge walk-in closet and the bathroom where the water ran in the bathtub and bubbles formed on its surface. Back in the bedroom, he dropped to his haunches and checked beneath the bed.

"Looking for the boogeyman?" Shelby taunted.

He straightened, his broad shoulders making the room seem so much smaller. "It's my job."

A twang of regret tugged at her belly. She was just a job to him. Not that she cared. When she left the Winston Estate, she'd forget about him before she drove off the grounds.

Liar.

How could she forget looking into his face when he'd carried her from the burning home? She'd thought he was her guardian angel.

Now he was just another reminder of the threat to

her and of her need to be aware and ready should someone try to kidnap her again.

"Are you finished?" she asked.

"No." He nodded toward the door on the other side
of her room. "You need to leave that door unlocked."

Shelby frowned. "I would think you'd want me to
lock all doors. Why not this one?" She walked toward
it. "Is it another closet? Because if it is, I don't have
enough shoes in my entire collection to fill it."

She jerked open the door to another bedroom. The
walls were painted a rich cream with white crown
molding. A king-size bed stood on one side of the room
with a simple ebony headboard and matching nightstand. In a corner near a floor-to-ceiling window, a
black lounge chair sat beneath a wrought iron floor
lamp. The artwork on the walls showed black-and-
white images of river and lake scenes.

Shelby frowned and turned back toward Maddie.
"I don't need two rooms, you know. There's only one
of me."

Daniel's lips twitched unmistakably this time.
"That's not another room for you."

"Then who is it for?" Even as she said the words, a
warm shiver rippled across Shelby's body and her pulse
beat a rapid staccato against her eardrums.

Maddie answered, "Mrs. Winston asked Daniel to
move his things from the guest house into the main
house to be closer to you. He'll be staying in the room
adjoining yours."

Shelby's heart flipped and slammed into her ribs.
How could she sleep knowing Daniel would be in the
room next to her? The man exuded testosterone the
way flowers gave off fragrance.

She opened her mouth to protest, but Maddie had turned her back and was headed out the door. "If you'll excuse me, I need to check on supper." Maddie left the room, hurrying down the hallway.

Shelby was left alone with her bodyguard.

Daniel fought the grin threatening to overtake his entire face. He found that he liked tormenting the young woman. The color rising in her cheeks and her flashing blue eyes made him want to grab her and kiss her before she walked away.

Shelby's mouth sagged open and then snapped shut. "I'm sorry, but this arrangement is not acceptable."

"I normally stay in the guest house at night. Mrs. Winston thinks it would be better for me to stay closer, especially since the bombing this afternoon." Daniel crossed his arms over his chest. "Trust me, I'm no happier about the arrangement than you are. I much prefer solving crimes than babysitting spoiled heiresses."

The pink in her cheeks deepened and she glared at him. "I'm not an heiress, and I'm not spoiled."

Daniel raised his eyebrows challengingly without saying a word.

"I'm not." Shelby stamped her foot and stared down at it, her eyes widening. "I'm not," she repeated. This time, she didn't stamp her foot. "I work hard, I support myself financially and I'm trying to further my education so that I can improve my skillset and my life."

With her shoulders thrown back and her chest pushed out, she was a fiery goddess and far too attractive. Straightening his spine, he dismissed her with a soft snort. "Nice speech." He turned away. "There are no monsters under your bed at this time. Please, enjoy your bath." He walked to the connecting door and turned in the threshold. "If you need me, all you have to do is call out my name." His lips quirked up at the corners as he pulled the door closed behind him.

"Jerk," she said to the closed door.

"I heard that," came his muffled response.

"I'd say it to your face," she said, louder.

"I know."

Alone and fuming over the bodyguard's low opinion of her, Shelby considered throwing something at the door. One glance around frustrated her even more. She'd feel guilty if she broke any of the fine porcelain statues or if she ruined the pretty white lacy pillows.

The sound of running water reminded her of the bath. Shelby turned away from the connecting door and hurried to shut off the water before it overflowed the enormous gleaming white bathtub. For the moment, she ignored the bath, stripped out of her clothing and stepped into the granite-lined shower that was big enough for two people.

As soon as that thought crossed her mind, she envisioned a naked Daniel standing beside her under the second showerhead, water running over broad muscles and down tight abs. Her body heated and she switched the handle back toward cold.

What was it about him that made her feel off-balance and out of whack? Then again, everything about her current situation did that. But Daniel's insistence on being close had her more on edge than anything else. She could put up with living in the mansion for the short-term, and even wanted to get to know her uncles. But the bodyguard made her skin twitch and places low in her belly ache for something she had never ached for in the past.

Sure, she'd had her share of experimenting with sex with men her own age, but none of them seemed as raw and dangerous as Daniel.

After she'd cleaned her body with scented soap, she scrubbed her hair with herbal-scented shampoo, applied conditioner, rinsed and climbed out of the shower.

The tub full of water and bubbles called to her, the soft-scented bath salts filling the air with subtle fragrance. What would it hurt to soak for a while? After being tied to a chair for the better part of the past two weeks, stretching out in warm, perfumed water sounded like pure heaven.

Wrapping her hair in a large fluffy towel, she pressed the button on the side of the tub that activated the jets lining the sides. The water roiled, creating more bubbles. Shelby slid into the warm water and stretched her legs along the bottom of the tub, positioning herself in front of strategic jets and redistributing the bubbles to cover herself should anyone walk in uninvited.

Again, her core tightened and throbbed.

If she called out from the bathroom, would Daniel hear her through two doors? Her nipples peaked through the bubbles. Why couldn't she get the man off her mind? Daniel had told her he wasn't thrilled with his assignment. He obviously wasn't interested in her or the fact that she was naked in the room beside his.

Shelby lay still, letting the jets and warm water do their thing to relax her and let the soreness of two weeks of captivity leach from her muscles. With her eyes closed, she pushed all thoughts out of her head except for the amazing way her body felt. She leaned back and let go of a long sigh.

Moments later, sleep claimed her and she slipped into the nightmare.

She was back in the parking lot at the college, juggling her books to get her key out. Dark figures floated out of the trees and surrounded her, shoving her into the dark interior of a van.

A hand clamped over her mouth, stifling her scream. She struggled, but couldn't break the hold on her arms. Shelby kicked out, but only hit air and water.

Her mouth and nose covered by meaty fingers, she couldn't breathe, couldn't get air to her lungs and felt herself blacking out.

A moan rose up her throat. One of the men backhanded her cheek. Another moan escaped and she thrashed, trying to break the hold on her.

Then strong arms scooped her up and carried her away from the van.

She fought the arms, kicking, struggling, desperate to get away and back to her grandfather.

"Shh…it's okay," a deep male voice whispered into her ear. "Open your eyes, Shelby."

"It won't help. It's dark," she muttered.

The arms lowered her into a bed so soft, she felt as if she floated on clouds. It wrapped around her, warming her wet body.

"Shelby, open your eyes." A hand smoothed across her cheek.

She winced, afraid of being hit again. "My eyes are open," she insisted.

"No, they're not," the voice said. A thumb brushed gently across her eyelid. "Look at me."

Shelby blinked, her eyelids fluttering. Light filtered through her lashes as she focused on the face leaning over her. She wasn't in the parking lot of the university, but in a bed. She'd fallen asleep.

A glow from behind illuminated the highlights in his dark blond hair. Moss-green eyes stared down at her and he wore a gentle smile on his face. "See? You're safe. You were having a bad dream."

She leaned her face into his shoulder, breathing in the clean scent of his shirt. Her hands pressed into the solid wall of his chest and she felt safe and protected.

He held her, his warm hand stroking her back, skin against skin. After a while he stiffened and set her away from him. "This isn't a good idea."

Without his warm chest to lean against, a cool air-conditioned breeze brushed across her skin and she glanced down. The remaining fog of sleep whipped away and she pushed to a sitting position. "Holy hell, I'm naked!" She grabbed the comforter and pulled it up over her body. "Explain yourself," she demanded in the commanding tone she only used when she had to evict a rowdy customer from the bar.

The bodyguard chuckled, straightened and stood. "Let's get something straight, little girl—I never explain myself." He trailed a finger along the curve of her shoulder. "You might want to dry off with a towel. And next time you take a bath while recovering from a concussion, don't fall asleep. I'll do my best to protect you from bad guys, but unless you want me to be with you in your bathtub, I can't always protect you from drowning."

* * *

Daniel retreated to his room. As soon as he closed
the door between them, he heard a soft *whomp* against
the door. Probably a thrown pillow. He smiled.

"I'm not a little girl!" she shouted, the sound muffled by the door.

No, she wasn't a little girl. When he'd carried her
wet, sexy body to the bed, he'd been more than aware
of that fact. And he was glad he'd left her mad instead
of terrified, as she'd been when he'd found her, thrash-
ing in the tub, splashing water over the sides, deep in
a nightmare.

She must have been reliving her kidnapping and
captivity. Kept in a basement in the dark for two weeks
had to have played hell with her mind, not knowing
who was holding her, what they had planned for her
or if she'd ever see her family again.

Lucy, Thad's nurse fiancée, had been to his room,
removed the pieces of shrapnel lodged in his back and
applied antiseptic ointment.

He'd just dressed after showering off the stench of
smoke from the day before, when he'd heard her soft
moans. At first, he'd thought the sound was the wind in
the trees. When the moans continued and grew louder,
he'd pushed through the connecting door, afraid she
was under attack again and that he wouldn't get to her
in time to save her.

He'd run into the bathroom and found her caught
in a terrifying dream after having fallen asleep in the
bath. He'd reached in and scooped her out, holding her
naked body against his.

She'd fought, kicking and wiggling, her breasts rubbing against his knuckles, her thighs straining against

his hold, and he'd been so turned on by the sight of her body he could barely walk with her into the bedroom and lay her on the bed.

When he should have set her down and walked away, he couldn't. He'd stayed, holding her, his pants growing tighter by the minute.

Then she'd leaned into his chest, pressing her breasts against his shirt, her fingers curling into the fabric, holding him hostage.

Hell, he'd wanted to strip down and climb onto the bed with her.

Daniel paced the length of his room, his leg aching, the walls seeming to close in around him. He wasn't cut out to be a bodyguard to a woman like Shelby. The Secret Service was his life. He'd been all about the job, training hard, putting his life on the line daily. But this… Being with her constantly would only create more problems. He had to get Kate to see reason, assign someone else. Anyone but him.

His mind made up, Daniel unbuttoned the damp white dress shirt and ripped it from his shoulders, the scent of Shelby still clinging to him. How could he protect a woman he wanted to kiss, hold and make love to? She'd keep him distracted every moment of every day.

He pulled a black polo shirt over his head and tucked it into his pants. Then he marched toward the door and threw it open.

Patrick O'Hara walked toward him, his face drawn and haggard. When he spied Daniel, he smiled. "Mr. Henderson."

"Daniel," he said. "Call me Daniel."

Patrick held out his hand. "I want to thank you again for saving my granddaughter from that burning house."

He shook his head, tears welling in his eyes. "That girl means more to me than anything. I don't know what I would have done if I'd lost her."

Daniel took his hand, prepared to shake it, but was pulled into a firm hug.

"Thank you," Patrick said over his shoulder. "Thank you for everything you've done for her and for taking care of her now."

Guilt rose up in Daniel's chest. "You're welcome, but you don't have to thank me. I'd have done it for anyone in the same situation."

Patrick gripped his arms and held him at arm's length. "But it was Shelby, and for that, I'll be forever in your debt." The older man dropped his hands and stepped back. "I'm sorry, but for two weeks, I thought she was gone for good." He scrubbed his hand through his graying hair. "You've given her back to me." Patrick straightened. "Thank you."

Made uncomfortable by all the emotion in the man's face, Daniel cleared his throat. "If you'll excuse me, I need to check on something." Leaving Shelby's grandfather in the hallway, he hurried down the stairs to the main level and went in search of Kate. She had to find someone else to be Shelby's bodyguard.

His chest tightened when he stepped through the open door of Kate's office.

Kate sat at her desk. Debra sat in a chair to the side with a computer tablet resting on her big belly, writing on it with a stylus.

"I rescheduled your appearance at North Carolina State, apologizing for the inconvenience. They were understanding and concerned about today's bombing."

Kate looked as smooth and together as she normally

did. "I want you to cancel all my meetings for today. I want to spend time getting to know my granddaughter." She glanced up. "Daniel, good. I wanted to speak with you." She turned to Debra. "Do you mind?"

Debra rose with a smile. "I'll go make those calls." She left the room, closing the door behind her.

"Please, Daniel, have a seat."

He crossed the floor, but veered toward the window instead of the chair. "If you don't mind, I'd rather stand."

Kate nodded and pushed back, rising to stand beside him.

For a long moment, neither said a word.

Kate sighed. "It never ceases to amaze me that while our lives are so chaotic and stressful, the world around us continues on. The trees produce leaves, the sun shines and the birds sing." She laid a hand on his arm. "What's troubling you, Daniel?"

"I want you to find another bodyguard for your granddaughter." He hadn't planned on blurting it out like that, but there it was.

Kate's hand dropped to her side and she faced him. "Are you worried you might take another bullet?" She stared at him. "I will understand. You've put yourself on the line for me already and have the injuries to prove it. I know it's wrong of me to ask you to do it again."

Daniel shook his head. "It's not that. I'm not afraid of being shot at."

"Are you afraid you aren't recovered enough to do the job?"

"No." He pushed his hand through his hair. "I'm

not afraid of the job. I just don't think I'm the right man to protect her."

Kate snorted softly. "You're the only man I trust to protect her. You threw yourself in front of a shooter to save my life. Your dedication to duty and your selfless disregard for your own life make you the only person I know of who could protect Shelby the way she needs to be protected." Kate touched his arm again. "Please, Daniel. If she truly is my daughter's daughter, I owe her and her mother, God rest her soul, my promise to protect her."

"Do you have any doubt she's your granddaughter?" Daniel asked, staring down into the bright blue eyes so like Shelby's.

The former vice president's eyes misted. "I thought my daughter was dead. I never would have given her up willingly." She hung her head and turned away, her voice thick. "That was the darkest moment of my life. I didn't want to live."

Daniel's heart squeezed at the raw emotion.

Kate spun back toward him, tears trembling on her lashes. "I'll do anything to protect her. I want her to know how much I loved her mother, how much I could love *her* and how much I want to be a part of her life." She reached out to him, taking his hand. "Daniel, please help me to keep her safe. I've only just found her. I don't want to lose her."

Daniel didn't want to be affected by her plea, but he was. This woman was strong, gutsy and willing to take on any political battle to right a wrong. And when it came to her family, she'd lay down her own life to protect them. She was a real, genuine, good person and it seemed there were too few of those to go around. Especially in the world of politics.

Kate let go of his hand. "Of course, if you feel that strongly, I'll find someone else. But I won't feel as confident that he'll protect her like I know you will."

Daniel turned back to the window. The trees were still green, the sun was shining and nothing out there had changed. As Kate had said, the world would continue on despite their problems.

If he left Kate to find another bodyguard, she'd worry that her granddaughter wouldn't have the protection she needed. Whether or not that was true, Daniel couldn't disappoint Kate. And now that he'd saved her from a burning building and possibly from drowning in her bath, he had a responsibility to keep Shelby alive.

Would he trust someone else to be there when she needed him? And the thought of another bodyguard rushing in to save her when she lay naked in a bath didn't sit right with him.

"Daniel?"

He drew in a deep breath and turned. "Don't worry. I'll do the job."

Chapter 6

Shelby dressed in the same outfit she'd worn from the hospital, provided by her grandmother. The feel of luxurious cashmere beat the heck out of the blouse she'd worn for two weeks straight, but it still made her uncomfortable, knowing someone else had purchased the garments for her.

She was not a charity case, and she refused to be treated as such. More determined than ever to reclaim the life that had been interrupted so brutally, Shelby stepped out of the room and went in search of her grandfather.

She knocked on the door across the hall. After a moment, when there was no answer, she turned toward the staircase.

Before she took one step, a low sexy voice asked, "Going somewhere?"

Shelby gasped as a shadow detached itself from the wall beside the staircase and Daniel stepped into the light.

"Don't do that," she exclaimed, pressing a hand to her racing heart.

He spread his arms wide, all innocence. "Do what?"

"Scare me like that." She braced herself as she faced the man who'd upended her self-control and left her head spinning and desire rising like molten lava through the vent of a volcano. Heat rose up her cheeks as she recalled his hand stroking along her naked back and clamped around her rib cage and thighs as he'd carried her to her bed. The man had seen more of her than a bodyguard should ever see, and it made her hot all over knowing it. Why did he have to be so darned handsome and aggravating at the same time?

She pushed past him and marched toward the stairs. "I'm looking for my grandfather."

"He was headed into Mrs. Winston's office a moment ago. I'm sure he's still there. Is there something I can help you with?"

"No. I'm quite capable of helping myself."

"Good enough." He fell in step behind her.

She could feel the heat of his gaze burning into the back of her neck. Halfway down the stairs, she stopped and turned. "Do you have to follow me everywhere?"

"Yup," he said with too much cheer in his voice. "It's my job."

"Really? Inside this big ol' house I would think I'd be safe enough to walk around on my own."

"As you mentioned, it's a big house. I have to stay with you, just in case."

Shelby blew a sharp burst of air through her nose

like a bull in a fighting ring. "Are you always this irritating?"

"No." He grinned. "Sometimes I can be even more
irritating…when I try."

She turned and walked two more steps down.

He followed.

She stopped, then he stopped.

Giving up, she hurried down the steps. When she
reached the bottom, she heard voices coming from one
side of the open entryway. One of them sounded like
her grandfather. She headed that direction, slowing
when she came close to the half-closed door.

Shelby paused, her hand reaching out but not pushing the door open.

"I told you, I didn't know our daughter was alive,"
Kate Winston was saying. "If I had known, I'd have
gone after her. I loved her, and I was devastated when
I was told she'd died."

"So devastated you didn't bother to verify that she
really was dead?" Her grandfather sounded angry, disappointed and sad.

Shelby wanted to go to him and wrap her arms
around him. The man had given her so much love and
understanding all her life. She loved him so much and
couldn't stand to see him sad or angry.

Shelby started to open the door when Kate's voice
said softly, "My mother told me she'd died when she
was born. I had no reason to think she'd lie. Whatever
you might think, my mother loved me."

"You didn't bother to see the body for yourself?"

"I was in no condition to. I was heartbroken. After
carrying her for nine months, to lose her like that…

The doctors gave me a sedative. I don't remember much of anything the first week after she...was born."

"I find it very hard to believe."

"Believe what you want," Kate said, her voice growing more firm. "The fact is, I didn't get the chance to know my daughter and I'd give anything to have had that time with her. Now that I've found Shelby, I won't give up the chance to get to know my granddaughter."

"And you'll have time in your busy political schedule to get to know her? Rumor has it you are being groomed to run for president."

"It's true. But my family is more important than anything else. That includes Shelby."

"What if she doesn't want to get to know you?" her grandfather asked.

"Whatever our differences, I hope you will give her the choice."

"Shelby has a mind of her own. It will be up to her. I trust you will abide by her wishes."

Kate hesitated, then answered softly, "I will."

"You're eavesdropping." Daniel's warm breath stirred the hairs along the side of Shelby's neck.

A delicious shiver rippled down her spine and she squeezed her eyes shut. Then she stiffened her back, opened her eyes and knocked on the door.

"Come in," Kate called.

Shelby pushed the door open and entered.

Shelby's grandfather stood in the middle of the room. Kate stood behind her desk, as if using it as a shield. The air sizzled with their energy.

"Ah, Shelby, we were just discussing you." Kate rounded the desk and crossed to her, holding out her hands. "Are you feeling better? I can have a doctor stop by and check you over, if you'd like."

Shelby ignored the woman's outstretched hands. "I don't need a doctor."

Kate's arms fell to her sides and she smiled, though the effort looked forced. "I had Debra order clothes for you, but Maddie said you refused and wanted me to cancel. Is something wrong?"

"Yes. I'm not used to people ordering for me, doing things for me or otherwise running my life."

"I'm sorry, darling. I just wanted you to feel welcome and comfortable after what you've been through." Kate turned to Shelby's grandfather. "I can't imagine what you *both* went through."

Shelby closed her eyes and opened them again when they reminded her of being in the dark for so long. "I'm not fragile and I'm not going to fall apart, so, please, don't treat me like I will. I want to put it behind me and get on with my life."

"Of course." Kate's smile grew, becoming more natural. "Your grandfather was telling me you had a mind of your own. You remind me of him when he was eighteen." Her gaze softened and she cast a glance at Patrick. He didn't look away, their gazes seeming to connect as if with a shared memory. For a moment, they both appeared much younger than they were. It struck a chord in Shelby. Could it be there was still a spark left between them after forty years?

Pushing the thought aside, Shelby said, "I'd like to get back into my life, starting today."

Kate's brows rose. "So soon?"

Shelby's grandfather stepped forward. "Don't you want to take another day to recuperate?"

Shelby shook her head. "I can't sit around and do nothing. I'm two weeks behind in my schoolwork and I need to talk with my instructors to see what I can do to catch up."

"I know how important school is to you, Shelby." Her grandfather touched her arm. "But you've been through a lot."

Shelby held up her hand. "Enough. If one more person says I've been through a lot, I'll explode. The only way I can put this all behind me is to move forward, get back into my life and live it." She glanced at her grandfather. "You know me. I'm no good at sitting around."

Her grandfather smiled. "No, you're not."

"I need my books, class notes, assignments and my own clothes."

"I'll have someone sent out right away," Kate said.

"No. I'm going myself. I need to check on my car and talk to my instructors. If I hurry, I might catch them before they leave for the day."

"But is it safe for you to go?" Kate looked to Daniel.

His lips pressed into a straight line. "I can be with her every step of the way."

"You can take one of the cars," Kate offered.

Shelby put her foot down, determined to do it her way. "No, I won't be chauffeured around in a limousine."

"I need to go out to the bar and check on things there," Patrick said. "We can go in my vehicle."

"How long will you be staying?" Daniel asked.

Patrick scratched his chin. "I'm not sure."

"Then I'll take her in my vehicle. She needs to be at the Winston Estate at night. The security is tighter here."

Patrick nodded. "Fair enough." He stared at Shelby. "Do you want me to follow you to the university?"

"No, Granddad. I'll be fine with Daniel." Much as she hated admitting it, she felt protected with her bodyguard around. "You need to check on things back home."

His bar was his livelihood. He needed to be there to manage and keep it running as smoothly as possible. Shelby wondered how much time he'd spent away from it while she'd been missing. Probably more than the staff could handle on their own.

As if reading her mind, her grandfather reassured her, "The staff has been taking care of things fine without me, but I want to make sure they don't need any more supplies."

"Go on." She squeezed his hand. "I'll be okay."

Her grandfather hugged her. "Don't go disappearing on me again. I can't lose you twice. My old heart can't go through that again."

"Like you're old." Shelby snorted. "You were a kid when my mother was born, and my mother was a kid when I was born. That makes you pretty young for a grandfather."

And Kate Winston looked too young to be a grandmother. Perhaps if she'd been old and gray, Shelby would have been more accepting of her. But she was too darned young and looked every bit the formidable political candidate.

Before she'd learned Mrs. Winston was her grandmother, she'd admired her as the former vice president and had hoped she'd run for president. Now...

Shelby sighed. She had a hard time believing the woman hadn't known her daughter was alive. What mother didn't go to her daughter's funeral or ask to see her daughter, even if she was dead?

The jury was still out on Grandma Winston. The thought of calling her Grandma nearly made Shelby laugh out loud at the absurdity. "Come on. It's quite a way to go to get to Beth City and I want to get there before all the professors go home."

Daniel frowned. "Beth City?"

"You didn't think I was going to school here in Raleigh, did you?" She smiled at his disapproval. "I live on the Outer Banks. Beth City was the nearest school with the master's program I needed."

"Do be careful," Kate said. "We still don't know who is responsible for taking you in the first place."

"That's why we'll be taking the big guns, right?" Shelby rolled her eyes toward Daniel and then relented. "I'll be okay. It's broad daylight. I was abducted after dark in an empty parking lot. There will be students and faculty still milling about. If we get there before they all leave." She headed for the door. "Come on, Granddad. Mr. Henderson and I will walk you to your truck."

"I don't know. I think I'd like it better if you stayed here and let someone else do your running around for you," her grandfather said, second-guessing himself.

Shelby stopped in the middle of the room and propped her hands on her hips. "Let's all get one thing straight." Her gaze moved from one person to the next. "I did not escape one prison to be trapped in another. This estate is pretty and tastefully decorated, but if I can't come and go, I might as well be in that basement in the dark, tied to a chair." Her body shook with the force of a harsh tremor. "I can't live like that."

"But—" her grandfather started.

"Patrick," Kate cut in. "Let her go. Daniel will take good care of her."

Her grandfather glared at Kate. "You have three sons. Shelby is my only family. If I lose her…"

Shelby's eyes stung at the anguish in her grandfather's voice. She went to him and hugged him close. "You're not going to lose me. I promise." She turned back to Daniel. "And so does Daniel."

Daniel's brows furrowed and he stood tense, his hands balling into fists.

"Don't you?" Shelby pleaded with her eyes.

Finally he relaxed his hands and he nodded. "I'll do the best I can to keep her out of trouble."

Shelby's grandfather laughed. "You'll have your hands full. That girl is as sweet as they come, but trouble seems to follow her wherever she goes." He kissed Shelby's forehead. "Okay, then. Go to school, though what good it will do you at the bar, I don't know."

"Granddad, you were the one who told me a good bartender is an underpaid psychiatrist."

"Yeah, and you don't have to have a fancy degree to be a bartender."

"I know, but the bar might not always be there. I have to be able to support myself." She narrowed her eyes at him. "And you were the one who told me to get a degree."

"You'd have done it without me telling you to. Besides, you already have one."

"I could never have done it without your love and support and the tip money I make at O'Hara's. But a psychology degree won't buy me much. I have to go further and get my master's."

"I know. I know. I just like to yank your chain." Her grandfather smiled.

Maddie poked her head in the office door. "Mr. Kincannon is here to see you, Kate."

"Send him in, please," Kate said.

A tall brown-haired man with tinges of gray entered. "Ah, I see the young Ms. O'Hara is getting around. I trust you didn't receive any injuries from the explosion earlier?"

Shelby frowned at the man. "No, I did not." Her eyes narrowed. "Should I know you?"

Daniel stepped forward. "This is my boss, Jed Kincannon, director of the Secret Service."

The older man held out his hand.

Shelby took the hand, but she didn't get a good feeling when she shook it. She wondered how long it would be before she trusted a stranger again.

"Jed, do you have anything to tell me about the men who abducted my granddaughter?" Kate asked.

"Nothing yet," he replied.

"I have the feeling this is Cartel related. They use dirty tactics like this." She gave the man a direct stare. "Don't you have any undercover agents who have infiltrated the Cartel?"

"We don't have any leads at this moment."

"Nothing? Not even a motive? Why would someone want to hurt my granddaughter? Who would have dug deep enough to learn something even I didn't know?"

"I don't know." Kincannon shook his head. "And we have nothing."

"What about Richard Nelson?" Kate asked.

The director tilted his head. "What about him?"

"He's made several statements about eliminating the

opposition. I'm his competition in his campaign to secure the party nomination for the presidential election."

Kincannon seemed to consider her words. "That's a possibility. He wants to position."

"We've had this discussion before. I've toyed with the idea of backing out of the race, but I haven't made up my mind. And I don't want word of my decision, or indecision, to leave this room, is that understood?"

Shelby could see how the woman had built her reputation as a strong political candidate and opponent. She didn't mince words and she thought through everything.

Kincannon nodded. "My lips are sealed."

"As are mine," Daniel said.

Shelby almost smiled.

Kate didn't mess around. She demanded loyalty from the people around her, and they seemed willing and almost happy to give it to her.

Kate turned to Patrick and Shelby. "If someone is after me and my family because of my run for president of the United States, can you imagine if I were to actually go through with it?"

She shook her head. "Sometimes I wish I was that eighteen-year-old girl back on the Outer Banks. Before I was forced to marry the man my father chose for me, before I entered politics. My family wouldn't be under attack and I wouldn't have to worry about having a target painted on my back every time I step out my front door."

Patrick stared at her. "It was the life you chose."

Kate nodded. "Not really, but that's water under the bridge." She turned to Kincannon. "I've asked Daniel to provide for Shelby's security."

"What about you?" Kincannon asked.

"If this is an attack on my family because of my former position or my current politics, I want my family protected. After D'Angelis turned, Daniel's the only man from your agency I trust at this time."

"I have more trustworthy agents. Let me assign one to Ms. O'Hara."

Kate's lips pursed. "No. I want Daniel."

Kincannon stared from Kate to Daniel. "You're on board with the change in assignment?"

Daniel nodded.

A little thrill rippled through Shelby. Watching Kate Winston in action gave her a strange sense of pride. And then for Daniel to agree that he was okay with taking on the responsibility of being her bodyguard…

It shouldn't have given her that rush of heat through her body. But it did, and she couldn't fight what she couldn't control. "If you all have finished deciding what's best for me, I'd like to get out of here."

Kincannon frowned. "Where's she going?"

"To gather her school assignments and clothes," Kate said. "Then she's coming back to stay here with us until we get this figured out."

Kincannon seemed to digest that. "Okay, then. Daniel's on it. Do you want me to assign another bodyguard to you, Kate?"

"I'll hire my own, thank you." Kate faced Shelby. "I'll see you back here later tonight?"

"Yes, ma'am." Shelby turned and left before they started talking about her again as if she wasn't in the same room with them. As she left the front door of the mansion to climb into Daniel's SUV, she was struck again by how bright the sun shone and how green and colorful everything was. Being in the dark so long was like being blind. When she could finally see again, she couldn't seem to get enough.

Locked inside a mansion, no matter how beautiful, was not where she wanted to be. If Daniel was going to be her bodyguard, he'd have to get used to following her around or be left behind.

Daniel drove the SUV down the driveway and out onto the highway heading toward Beth City, wondering what the hell he'd done by agreeing to watch over the independent, young Shelby O'Hara. He'd have his hands full keeping up with her.

"I'll take you to the university and then we head back to the Winston Estate."

"What if I'm not ready to go straight back?" she countered.

"I want to be back by dark. It's hard enough watching out for bad guys in the daylight."

He noted Shelby didn't agree or disagree with his idea of heading right back to the estate where he could keep her in a defined area that was rigged with security cameras.

Out in the open, he had no way of knowing who might hit and when. His hands gripped the steering wheel as he navigated Raleigh traffic and finally made it out to the highway leading east to Beth City. He checked his rearview mirror periodically to make certain they weren't being followed. So far, so good.

Shelby pressed a button and lowered the window, letting the breeze blow through the car. She leaned her head toward the wind, her dark hair flying out behind her, her blue eyes gleaming in the sunlight.

Daniel could imagine Kate looking like this when she'd been the same age. He could see why the young Patrick O'Hara had fallen for her. Too bad their affair had gone so wrong. Both had been too young, too impetuous.

He'd seen the anguish in Kate's eyes when she'd learned her daughter hadn't died, but had lived to die before she got to meet her. No one could fake that. To have missed knowing your child, missed watching her grow up, her first steps, her first day at school, her first crush on a boy...

Daniel's mother had celebrated all his and his siblings' firsts, loving every minute of their lives and loving them unconditionally.

Had Kate's mother been that cruel, to tell her that her child had died? Why would she do that?

"Do you mind if I play some music?" Shelby asked.

Daniel shook his head. "Have at it."

She fiddled with the tuner until she found an oldies station.

"Really?" Daniel laughed. "I'd have pegged you for pop/rock."

She shook her head and smiled. "I live on a beach. This is my comfort music. It reminds me of home."

He could relate. His family home was on a beach much farther north and rockier than those found on the Outer Banks of North Carolina, but still, the music reminded him of home, as well.

"It was so dark and quiet where I was, all I had were the songs I remembered to keep me company." She glanced out the window, her mouth turning down, her eyes darkening. "I only sang the happy ones."

His chest tightened, imagining her tied up in a basement, alone and scared. His fists curled around the steering wheel. He wanted to be on the investigation team searching for the bastards who'd kidnapped her. When he found them, he'd be hard-pressed to control his anger and resist the desire to kill them for what they'd done.

"Are you angry at me?" Shelby asked.

Daniel glanced her way, shaking out of his thoughts. "No, why?"

"You looked like you wanted to kill someone."

"I was thinking about the men who kidnapped you."

"And you want to kill them?"

"Yes," he said through gritted teeth.

"What good would that do?"

"They'd be off the street and unable to hurt anyone else, for one."

She stared at him a moment, then said, "Despite what they did to me, I don't wish them dead."

"You're much nicer than I am."

Shelby sat back in her seat and gazed out the window at the road in front of them. "I'd want to know why they kidnapped me."

"You're related to a very influential and wealthy woman."

"But that's her. I'm not influential or wealthy."

"Yeah, but she's known for taking care of her family."

"Who would have known I was her granddaughter?" She laughed humorlessly. "*I* didn't know I was her granddaughter. I still find it hard to believe. Did they demand a ransom?"

"No." Daniel shook his head. "That's what has us

all stumped. They never demanded anything. Did your captors say anything to you?"

"Not a word. It was as if I was a dog at the pound, to be fed and locked up until it was time to euthanize me." She sighed. "Well, that was one of the thoughts I had at the time."

"Not a particularly good one."

"I know. Thus the beach songs."

"You were lying on the floor in the kitchen when I found you. How did you get there?"

She straightened, her lips curling. "I broke a brace off my chair and used it to break the zip tie binding my wrists." She glanced down as she rubbed the sores there. "I would have made it out if I'd run a little faster. But after sitting still for so long, my legs weren't cooperating." She smiled. "But I kicked one of my captors in the face and hit the other with a heavy flashlight."

Daniel's stomach tensed. She'd been kept in the dark both physically and mentally. It had to have been tough. But she'd been tougher. To have the inner strength to figure a way out of her predicament was a testament to her resilience.

Shelby wasn't what he'd thought the granddaughter of Kate Winston would be like. But then she'd been raised by her grandfather and thus she was much more down-to-earth. He found himself drawn even more to her, and not just because of her physical attributes—all of which he'd seen and admired, and many of which he'd touched and wouldn't mind touching again.

Shelby's head swiveled as they passed a road. "That was our turn."

Damn. He'd missed his turn off the highway just thinking about her. Being a bodyguard to Shelby was a mistake when all he could think about was getting his hands back on her delectable body.

Once again, he wondered why he'd agreed to continue on as her bodyguard. To be a good bodyguard, he needed to be impartial, focused and free of distraction. Shelby O'Hara had distraction in every ounce of her gorgeous body.

Chapter 7

Shelby sat on the other side of the SUV, her mind on the man driving instead of the assignments and classes she'd missed. When she should have been planning ahead on the catch-up work she'd have to hustle to complete, she was thinking about how thick Daniel's thighs were and wondering what they looked like beneath the denim of his jeans.

Hell, he'd seen her naked. She ought to have the same privilege. Not that she should be thinking about him that way at all, but she couldn't help it.

Her core heated and she squirmed in her seat, inches away from his big hands gripping the steering wheel. The same hands that had carried her from the bath to her bed, naked.

"So how did you become a bodyguard?"

"I work for the Secret Service. I was detailed out

to provide protection to former vice president Kate Winston."

"Secret Service. Sounds impressive." She tapped her fingers on the armrest. "And interesting. Are all Secret Service agents glorified bodyguards?"

His jaw tightened and his fingers curled around the steering wheel turned white around the knuckles.

She must have bruised his ego. She smiled inwardly, glad she'd gotten beneath his skin.

"Some of us work on investigations into threats against the president and vice president."

"Why aren't you working on the investigation? Did you make someone mad?"

His fingers loosened and he sighed. "I was injured when someone shot at Mrs. Winston. I've been sidelined from the investigation."

"You were injured? Is that why you limp?" Now she felt bad for poking fun at the man.

He nodded. "I took the bullets meant to kill your grandmother."

Shelby sat for a moment in silence, the full extent of what he was saying hitting hard. "Who would have it in for her and why?"

"If we had the answers, wouldn't we have caught him by now?"

"I suppose." She glanced out the window as they passed houses and businesses. "I don't understand why people have to be so callous and angry all the time."

"Being a part of the Winston family, with all their wealth and property, has its perks."

"And apparently its price." Shelby pushed a hand through her hair and stared forward. "I didn't ask for it."

"No, you didn't. But you can't deny it. You look just

like a younger version of Kate. Anyone with a pair of eyes could see it."

As they drove onto the university campus, Shelby stared at her reflection in the side mirror. She did look a little like her grandmother and a lot like the pictures of the younger Kate Winston.

Campus looked the same as it did the day she'd entered the library to research information for her paper. The sun was just as bright, the trees weren't much different and the buildings were all still there.

The only thing that had changed was her. Two weeks ago, the most important thing in her life was getting a good education.

Her grandfather had done everything in his power to give her all the opportunities to improve her life. Despite his argument earlier that day about not needing an education to be a bartender, he'd been the first one to kick her butt and remind her of how important it was to get a degree that would provide a livable income. He'd drilled it into her head that she had to be able to support herself and anyone else who might come along. That *anyone else* being any children she might bring into the world.

Her grandfather worried that she wouldn't be able to support herself when he was gone. He'd admitted he'd spoiled her mother and she'd been less than responsible when she'd been growing up, as evidenced by her pregnancy at age eighteen.

He'd raised Shelby to be more responsible. She'd helped out at the grill from a young age, earning her own spending money. Nothing was free in life, he'd told her. And she alone was responsible for her own actions.

She didn't mind working, and she loved her grandfather more than anyone in the world because deep inside she knew he loved her, too. And she'd almost lost him. Or rather, they'd almost lost each other. With her life back in her own hands, she vowed never to be so vulnerable again.

She pointed to a brick structure, "Pull up beside that building. I'll just run in and see if my professor is there."

When she reached for the door handle, his hand snaked out and grabbed her arm. "*We* will go inside the building together."

His unrelenting grip on her arm left her no choice.

"Seriously? Look around you. There are students everywhere, and faculty and staff. I can make it to my professor's office and back with no problem."

"If it's all the same to you, I'd rather go with you."

"It's not all the same to me. I don't need a bodyguard to lead me around on a leash." Shelby yanked her arm free and pushed the door open, jumping out. She set off at a good pace, hoping to reach the building and duck inside before he could catch up.

She hadn't gone five steps before Daniel was out of the car and at her side, matching her pace. Students passed on each side of her.

Each time one walked by, Daniel glared and moved closer to Shelby.

Finally Shelby stopped and faced him. "You can't do this. You're scaring the other students."

"Do you realize how close they are getting? Anyone that close could jam a knife into you and you wouldn't see it coming."

"They're students, damn it, not terrorists." Shelby

stomped away from him and pushed through the door into the building.

Once inside, she mounted the stairs in the stairwell to the third floor and hurried toward her professor's office.

Daniel dogged her footsteps, never more than a few steps behind, his limp more pronounced after climbing the stairs.

When they reached the office, Shelby faced Daniel. "I'm going inside. Alone."

He frowned. "I'd rather check it out before you go in."

"Too bad. I'll take my chances. You're staying out here."

"But—"

She poked a finger into his chest. "Stay."

His frown deepened. "I'm not a dog."

"I know. A dog would have a much more obedient disposition." Shelby slipped through the wood-paneled door into the professor's office and closed it behind her. She waited on the other side, fully expecting Daniel to jerk the door open and follow her inside. When he didn't, she was almost disappointed, then she shook her head and turned.

The professor wasn't in, but his teaching assistant was.

Shelby wrote down all the assignments and promised the assistant she'd email the professor with her excuse.

She was sure most professors had heard every excuse in the books, but being kidnapped and held for two weeks had to be new, ranking right up there with being taken by aliens. And they might not believe her, since Kate's team had kept the abduction below the radar from news and media sources.

Once she had a list of the assigned work, she braced herself for her next encounter with Daniel.

When she stepped out into the hallway, Daniel stood surrounded by several young, college coeds. And the jerk was smiling at them.

One batted her eyes and took his hand, penning her phone number on his palm. When she'd replaced her pen in her purse, she lifted her thumb to her ear and her pinky to her mouth and mouthed the words *call me*.

Shelby's fingers curled into tight fists, her fingernails digging into her skin. She walked away without looking back. It wasn't as if he was her boyfriend. She was the job to him.

So what if he'd seen her naked? As a Secret Service agent he'd probably seen lots of naked women. A girl on every job, like James Bond.

She heard him behind her say, "Sorry, ladies, I have to go."

He had a job to do.

Her.

Shelby's teeth ground together. As she passed the elevator the doors were closing. She ducked in before they closed all the way. Daniel ran the last couple steps, but didn't make it in time to jam his hand between the doors and stop its progress.

Thankfully, the elevator was going down. But it stopped at the second floor. Damn.

If she gauged it right, Daniel would assume she would get off on the ground floor. What he didn't realize was that there was a walkway across to the next building on campus from the second floor. And the entrances to that building led to the parking lot where she'd left her car.

Her grandfather had left it there, more worried about her return than bringing her car home. She kept a spare key in a magnetic box on the undercarriage of the vehicle. If she could get there before Daniel, she would take herself to the Outer Banks and collect her own clothing. Maybe she could help her grandfather out for a few hours at O'Hara's Bar and Grill.

She stepped off the elevator and crossed the glassed-in walkway to the next building and took the stairs to the exit, all the while glancing over her shoulder for Daniel. Once outside the building, she hurried toward her car, sitting where it had been the night she'd been attacked.

The closer she got to the car, the faster her heart beat. She told herself there was nothing to worry about. The sun shone down on her, there were other people in the parking lot and she wasn't a lone student asking to be abducted in an empty parking lot.

A white SUV backed out of a parking space, blocking her path to her car.

Shelby stopped and waited for the vehicle to move on.

The longer it took to complete the reverse, the more impatient she became. She glanced behind her, worried Daniel would figure it out and come after her before she reached her car.

The SUV turned, still backing toward her. Then when the driver should have shifted into drive, it continued backward, sliding up alongside the position where Shelby stood.

A door swung open.

Something clicked inside her, her heart rate sky-rocketed and her senses jumped to full alert. Shelby backed up a step, turned and ran, daring only one glance over her shoulder.

A man in a black ski mask leaped out of the vehicle and gave chase.

Heart racing, she ran for her life, the nightmare happening all over again. "Help!" she cried.

Students stopped and stared, too shocked by what was happening to be of any use.

"Help!" Shelby cried, adrenaline the only fuel powering her legs. She refused to be caught; she couldn't go back to a dark cellar where all she'd had were her thoughts to keep her from going insane.

She ran around a vehicle and headed for the building she'd just exited. Pushing through the glass doorway, she ran into a solid wall of muscle.

Shelby screamed and fought, every instinct geared for survival.

"Shelby, it's me!" Daniel yelled. "Stop fighting."

When she realized it was Daniel, she fell against him, wrapping her arms around his waist. "Don't let them take me."

"Shh…it's okay." His arms circled her, drawing her close. His hands ran down her back, stroking her to calm. "Now, tell me what you're talking about." He pushed her to arm's length and stared into her face.

"A man in a ski mask." She pointed toward the door as the white SUV raced past. "He came out of that SUV."

Daniel shoved her to the side and sprinted out the door. Shelby followed behind him, refusing to let him out of her sight.

He didn't go far before he stopped. "Damn. No license plate." Daniel pulled his cell phone out of his pocket and hit one of his contact numbers. "Why the hell did you run from me?" He glared at her as he put the phone to his ear. "How can I protect you if you don't cooperate?"

"I didn't think it would happen in broad daylight." Shelby stood like a recalcitrant child, her head hanging low. "Why is this happening to me?"

He shook his head, the anger melting from his face. He gathered her against him with one arm, while he held the phone to his ear. "Do us both a favor and don't run from me. I might not find you in time if it happens again."

Shelby nodded, thankful for his arm around her and completely terrified by the thought that it *could* happen.

Again.

When Jed Kincannon picked up on the other end, Daniel didn't waste time on pleasantries. "Henderson here. There's been another attempt to kidnap Kate Winston's granddaughter." He gave the details and a description of the white SUV. "It didn't have a license plate."

"I'll get on the horn with the local police immediately. Stay with the girl," Kincannon said. "You're headed back to the Winston Estate?"

He could feel Shelby trembling against him and his arm tightened around her. "Yes, sir." Damn right he was taking her back where there were pretty stiff security measures in place, and not only would it be difficult for someone to get in, it would be almost impossible for someone to leave unnoticed.

"Good," Kincannon said. "Keep her there as much as possible."

Daniel wanted to laugh at the man. That would be like caging a wild cat. She'd eventually find her way out and he'd be running to keep up with her. His bum knee throbbed in anticipation. Daniel clicked the off button and pocketed the phone. "Come on. We should be getting back to the estate."

"I'm not going back," she said into his shirt, the tremors subsiding. She pushed back and stared up into his eyes. "I'm going home."

"Like hell you are. It's not safe."

Her lips pressed into a thin line. "I'm going home to get my own clothes. Then you can take me back to the Winston Estate."

He didn't like the idea of driving all the way over to the Outer Banks. It would take a couple of hours to get there from where they were and even longer to get back to Raleigh. "It'll put us getting back after dark."

"I'm not going back without my own clothes. I'll take my own car if I have to."

Anger and frustration mixed and boiled over. "You were almost kidnapped again. Don't you get it?"

She stared up at him. "Yes, I get it. I was stupid to run away from you."

"Then why did you do it?"

She looked away. "You're pushy, and I'm not used to someone telling me what to do and following me around like I'm a child to be coddled."

"Then stop acting like a child." He gripped her chin in his fingers and tipped her head up. "I can't help you if you don't let me." With her face turned up to him and her lips only inches from his, he realized his error too late. All the anger at having been duped, followed by the surge of emotion he'd experienced when he'd seen her running toward him with fear and desperation in her eyes welled up in him and he took it out on her. He pressed his lips to hers in a searing kiss, one that took his breath away and left him dizzy with the intensity.

When he broke away, he whispered against her lips, "Don't run from me."

She braced her hands on his chest, curling her fingers into his shirt, clinging to him.

"Promise." His hands slid over her shoulders to grip her arms. "Promise you won't run from me," he said through gritted teeth.

"I promise," she whispered. Then her hands circled the back of his neck, bringing his lips back to hers. She gave as good as she got, her tongue pushing past his lips to take his in a long, slow glide. Her hips pressed against his as she moved closer, her calf curling around the back of his leg.

They could have been anywhere, but he felt as though they were alone on a deserted island, only him and Shelby.

A horn honked, shaking him out of the dream he'd been in, waking him to reality. They were standing in a parking lot. People were moving around them and anyone could have run them over and they would never have seen it coming.

"Come on." He grabbed her hand and dragged her back to the other building's parking lot.

She ran to keep up, her fingers wrapped in his. When they reached his SUV, he gave it a quick once-over, checking for bombs, before he allowed her to get in. Given her track record, a bomb could happen again, just like a kidnapping had almost succeeded.

He shivered at the thought. Even more than his promise to Patrick to keep her safe, he couldn't live with himself if he lost her.

"Where are we going?" she asked as she buckled her seat belt across her lap and settled back against the leather seats.

He shifted into Reverse, backed out of the parking space and drove toward the exit, his focus on the road, the vehicles around him and everything else but that kiss. "We're going to the Outer Banks, damn it."

Ah, who was he kidding? He couldn't think of anything *but* the kiss.

Chapter 8

Shelby leaned forward as they crossed the Washington Baum Bridge onto the strip of land known as the Outer Banks. With her window lowered, she breathed in the salty tang of the air, her chest swelling with love for the island, love for the long stretches of beach and this crazy touristy piece of heaven.

The sun was low in the western sky, making the sky orange and the water glisten like a thousand black, sparkling diamonds.

"I love this place," she said out loud, not expecting any response from Daniel. "It's home to me."

Daniel had driven all the way from the university without uttering a single word.

Shelby had been hesitant to break the silence, figuring he was still mad about her attempt to escape him. She wanted to be mad back. After all, she was more or less on a short leash with the bodyguard, unable to take a step without his approval or clearance.

Mad as she should have been, she couldn't wipe that kiss out of her mind. When she'd been thinking about him naked, she hadn't imagined how just a kiss would fry every brain cell in her head and leave her lips tingling for the next hour. Hell, they still tingled.

Sure, she'd dated guys, had sex with a couple of them, but none of them had kissed her like that and left her wanting so much more.

She sat as far away from him as possible in the confines of his SUV, running her tongue over her lips, tasting him there, and as she wondered what had triggered the kiss, one thing became perfectly clear. As much as she'd been thinking about him, he'd also been thinking about her.

Heat filled her insides, surging into places that shouldn't be feeling warm while stuck in a car with a surly bodyguard for the next few hours.

When they crossed the bridge and she could see the Atlantic Ocean ahead, she felt a sense of relief, of coming home and excitement.

"There were a couple of times I didn't think I'd see this place again," she said, her fingers gripping the armrest, emotion swelling in her throat.

Daniel glanced her way. "Seems like you did your best to make it happen."

She nodded. "I couldn't give up. I knew my grandfather would be beside himself with worry. If for no other reason, I had to make it back for him." She smiled. "But now that I'm here, I'm glad I made it back for me, too. I love the smell of salt, the beautiful sunrises you can only get here on the edge of the ocean."

Daniel turned south along the long stretch of land that made up the Outer Banks, passing tourist shops, restaurants, hotels, cottages and all the places Shelby knew by heart. She'd ridden her bicycle past them when she was too young to drive and driven past them every day she went to school or on those rare occasions when she went to Raleigh to do some shopping at the big department stores.

She loved this place where people came to relax and vacation away from the stress of the bigger cities.

When she spotted the roofline of O'Hara's Bar and Grill, excitement filled her and she could hardly wait for Daniel to park the SUV before she threw open the door and jumped out.

"Shelby," Daniel said, his voice stern, brooking no argument.

She stopped and waited for him to join her, aware he'd saved her twice in the past two days, and she owed him something for that.

When she stepped into the bar, the waitresses and bus boys stopped what they were doing and rushed over to her, exclaiming and hugging.

"Shelby, oh, dear, sweet Jesus," Lana Innman cried. "We were all so worried about you. You grandfather has been beside himself. How are you? Are you okay?"

Shelby's heart swelled at the welcome and she blinked back ready tears. "I'm fine, just glad to be back."

Marisa Webber joined the group hug. "Patrick said you'd been found, but I couldn't believe it without seeing you with my own eyes." She sniffed and brushed tears from her cheek. "We'd almost given up hope."

"Yes, we had. Almost. But I knew you were tough

and you wouldn't let anyone keep you down long." Lana hugged her again and glanced across at Daniel. "Wow. Who's the hunk?"

Shelby bristled. "This is Daniel. He's my..." she struggled with calling him her bodyguard, not wanting to sound like she was all that important.

"I'm her friend," he finished for her, saving her the embarrassment.

With a grateful smile at him, she repeated, "That's right, he's my friend."

"Just a friend?" Marisa asked. "If that's all, can I have his number?"

Normally Shelby couldn't be mad at Marisa; she flirted with all the male customers. She was kind-hearted and fun loving and didn't have a mean bone in her body. But after Daniel's kiss, Shelby had a hard time taking Marisa's flirting lightly.

Patrick O'Hara came out of the back office, grinning from ear to ear. "I told you she was okay. Now move, so I can get a hug in there."

The staff stepped back and let Patrick in. He engulfed her in a bear hug. "I can't seem to get enough of these." He kissed the top of her head, the way he had when she'd been a little girl. "I'm so glad you're back."

"We only came in to collect her things," Daniel said.

"I'm glad. I was about to go through your bedroom and would probably have gotten the wrong items."

"Don't worry. I'm here now, and I can get what I need." Shelby kissed her grandfather's cheek. "Don't forget you need to be back at the Winston Estate sooner rather than later."

"I will, as soon as I put together the order list for tomorrow."

"Don't take too long." Shelby hugged a couple of the others, then broke free and headed for the back exit and the staircase that led up to their apartment above the bar.

Daniel grabbed her arm before she put her foot on the first step. "Let me go first."

"Fair enough." She handed him her key and followed him up the stairs. "The lock can stick a little. You have to wiggle the door when you put the key in it."

He inserted the key and attempted to twist it in the lock. As she'd predicted, it didn't work.

"Like this," Shelby reached around him and wrapped one hand around his holding the doorknob and the other over his fingers and turned the key, wiggling the handle at the same time.

When she touched him, a jolt of electric awareness burned through her.

As soon as the handle turned and the door opened, she jerked her hands away and moved back. In her hurry, she forgot she was so near to the edge of the landing. She teetered on the steps and nearly fell.

Daniel slipped an arm around her waist and crushed her to his chest. "Steady there," he whispered into her hair, his mouth touching her temple.

Her pulse slammed against her veins, shooting red-hot blood through her body.

Though she'd gotten her feet under her, he didn't let go, holding her longer than was necessary, and she was glad. Had he let go, her knees would have given way and she'd have melted like a puddle of goo at his feet.

"Are you okay?" he asked, his lips brushing against her earlobe.

Hell, no, she wasn't okay. The man made her turn to mush whenever they touched.

Digging deep, she summoned enough willpower to pull herself together and look up at him. "I'm…"

That was her second mistake. In the fading light, she stared into his smoldering green eyes and lost herself all over again. She leaned up on her toes and pressed her lips to his.

He cupped the back of her head and sealed the kiss with one of his own, his mouth consuming her, his tongue thrusting between her teeth to caress hers.

When at last he lifted his head, he dragged in a deep breath and stepped through the door, pulling her behind him. "Wait here," he commanded.

Wait? Her body on fire, she stood rooted to the spot, afraid if she moved, she'd collapse.

In the span of a few minutes, Daniel had searched the entire two-bedroom apartment.

But those few minutes were barely enough for her to come back to earth and get a grip on her rioting emotions.

"Get your things," he said, his voice stern. "We're going back to Raleigh."

She'd been ready to march into her room and do just that, but having him come back at her as though what they'd shared hadn't happened was a slap in the face. Anger rocketed up inside her.

"What just happened here?" she demanded.

His gaze met hers briefly and he looked away. "Nothing."

"Are you telling me that kiss meant nothing?"

He faced her, and for a long moment, he stared down at her, a muscle ticking in his jaw. "Really, Miss

O'Hara, I'm just doing my job." He turned and walked toward the door, where he stopped and glanced down at his watch then back up to her. "Five minutes."

Daniel waited outside the apartment door, sucking in fresh air and sanity. The kiss had rocked him deeply and he had been far too tempted to drag her into the apartment and take it ten steps further. And, damn it, that was the worst thing he could do.

He was on the job, not on vacation. He wasn't supposed to kiss the woman he should be protecting. It violated every ethic in his books. As a bodyguard, he was supposed to remain detached and observant. When he'd kissed Shelby, he'd lost track of everything. If someone had decided to shoot at them, they'd have had plenty of opportunity to kill.

The best way to end this was to make a clean, if ugly, break. Piss her off and she'd never get close enough for him to be tempted to kiss her again.

By the sound of drawers and doors slamming and the curse words coming from inside the apartment, he'd accomplished his mission.

That didn't do anything to lessen his desire for her. He'd have to deal with it. No more kissing the girl.

After five minutes on the nose, she emerged from her bedroom, a duffel bag slung over her shoulder. She breezed past him and clomped down the stairs, her eyes blazing and her back ramrod straight.

Oh, yeah. She was mad. And damn if she wasn't even sexier.

Swallowing a groan, he followed her down the stairs.

A few steps ahead of him, she entered the back door, the spring slamming it shut between them.

He had his hand on the handle to open the door when he heard a piercing scream.

Daniel ripped open the door and ran in. At first, he didn't see Shelby. She couldn't have gotten that far ahead of him. He rounded the corner into the kitchen and found a group of the staff gathered in a tight circle.

Daniel pushed through, zeroing in on Shelby's light brown hair. "Shelby, are you okay?"

She shot him an irritated glance. "I'm fine, but Lana isn't." Shelby held the woman's hands tight, bright red blood dripped from both of them.

Patrick O'Hara hurried through from another door, his face pale, the lines around his eyes and mouth deeper. "Here's the first-aid kit."

"Someone give me the gauze and surgical tape. I can't let up on the pressure until we can apply more."

Lana's face was pale and tears streaked down her cheeks. "I can't believe I was so stupid. I knew there was a broken glass in the dishwater, but I wasn't careful."

"We'll get you fixed up enough to stop the bleeding," Shelby reassured her. "But you're going to need stitches."

Lana swayed. "I'm feeling kind of dizzy."

"Get her a chair."

One of the busboys ran out to the dining area and returned with a chair. Daniel seated Lana, then took the first-aid kit from Patrick. He pulled out a roll of gauze and medical adhesive tape. He made a tight pad of gauze and applied tape on two sides. "Can you stand long enough to dip your hand under clean water?"

Lana nodded. "I think so."

He eased them toward the sink.

Marisa turned on the cold water and Shelby held Lana's hand beneath the steady stream. "I'm going to let go. Look at me, not your hand. I don't want to pick you up off the floor." She smiled. "Come on, Lana, you're tough. You can do this."

"Okay, Shelby, just do it." She stared at Shelby as they pushed her hand beneath the water.

Once Shelby let go, the blood flowed heavily.

Daniel pulled her hand from the water and clamped the wad of gauze over the cut and taped it down. He added another wad of gauze and more tape. "She needs those stitches."

Shelby washed the blood from her hands and found a clean dish towel for Lana to hold under her hand. "We can take her."

"No, let me. As the owner, I should take her." Patrick hooked Lana's arm and guided her toward the exit. He paused and turned back to Shelby. "I just let Kayla go home sick and we have a group scheduled to come in. They're going to be shorthanded."

"I'll stay and help out." Shelby shot a glance at Daniel, daring him to argue.

He washed the blood off his hands, shaking his head. "We're not staying."

"I'm not leaving. Unless you plan to hog-tie me and throw me in the back of your car, I'm not going anywhere."

Marisa whooped. "Yeah, baby. I gotta see this."

Daniel's adrenaline spiked and he fought to control the urge to do just what she'd said. With a deep breath, he resisted and played on her father's fears. "Mr. O'Hara?"

Patrick shook his head. "No, sweetheart, you need to go with Daniel." Her grandfather frowned. "I don't want to leave you, knowing you could disappear again."

"Go, Granddad." Shelby touched his arm and Lana's. "I'm fine, and I'll be here when you get back. Take care of Lana. She needs you now."

Patrick's gaze went to Daniel. "Don't let anything happen to my girl, will ya?"

Short of dragging Shelby out of the bar, Daniel wasn't convincing her to leave until her grandfather returned. Resigning himself to waiting this one out, he nodded at Patrick. "I'll do my best."

The older man's eyes narrowed. "Do better. She's the only family I have left."

"Yes, sir."

"Come on, Lana, let's get you sewn up before you bleed all over the place." He winked at her and led her out of the bar.

Ignoring Daniel, Shelby clapped her hands together. "Come on, people. We have a party arriving in twenty minutes. Let's get this place cleaned up and ready."

The waitresses, busboys and bartender hurried back to their duties. Shelby snagged a mop and a bucket of cleaner and headed for the kitchen.

Daniel followed.

"If you're going to hang around, you might as well help." She shoved the mop into his hands, stepped over the puddle of blood on the floor and, using a strainer, scooped the broken glass out of the sink and deposited it in the trash.

While she cleaned the dishes, Daniel mopped the floor, thinking there was no glory in being a Secret Service agent. Once again, he wondered what he'd been thinking when he'd agreed to be Shelby's bodyguard.

Trouble. With a capital *T.*

As expected, a group of thirty men from a rowing team out of D.C. converged on O'Hara's, shouting, laughing and raising good-natured hell.

Daniel helped by bussing tables while keeping a close eye on Shelby. He studied all the men, searching each face for a clue as to his intention.

Most of them wore polo shirts with their club logo on them. They were healthy, muscular men with innocent faces out to have a good time. For the most part.

Daniel wished Shelby was serving behind the bar. As she wove her way between the tables, any one of the men could attack and he'd be too late to help her.

He tried following her around, but that only made her mad, and she told him to back off.

At one table, she smiled and chatted with several of the rowers while serving fresh drinks and collecting the empties. When she turned back toward the bar, she tripped and would have fallen, but one man reached out and yanked her onto his lap, saving her, but not the contents of her tray.

Bottles and mugs toppled to the floor. Only one broke; the rest remained intact. Rubber tub in hand, Daniel hurried to her side.

"Oops." Shelby laughed. "Thanks for the save, but you can let me up now."

The man who'd pulled her into his lap laughed and refused to let go of her, his buddies egging him on.

Shelby retained her ever-present smile. "You really should let me up." With a glance at Daniel, she looked back at the man. "My boyfriend doesn't like it when other guys touch me."

The man immediately let go. "Sorry, dude. Didn't mean to poach."

Daniel's fingers clenched around the tub he'd been about to throw at the man. He still wanted to throw it, but he held back with a considerable amount of effort.

Shelby's lips twisted into a crooked smile. "See? He gets all hot and bothered when other guys so much as look at me, don't you, baby?" She kissed his cheek and slid a hand along his shoulder as she passed by him.

The guy in chair held up his hands, apparently seeing the danger in Daniel's eyes. "Like I said, man, I didn't know."

After a moment, Daniel shrugged. "No harm, no foul." He bent to clean up the bottles and mugs. When he had the mess cleared, he went to find Shelby.

She wasn't in the bar.

His pulse ratcheting upward, he hurried for the kitchen. Not there either, nor was the cook or anyone else.

The back door stood open as if someone had gone out in a hurry.

Daniel slammed the tub of bottles and mugs on a counter and ran for the back door.

Outside, the cook was tossing a heavy bag of trash into the Dumpster.

"Where's Shelby?" Daniel demanded.

The young man lost control of the bag he'd been hefting up into the trash container and it crashed back behind him, breaking open. "Well, damn." He glared at Daniel over the mess. "Don't sneak up on me like that."

"Shelby? Where is she?"

"How should I know? You're the one who's been following her around all night."

Daniel glanced left then right. Nothing moved in back of the building and there was no sign of Shelby. He ran back into the building and down the hallway toward the bar. A door opened immediately to his right and someone stepped out of the ladies' room and smacked into him. Reaching out, he grabbed the woman to keep her from falling.

His hands wrapped around Shelby's arms. As soon as he realized it was her, he crushed her against his chest. "Where the hell have you been?"

"To the bathroom," she said breezily.

"You just about gave me a freakin' heart attack."

"I didn't go far," she whispered, her mouth close to his, her breath warming his skin.

With her body pressed to his, his adrenaline still running high, he couldn't hold back. "Woman, you're making me crazy." He crushed her lips with his in a brutal kiss. His fingers knotted in her hair and he tugged, tipping her head back more so that he could trail his mouth along her jawline and down the side of her throat to that place where her pulse raced beneath her delicate skin.

Shelby's hands circled the back of his neck, drawing him closer, her calf rising up the side of his leg, curling around. "Missed me, huh?"

Chapter 9

Shelby could have kicked herself.

From hot and fiery to cold and distant, Daniel pushed Shelby away and stepped back. "That shouldn't have happened."

"But it did and you can't take it back." Her lips curled upward in a smirk. "You wanted to kiss me. Admit it."

He stared at her for a long time. Then he pushed his hand through his hair and turned his back to her. "We'd better get back to work."

She grabbed his arm. "Would it hurt so much to admit you find me attractive?"

He whipped around, his eyes blazing. "It wouldn't matter. You're in a different stratosphere entirely. I'm your bodyguard, not your lover. Don't get the two confused."

FREE Merchandise is 'in the Cards' for you!

Dear Reader,

We're giving away FREE MERCHANDISE!

Seriously, we'd like to reward you for reading this novel by giving you **FREE MERCHANDISE** worth over $25. And no purchase is necessary!

You see the Jack of Hearts sticker above? Paste that sticker in the box on the Free Merchandise Voucher inside. Return the Voucher promptly...and we'll send you valuable Free Merchandise!

Thanks again for reading one of our novels—and enjoy your Free Merchandise with our compliments!

Pam Powers

Pam Powers

P.S. Look inside to see what Free Merchandise is **"in the cards"** for you!

FM-SUS-13

We'd like to send you two free books to introduce you to the Suspense Collection. These books are worth over $15, but they are yours to keep absolutely FREE! We'll even send you 2 wonderful surprise gifts. You can't lose!

REMEMBER: Your Free Merchandise, consisting of **2 Free Books** and **2 Free Gifts**, is worth over $25.00! No purchase is necessary, so please send for your Free Merchandise today.

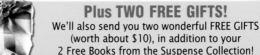

"What do you mean, I'm in a different stratosphere? We're both human. What's so different about you versus me?"

"You're the granddaughter of the former vice president of the United States, for the love of God."

Shelby's eyes widened. "Really? That's what's got your shorts in a twist?" She shook her head. "I'm the granddaughter of a man who owns a bar. I don't live in a mansion, I'm not a debutante with a purse for every outfit and a room full of shoes. I'm Shelby O'Hara."

"And I'm your bodyguard. Nothing else."

"Damn right it's nothing else. And I thought you were down-to-earth and a straight shooter. But I believe you're something of a snob." She pushed past him and marched back into the bar. "Just stay out of my way. I have work to do."

Much as he'd like to stay out of her way, he couldn't. Not when the danger was real. If the first kidnapping hadn't convinced her, the second attempt sure as hell had convinced him.

He spent the rest of the evening jumping at every loud noise, dogging every one of Shelby's footsteps and hating that all the guys in the bar were falling in love with the petite brunette with the perpetual smile for everyone but him.

The more he frowned, the brighter her smile grew, to the point he wanted to throw her over his shoulder like a caveman and take her back to the Winston Estate just to put an end to his agony.

Near eleven o'clock, Patrick O'Hara returned to the bar, having taken Lana to a twenty-four-hour clinic for the stitches and dropped her off at her house on the way back.

Patrick hugged his granddaughter as soon as he walked through the door. "I was worried sick the entire time I was gone, thinking I'd get back to find you had disappeared again." He kissed her forehead and she hugged him again.

"I'm not going anywhere. We had a good night and nothing out of the ordinary happened."

Daniel noted that Shelby hadn't bothered to tell her grandfather what had happened at the university. Had she informed him of the near miss, he'd have been even more determined to stick to her like glue, something Daniel had discovered Shelby didn't like. She was an independent young woman, sometimes too independent for her own good. His job was hard enough keeping her safe without worrying about her taking off because she was mad at him for something.

Thankfully, the rowing team had to be up at the crack of dawn to work out. One by one, they filed out of the bar, leaving it nearly empty.

"You two can head back to the Winston Estate now. I'll be right behind you as soon as I give the order list to Marisa."

"Are you sure?" Shelby wiped her hands on a towel and tossed it on the bar. "I can stay and help clean up."

"No, the staff handled it fine while you were gone. I'm sure they can do it again."

Her brows furrowed. "Don't think you're going to get rid of me altogether. This arrangement is only temporary."

"I hope so, dear. The sooner they figure out who was responsible and lock him up, the sooner you won't have to have a bodyguard and the better I'll feel. Now get going so I can finish up."

When Patrick put it that way, Daniel didn't know how he felt. On one hand, he'd be free of babysitting duties. On the other, he'd have no need to be around Shelby. They'd part ways and that would be the end of it. A Secret Service agent's life wasn't geared toward long-term relationships. "You heard your grandfather. You're slowing him down." Daniel hooked Shelby's arm and guided her to the exit and his vehicle.

Shelby jerked her arm free. "You don't have to be so pushy, bodyguard."

He prayed she'd stay mad. After the fiery kiss in the hallway, he wasn't sure he could keep his distance. "I do if I want to get you back to the Winstons' place before dawn. As it is, it'll be nearly one in the morning before we arrive."

"Well, then, let's get crackin'." She led the way out the door to Daniel's SUV.

When she placed her hand on the door handle, he stopped her. "Let me check first."

Shelby stood back while Daniel shone a pocket flashlight under the car. He opened the hood and checked inside the engine compartment for anything that didn't belong. When he was satisfied there weren't any explosive devices attached to the vehicle, he waved a hand toward the passenger seat. "Your chariot awaits, princess."

Her lips thinned. "I'm not a princess. I'm a waitress." She got in and slammed the door shut.

Daniel hid a grin as he slid into the driver's seat and buckled his seat belt.

The long drive back to Raleigh was completed in silence. Shelby fell asleep against the window, the shadows beneath her eyes more pronounced.

Daniel had to remind himself she'd only been free from her captors for a little more than a day. A lot had happened in that time frame. She was exhausted. When she wasn't mad, her face softened and her lips relaxed, full and pink and completely kissable.

Daniel forced himself to concentrate on the road ahead. If he wasn't careful, he'd drive into the ditch. He stayed alert by going over everything that had happened. D'Angelis had told them enough to save the girl before he died. But he'd died in custody. Someone at the police station had to have poisoned him.

D'Angelis had been a Secret Service agent like Daniel, with one huge difference: he'd gone bad. Sold out to the highest bidder, and it was suspected he'd worked for the Cartel. If there were dirty agents in the Secret Service, there could be dirty cops at the police station. But who had access to the man? Who could have slipped him the poison between the time he was brought from his cell and the time he died?

Daniel's grip tightened on the steering wheel. He didn't know who to trust anymore. Anyone could be after Shelby. If he asked Kate to find a different agent to provide for her safety, he couldn't be certain that agent was a good agent.

The only reason he could come up with that would make someone target Shelby was her connection to Kate Winston. And who would have known Kate's daughter had survived? For all these years, Kate had presumed her child was dead. The only others who knew about her pregnancy were her mother, father and the hospital staff who helped deliver the baby. And, of course, her grandfather.

Daniel pulled up to the gate of the Winston Estate,

no closer to the truth than when he'd left and a whole lot more frustrated by a couple of incredibly hot kisses.

He parked at the front of the house. As late as it was, he didn't want to make Shelby walk any farther than she had to. She was still asleep when he rounded the car, grabbed her duffel bag out of the backseat, looped it over his shoulder, then opened her door.

She tipped slightly until her seat belt caught her and kept her from falling out.

Daniel reached across her lap and unbuckled her belt, then gathered her in his arms and carried her up the steps to the big house.

The door opened as soon as he stopped in front of it and Kate Winston stood there in her bathrobe, her face clean of makeup. "I was beginning to worry, until Patrick texted me to say you were on your way back. Any mishaps?"

"Not on the trip back. Let me get her up the stairs and then we'll talk."

"I can get there myself." Shelby's eyes blinked open and she stared up at him. "Put me down."

"Are you sure, dear?" Kate asked. "You look so very tired."

"I can walk." Shelby pushed at Daniel and he set her on her feet, keeping one of his arms behind her back to steady her.

"Let me check your room before you go up," Daniel insisted.

"I'm sure it's the same as I left it. You and Mrs. Winston need to talk, and I need a shower. I can manage on my own."

Daniel hesitated. "I'd rather not leave it up to chance."

"And I'd rather be alone," she said. "I'll be sure to scream if there's a monster under my bed."

Kate touched Daniel's arm. "Thad was here earlier. I had him check things in Shelby's room. I'm sure she'll be fine."

Shelby cocked an eyebrow. "See? Even the lady of the house thinks it's safe here. If it isn't, I might as well go back to *my* home."

With a smile, Kate took Daniel's arm. "Let her have her peace. Shelby, honey, do you need help getting up the stairs?"

"No." Shelby took the duffel bag from Daniel and set off across the foyer toward the stairs, her gait more wobbly than Daniel liked. She made it to the stairs and gripped the rail all the way up, half carrying, half dragging the duffel bag. The whole time Daniel watched, wanting to go after her and carry her and that damned bag up to her room.

"Come, Daniel," Kate said. "I want to know everything that happened today."

Daniel followed Kate into her study, determined to tell her only the things pertinent to the case. Kate didn't need to know he'd kissed her granddaughter.

What would she do if she did know? Have him reassigned?

Without knowing who to trust, he couldn't leave Shelby in someone else's hands.

Shelby had to drag herself up the stairs. The nap she'd had in the car had done little to banish the exhaustion she was feeling. Working at the bar had been a stretch after two weeks in hell with no exercise. Though it had felt good to be back to normal, she'd been tense and jumpy all night. Partly because she wasn't sure who to trust in the crowd at the bar and partly because of Daniel watching her.

Her lips still tingled from the kiss on the landing outside her apartment and the kiss in the hallway outside the bathroom in the bar. She'd kissed a few boys in her life, but nothing had compared to what she'd experienced with Daniel. Not only had it been good, it had sparked desire so strong, she'd almost forgotten where she was.

She moaned softly. The thought of kissing Daniel heated her blood and pushed her exhaustion aside. Now that she was awake, her body recalled the way it felt pressed against his. He'd been hard with desire, of that she was certain, and it made her hot and bothered all over.

A cool shower and her own nightgown would help her settle in for a good night's sleep.

Dropping her bag on the floor, she rummaged inside until she found clean panties and her favorite baby-doll nightie. She'd bought it on a whim and hardly wore it. Living in the apartment over the bar, she'd always worn an old T-shirt and stretchy shorts to bed.

Living in the Winstons' mansion made her more conscious of everything she wore, including her nightclothes. At home, instead of grabbing the ratty T-shirt she normally wore to bed, she'd dug the pretty teal nightgown out of her drawer. Now she almost changed her mind and scrounged for a T-shirt, but one glance at the connecting door made her hold on to the gown.

The man had some serious commitment issues and prejudices against people with a lot of money, not that she was one of them. Shelby had served all kinds at the bar and they all put their pants on the same way. Her connection to Kate Winston was an accident of birth. She was not connected to Kate's bank account and wouldn't want to be, even if she was asked.

Shelby had inherited her grandfather's sense of responsibility and drive. If she made it in this world, it would be because of hard work and her intelligence, not because she'd been born into wealth.

Gown in hand, she entered the bathroom and shut the door behind her. The bathroom was bigger than her bedroom back home and almost as big as the living room. The counters and shower were made of a beautiful white granite with brown and black speckles. The floor was covered in white marble tile and the fixtures were a shiny gold.

She glanced at the bathtub she'd used the day before and her cheeks heated. That was the first time Daniel had seen her naked.

And the last time he would, she decided. He'd have to beg her to make love to him after he'd been so callous earlier. Even then, she'd tell him where he could get off.

She stripped out of the clothing Kate had given her, now rumpled and stained from waiting tables at the bar. She glanced down at the sweater with regret. It was nice and she'd hate it if the stains wouldn't come out.

She filled the sink with water, applied some of the hand soap to the spots and then let it soak.

Stripping off her undergarments, she couldn't help but think of Daniel sleeping in the room on the other side of her bedroom. All she had to do was walk over there, open the door and let herself in.

Her core tightened, electric tingles spreading through

her body, angling downward. She jerked the handle on the shower, setting it on cool and stepped beneath the spray. The chill of the water made her catch her breath, and her wrists stung when the water hit the sores she'd created scraping the zip tie off. Both shocked her back to sanity.

Daniel was off-limits. He was her bodyguard, a Secret Service agent and a damned good kisser. But that was all. He wasn't the stuff relationships were made of. He'd told her that in no uncertain terms.

Knowing him only a day was not long enough to form an attachment to her guardian angel, the man who'd pulled her from a burning building. Hell, a fireman could have done the same and she wouldn't be drooling over him or wishing he'd kiss her again.

She should be worrying more about catching up on homework or about who was trying to kidnap her and less about getting in bed with the government agent. She squirted a little of the beautifully scented shampoo on her hand and applied it to her hair, scrubbing hard, as if she could scrub the images and thoughts about Daniel out of her head.

Not likely.

With quick efficiency, Shelby washed her body and rinsed her hair and skin, careful to avoid touching the bump on her forehead. Then she shut off the water. The towel she wrapped herself in was thick and luxurious, like everything else in the mansion. All the towels they had back home on the Outer Banks had been well worn and washed. They were thin, some threadbare. It wasn't that she and her grandfather were poor, they just hadn't found a need to replace things that worked just fine.

Shelby tossed the towel over the rack and slipped into her nightgown and bikini panties.

A sound in the bedroom made her jump.

"Daniel?" she called out.

No answer.

She grabbed the metal toothbrush holder and eased toward the door. "Daniel?" she called out, louder this time, her heart lodged in her throat.

As the bathroom doorknob turned, she remembered that she hadn't locked it and dived for the handle and the locking mechanism, twisting hard.

She got it locked. With her pulse slamming against her veins, she stood in her nightgown, holding the toothbrush holder and wondered what the hell to do next.

Chapter 10

Daniel paced in front of Kate's desk. "I don't like what's happening. The attack at the school made it clear that Shelby is still a target. Whoever is after her won't stop until they've caught her and used her for whatever they hope to accomplish."

Kate sat in the leather chair in her robe, looking no less regal than if she wore one of her tailored gray suits. "I don't know what else to do. She's at risk because of me. Until I know who they are or what they want, I can't do anything about it." She rested her face in her hands. "All I can do is pray that you're always there to keep her safe."

"She's got a mind of her own and she's not afraid to use it."

Kate smiled. "She's like her grandfather. Stubborn man."

"The point is, she doesn't take kindly to being followed around and putting her life in someone else's hands."

"For the time being, she'll have to get used to it. She's not safe." Kate stood and cinched the robe at her waist. "It's late, Daniel. Even a good bodyguard needs his rest. Go to bed. We can worry about this again in the morning."

He was ready. The few minutes he'd been talking to Kate, he'd been farther from Shelby than he'd been since he was assigned to protect her. His instincts were to go to her and make sure she was all right. Not that much could happen to her in the relative security of the Winston Estate. Still, he didn't trust anyone but himself to ensure her safety.

Kate drifted off toward the kitchen for a cup of tea while Daniel hurried up the curving staircase and along the landing to the door to Shelby's bedroom. He leaned his ear against the thick wood paneling and heard nothing. He tested the door. It was unlocked, and he debated whether or not to knock or barge in and demand she lock the door. Instead, he opened the door, reached in and twisted the lock, then closed the door again. No use alarming her. She was probably already asleep. Daniel went to his own room to get ready for bed.

As he closed his door behind him, he heard a noise from Shelby's room.

He crossed to the connecting door and listened.

The noise sounded again…and he could swear he heard Shelby calling his name. He could be mistaken; the sound was so soft he could have imagined it.

Then the noise sounded again and Shelby's voice called out, louder this time.

He tried the door and discovered it was locked and cursed himself for locking the other door before checking to see if Shelby was okay. Pulling his weapon from the holster beneath his jacket, he performed a hard side kick with his heel close to the locking mechanism. The door frame splintered, but the door didn't give. He kicked again and the door flew open, the frame shattering.

"Daniel?" Shelby called out from inside the bathroom. "Please tell me that was you," she said, her voice breaking as if it caught on a sob.

"It's me," he responded, arriving at the door to the bathroom as she opened it and threw herself into his arms. He caught her and held her against his body with his free hand, his gaze panning the room. Nothing moved; the room was empty except for the two of them.

"What happened?" he asked.

"I'd just gotten out of the shower when I heard a noise in my room. Then the doorknob twisted. I got to it in time to lock it." She looked up, her eyes wide, her fingers digging into his shirt. "Please tell me it was you."

He shook his head. "Sorry, sweetheart, it wasn't."

Shelby closed her eyes and pressed her forehead to his shirt. "I could have been imagining it. With all that's happened, my mind could be playing tricks on me."

He didn't believe it for a minute. "Had you locked your bedroom door?"

She nodded. "I'm pretty sure I did."

"Wait here."

Her fingers tightened on his shirt. "I'd rather not."

With her tucked in the curve of his arm, he led her through the connecting doorway to his bedroom door. He gripped her arms and moved her to the side of the door. "Lock this behind me and don't open it until I tell you to."

Opening the door, he pointed his weapon out into the hallway, then poked his head out, glancing in one direction and then the other. The hallway came to a dead end to the left, and the right led toward the staircase. No one stirred; nothing moved.

Carefully turning the knobs on the other doors in the hallway, he checked inside. Two of the rooms were empty. The room Patrick was to stay in was empty, as well. Daniel hurried down the hallway to the staircase and stared down at the floor below.

Kate Winston walked toward the stairs, carrying a cup. She glanced up and gasped. "Daniel? Is something wrong? I thought I heard a crashing sound."

"I don't know."

"There must be, or you wouldn't be carrying a gun." She looked around her and back up to him. "Is Shelby all right?"

"Yes. If you don't mind, I'll do a security check of the house."

"Please, by all means." She waited at the bottom of the stairs as he checked the other rooms on the second floor. When he returned, she met him halfway up the stairs. "Anything I can do?"

He shook his head. "No. I'll finish my check. You can go to bed. Your room is clear."

"Thank you, Daniel."

The sound of a key scraping in the lock on the front door echoed across the foyer, Daniel turned toward the sound.

The ornate door opened and Patrick O'Hara entered, closing the door quietly behind him. When he turned, he started. "Oh. I'm sorry, did I wake you?" His gaze went to Kate, his look one of longing.

"No, we were up." Kate held up her cup, descending the stairs. "Can I interest you in a cup of tea? Daniel was doing a last-minute check of the house."

"Shelby?" Patrick asked.

"In my bedroom for the moment. She's okay." Daniel descended to the first floor. "I'll only be a few minutes." He left Kate and Patrick in the foyer and checked all the rooms on the main floor, testing the windows and door locks to ensure they were secure. When he passed the kitchen on his way back to the stairs, he saw that Patrick and Kate sat at the bar, talking softly, mugs of steaming tea in front of them.

Daniel hurried back up the stairs and knocked softly on his bedroom door. "Shelby, it's me, Daniel."

She opened the door.

He stepped inside and closed the door behind him, then opened his arms.

Shelby went to him, burying her face against his chest, her body fitting close to his. She wore nothing but a sheer nightgown that barely covered her bottom, and he could see teasing shadows of her breasts beneath the thin fabric.

Holy hell. If he'd thought he could resist her, he was

sorely mistaken. Once he had his arms around her, there was no going back.

She ran her hands across his chest and around his middle, hugging him closer, her hips pressed against his.

His groin tightened, blood rushing to his head and lower to his throbbing member. The warmth of her skin beneath the sheer nightgown burned through, igniting flames inside him.

He lifted a hand to the back of her head, twisting his fingers in her hair, tugging her head back. "I didn't want this to happen."

"So why are you letting it?" She lifted her full, plump lips toward his.

"I can't help myself." He took her mouth, crashing down on her, thrusting through her teeth to caress her tongue with his. She tasted minty and fresh, warm and wet.

He reached down, cupped her bottom and lifted with one hand, the other still holding his pistol.

Her legs curled naturally around his waist and her arms went around his neck.

Her silky panties and his denim pants were all that stood between them.

Without breaking their kiss, he walked her to the bed and let her slide down his front to her feet.

Shelby pulled the weapon from his hand. "Can we set this aside?"

"I don't know. I think I'm in dangerous territory."

"Damn right you are." She shoved his jacket over his shoulders and he let it drop to the floor. When she reached for the buckles on his shoulder holster, he shoved her hands aside and worked them himself.

Meanwhile, she unbuttoned his trousers and ran the zipper downward, releasing his member into her palm.

Daniel jerked the holster off and tossed it onto a nearby chair. Then his hands slipped beneath her nightgown, cupping the full roundness of both breasts—so warm, soft and tipped with the tightest buds. He pushed the gown upward and claimed one of the rounded orbs, sucking it between his lips and tonguing the intriguing tip.

Her back arched, her hand pressing against the back of his head, urging him to suck the nipple deeper into his mouth.

He complied, licking the areola, nibbling the bud with the edges of his teeth while his hands roved over her waist and down to the elastic on her panties. Sliding his fingers beneath the fabric, he cupped her bottom, tracing the line between her cheeks.

Her hands grew restless, shoving his trousers down his legs.

He stopped her long enough to unearth his wallet from his back pocket and toss it on the bed. Then Daniel toed off his shoes and stepped out of the pants, kicking them to the side. He yanked his shirt up over his head and threw it across the end of the bed. Impatient to reveal all of her, he grabbed the hem of her nightgown and tugged it up over her head.

The gown flew across the room and he stepped back, his hungry gaze raking over her naked body, the panties the only thing in the way of him feasting on her.

The longer he stared, the brighter the pink in her cheeks became. She raised her hands to cover herself.

He caught her wrists. "Don't."

"Then quit staring and do something."

He laughed, dragged her into his arms and reveled in the feel of her breasts pressing against his chest. "Bossy much?"

"Don't make me wait. I'm on fire." She slipped out of his embrace and scooted up onto the bed.

Staring down at her delectable body, Daniel knew he was doomed. "This goes against all the rules."

"I'm betting you follow all the rules."

"I do." This woman had him so tied in knots, he couldn't back away.

Rules be damned.

The fire in his eyes had Shelby's body burning. She caught the elastic of her panties, slipping them down her legs in a long, sensuous move designed to leave Daniel panting. "In this case, I think you can break them." She let her knees fall to the sides.

Her entrance was slick and drenched with her juices. All she needed was him inside her, filling her.

He crawled up between her legs and kissed a path along the inside of her thigh to the center, the feathery-soft touches of his lips sending tingling electric shocks throughout her body.

Shelby ran her fingers down through the curls covering her mons, sliding a finger between her folds. She wanted him there.

Daniel tongued the tips of her fingers, pushing them aside to access the tiny strip of flesh packed with a plethora of nerves.

On the first flick, she moaned, her back arching off the mattress.

The second one had her grabbing his hair, her fingers digging into his scalp. "Oh, my," she whispered, her voice choked with desire.

Daniel slid two fingers into her and tongued her nubbin at the same time, catapulting her to the edge. "Yes! Oh, my, yes!"

He focused on that spot, flicking and tonguing until she hurtled over the edge, her body growing rigid, her insides a cascade of sensations, rippling over and over one another. Just when she thought she could die like this and be happy, Daniel moved away. "No!" she moaned.

"I'm not going anywhere." He reached for his wallet, extracted a foil packet and tore it open. In seconds he'd rolled the condom down over himself and slid up between her legs, his shaft poised at her opening. "Here's to breaking all the rules." He thrust deep, her channel stretching to accommodate his girth.

Shelby pushed up, meeting his thrust and urging him deeper, the sensations exploding throughout her. She gripped his hips, guiding him out, then back in. Soon he settled into a smooth, steady rhythm, pumping in and out, increasing in speed with the tension in his body.

One final thrust and he held still, his member throbbing inside her.

Shelby wrapped her legs around him, her heels digging into his buttocks, holding him as close as he could possibly get. At that moment, they were one, connected in the most beautiful way.

After a while, he rolled her onto her side and fell to the mattress beside her, maintaining their intimate bond.

Lying in the crook of his arms, she couldn't think of a place she'd rather be. The lack of sleep and the strain of being kidnapped and targeted again, not to

mention the two weeks in captivity, pulled at her eyelids and she gave in, feeling safe and protected in her
bodyguard's arms. If only real life didn't intrude, she'd
be happy to stay like this forever.

Daniel held Shelby, her body pressed against his
side. She fit perfectly in his arms, her soft brown hair
brushing against his skin, her breath warming him.

For a long time, he refused to think, to let the logi-
cal side of his brain spoil the moment. But as Shelby's
breathing grew steady and deep, he had to face the
facts—he'd screwed up. He'd had sex with the woman
he was assigned to protect. It went against every rule
in the books. He'd lost perspective, lost his self-control
and, if he didn't get back on track, he'd lose his focus.

And if he lost focus, Shelby's life would be at risk.

Daniel extricated himself from the bed, sliding his
arm out from under Shelby's head. Bending over her,
he brushed his mouth across her swollen lips, tasting
her one last time before he steeled his resolve and got
his head back on straight.

At twenty-three, she was tough, independent and
completely irresistible.

And she was the former vice president's granddaughter. Out of his social league.

And the most important detail was that she was
Daniel's job.

He lifted her in his arms, careful not to wake her,
and carried her into her room, laying her on her bed.

She snuggled into the sheets without opening her
eyes.

Daniel wanted to crawl in bed with her. Instead

he stepped away, ensured her door was locked and checked that the latch on her window was secure and then left.

When he reached the connecting door to his room, he heard a soft knock. He tensed, his body on full alert.

"Shelby?" Patrick O'Hara's voice called out.

Shelby stirred, her eyelids flickering open. "Grand-dad?"

"Are you all right in there?"

She sat up, the sheet falling down around her waist. Her eyes widened as she came fully awake. Her glance shot to the pillow beside her and then around the room, landing on Daniel where he stood in the doorway.

"Shelby?" her grandfather called out again. "I was just heading to bed and I thought I heard a noise or something. Are you all right?"

"I'm all right, Granddad, just tired."

"Oh, okay. Goodnight, sweetheart. I'll see you in the morning."

Her gaze never strayed from Daniel, her eyes narrowing in confusion.

He felt pinned to the wall, but he couldn't reassure her when he needed to put distance between them. Without a word of explanation, and using every ounce of resistance he could muster, he pulled the door closed between them. He couldn't lock it since the frame had been destroyed.

Walking away was the right thing to do, but it didn't make it any easier. Shelby would be mad, and she had a right to be. He'd been a jerk to take advantage of her. But he'd be more of a jerk if he continued down that same path. Ultimately, the job would end and he'd move on to his next assignment. Leaving Shelby behind.

As much as he'd resisted being her bodyguard in the first place, he didn't relish leaving her in the end.

Chapter 11

Daniel tried to sleep, but knowing Shelby was only a few short steps away left him wide-awake, and full-on frustrated.

When the early light of dawn crept through his window, he knew he had to get out, breathe fresh air and clear his foggy brain.

He pulled on shorts and running shoes and headed downstairs and out of the house. He slipped through the gate, making certain it closed securely behind him. Only those with a need to know had the security code to enter, but anyone could get out with a single push of a button. He made a note to talk to Kate about other options that were more secure.

Ignoring the ever-present pain in his leg, he half jogged and half walked a mile before turning back. He didn't want to be too far away from the estate should anything happen. With Shelby asleep in her locked bedroom, she should be all right for a while. And he needed the exercise, or his injuries from that fateful day of protecting Kate would never heal.

The sun had yet to rise on his return. When he was within a hundred yards of the gate, he stopped to tie a shoelace that had come undone.

Leaning against a tree, he bent, tied his shoe and happened to look up just as someone exited the Winston Estate on foot, wearing shorts, a T-shirt and a baseball cap. Despite the hat, Daniel knew who it was and anger spiked in him.

Did she *want* to be kidnapped again?

Shelby turned away from him and set off at a jog.

Adrenaline spiked and Daniel took off after her.

At a crossroad, she turned right and disappeared around the corner.

Still a good fifty yards behind her, Daniel ignored the pain in his knee and sped up, concerned. Shelby was out on her own, now on a busier street and no one around to keep her from being taken.

Daniel raced for the corner. Before he reached it, a large white SUV like the one that had been at the university the day before sped by, heading the same direction as Shelby.

Sprinting as fast as he could go, Daniel rounded the corner without slowing, in time to see SUV's brake lights flash and the vehicle slow next to Shelby.

His heart thundering, Daniel yelled, "Shelby, run!"

Shelby had already noticed the danger and stopped on the sidewalk.

Move, Daniel willed her, still running to reach her in time.

As the vehicle slowed beside her, Shelby spun and ran back toward Daniel.

Without a gun or any other type of weapon, Daniel would only be able to shield her with his body. But he'd throw himself in the line of fire before he'd let a single bullet hit Shelby.

The SUV whipped into Reverse and backed up after Shelby's running figure.

Daniel reached her before the SUV, grabbed her hand and ran with her, dragging her faster and faster.

The SUV swerved in an attempt to hit them.

Daniel veered away from the road and headed through a stand of trees between two large houses. As he and Shelby emerged on the other side of the trees, the SUV was there, heading directly for Daniel.

Daniel had to let go of Shelby or risk her getting hit along with him.

Pushing her one way, Daniel dived in the opposite direction, narrowly missing the crush of the SUV's tires.

Shelby staggered and fell to the ground.

As Daniel picked himself up off the pavement, a man wearing a ski mask leaped down from the SUV and ran toward Shelby.

She lay on the ground, motionless.

When the man reached out to grab her, she exploded from the ground, kicked the man in the face and rolled out of reach.

About the time the man reached for her again, the back door opened and another man with a ski mask leaped out. Daniel arrived at the SUV at that moment and slammed the man into the side of the vehicle.

Startled by the attack, the man swung, his fist connecting with Daniel's jaw. Daniel's head whipped back, but he balled his fists and aimed for the man's belly, landing a hard one to the guy's breadbasket. He doubled over.

A scream behind him gave Daniel the necessary incentive to end the argument sooner. He raised his knee with a hard jerk, hitting the man in the nose. He went down, holding on to his face, blood streaming from beneath the dark ski mask.

Daniel spun toward the other guy.

He had Shelby in a headlock.

"One step closer and I'll break her neck," the guy growled.

"I'll give you one chance to let her go," Daniel bluffed, wondering how the hell he'd get Shelby away from the gorilla.

Shelby's face was red and she clawed at the meaty arm wrapped tightly around her throat.

At a standoff, Daniel edged closer.

Shelby went limp and collapsed in her captor's arms. She'd done nothing to deserve this. She was an innocent pawn in a game of politics and deception.

His heart in his throat, Daniel lunged for the man, rage driving him forward.

As he reached them, Shelby jabbed her elbow into her captor's groin. The man let her go and grabbed for his crotch. Daniel slammed his knee into the man's face and shoved him backward; he tripped over the curb and fell on his backside.

Daniel gripped Shelby's hand and ran back the way he'd come, dragging her along with him, praying she had the strength to keep up. If the men who'd threatened them followed, he wasn't sure he'd be so lucky to get her away the next time.

Shelby ran next to Daniel, gulping air into her lungs and shooting glances over her shoulder to gauge whether or not the bad guys were still following. The man she'd bested helped the one with the broken nose into the SUV. The driver sent the vehicle up over the curb in his effort to get away.

Daniel didn't let her stop until they'd reached the entrance to the Winston Estate. He punched the code into the keypad and the gate opened. Once he'd shoved her through, he hit the close button and the gate slammed shut behind them.

Shelby collapsed on the ground and lay there for a full two minutes until her breathing returned to normal. The adrenaline still spiking through her veins made her sit up. "Thank you," she said.

Daniel paced away, the color high in his cheeks. His eyes blazed and he breathed through his nose like an angry bull. He stopped in front of her, towering over her. "I don't know what was going through your head. I'm not here to make sure you have a good time. I'm not here to make love to you. My primary goal in this assignment is to keep you safe. If you insist on pulling stupid stunts like that, you can find yourself another damn bodyguard." He stalked away, leaving her on the ground by the gate.

She rolled to her feet and went after him. "Really? You think I *asked* to be grabbed off the street? You think I *planned* on having a secret identity connected to the former vice president of the freakin' United

States?" She grabbed his arm, forcing him to stop, though he refused to face her.

She marched around in front him and stood with her arms crossed over her chest. "I didn't want a bodyguard in the first place." Jabbing a finger into his chest, she went on, "And I sure as hell don't want one who has a problem with sticking around. You couldn't get up and get out of my bed fast enough." He stood rock solid, his face poker straight, his flashing green eyes the only indication she was making him angrier.

"What's wrong with you? Are you afraid you might like me? Afraid you're not good enough for me? 'Cause let me tell you, bubba, you aren't. I need a man who doesn't judge anyone based on their lineage. A man who will love me no matter who my parents or grandparents are or what they did." On a roll, unable to stop her tirade now that she'd started, she poked him again. "You know what you are? A scaredy cat. A big ol' scaredy cat."

He grabbed her finger and yanked her hard, slamming her against his chest. He caught her lips with his in a crushing kiss that stole her breath away and made her head spin.

When he shoved her away from him, she reeled backward.

He poked a finger into her chest. "For the record, I didn't ask for this assignment. I was stuck with it. For the record, I don't like babysitting little girls who don't know what's best for them. And for the record, I didn't run away from you. Did you ever think I might have left because I didn't want to make love to you again?"

That hurt like a punch to the gut. Shelby fought to keep from doubling over at the slam. "Good. Because

I don't want you touching me." Damn. She tried to stop it, but her eyes teared up and her bottom lip trembled. "Ever again."

Daniel stared at her, his jaw hard, his face impassive. Finally he eased her back into his arms and pressed his cheek against her hair. "You scared the crap out of me."

"I thought you didn't care."

"I don't want to." He stroked her soft brown hair, twisting his fingers in the silken strands.

"But you do."

"Yes." He sighed and took her hand in his. "Let's get you back to the house."

With her hand tucked in his big, warm one, Shelby leaned against him as they walked back to the mansion.

Kate met them in the foyer, her brows coming together in a worried frown. "What's wrong?" She glanced at Shelby's legs. "Why are your knees skinned?"

Shelby hadn't realized she'd been hurt. The adrenaline rush and near miss had blocked the pain. "I fell."

"The hell she did. She was attacked again," Daniel said.

"Dear God." Kate wrapped her arms around Shelby. "Are you okay? Should I call the doctor?"

Shelby hadn't been hugged by a female relative since her mother died and she'd been almost too young to remember. Kate's hug was warm, welcoming and seemed genuinely heartfelt.

After nearly being taken again, Shelby let the woman hug her. She liked the way Kate Winston smelled of honeysuckle, and she was warm and soft. She could see how a man from the Outer Banks could have fallen for the pretty socialite.

"Shelby?" Her grandfather hurried down the stairs, dressed in jeans and a polo shirt. "What's going on?"

The front door opened and Thad entered, followed by Jed Kincannon.

Thad smiled. "Looks like I'm just in time for the party. What's going on?"

Everyone started talking at once. Shelby's head began to ache and her skinned knees stung.

Daniel whistled to get everyone's attention. "We aren't accomplishing a thing." He curved his arm around Shelby's waist. "We're going to clean up."

"Yes, yes. Of course. Shelby's injuries need tending to." Kate waved toward the hallway. "Let's take this discussion into the kitchen while Daniel takes care of Shelby. I'll make breakfast, and we can talk about what we want to do."

"Are you sure you don't need me to help?" Patrick asked.

Shelby smiled. "You patched up all of my skinned knees as a kid, but I think I can handle this on my own." She leaned close and kissed her grandfather's cheek. "I love you, Granddad."

"Not as much as I love you, little girl." He patted her shoulder and followed Kate toward the kitchen.

Shelby had always been the only woman in her grandfather's life, and he'd never dated anyone that she knew of. She'd assumed he hadn't dated because he'd been too busy raising his daughter and then his granddaughter. Could it be that he had never gotten over his first love?

Shelby stared after her grandfather's retreating figure. A little nip of jealousy was quickly overridden by the thought that her grandfather might still be in love with the beautiful and powerful Kate Winston. How sad. With her in her mansion and him in his bar on the Outer Banks, they couldn't be farther apart.

Her heart aching for her grandfather, Shelby turned to follow Daniel.

"Wait," Thad said. "You'll need the first-aid kit." Thad ran to the kitchen and returned with a red-and-white box.

"Thank you." Shelby reached for it, but Daniel got there first. She frowned. "I'm not an invalid, you know."

"I know, but I'd rather you concentrated on getting up the stairs unscathed."

"Again, I think I can handle climbing and carrying a little box."

Daniel gave her lopsided smile. "Are you always this argumentative?"

Patrick snorted from the hallway. "She can be a pill sometimes."

"You're not helping, Granddad," Shelby shot back, crossing her arms as she turned on Daniel. "Are you always this domineering?"

"Let's agree you're argumentative and I'm domineering and maybe we'll get cleaned up sometime today. We have bigger fish to fry, and arguing down here isn't getting the oil hot."

Shelby started to give him a scathing reply, thought better of it and clamped her lips shut.

Daniel led the way to her room where she sat on the edge of the big tub in the bathroom while he cleaned the gravel from her skinned knees and applied ointment and bandages. His hand lingered on her thigh and she held her breath, waiting for him to lean close and claim a kiss.

When he didn't, she wanted to scream with frustration. Instead, she turned the tables on him. "My turn." She took the kit and stood. "Sit."

"I can manage on my own."

She gave him a meaningful stare and pointed to the edge of the tub. "Sit."

With that gorgeous lopsided grin that made her go weak at the knees, he sat.

She wet a clean washcloth and dabbed at a gash on his cheek where he'd been punched. "You're going to have a bruise."

"I'll live," he said, his smile slipping as she leaned closer. "You don't have to get so close."

"Yes, I do." She straddled his lap and sat with a smile. "I haven't properly thanked you for saving me." Shelby applied ointment to his cheek.

He caught her wrist in his hand and stared at her hard. "Don't make this any harder than it has to be."

"What do you mean?"

"When the threat is gone, you won't need my protection. I'll be reassigned."

Her heart fluttered. She'd already come to that conclusion, but hearing him say it drove it home. Forcing a smile, she shook her hand free. "I know that. In the meantime, let me take care of you for once."

His lips tightened, but he let go of her wrist. She applied a butterfly bandage to pull the edges of wound together and taped a gauze pad over it. "There. That shouldn't leave much of a scar." With her thighs rubbing against his, she could tell her position in his lap was having the desired effect. She patted his bandage softly and shifted her gaze to his mouth, tilting forward until her lips hovered over his. "Thank you for coming to my rescue." She swept her mouth across his, her lips barely skimming his.

He sat like stone for an excruciatingly long moment, his hands bunching into fists.

Shelby thought he'd mastered his self-control and that she'd overstepped her bounds.

Then he cupped the back of her head and kissed her hard, his tongue sweeping into her mouth, claiming her in a dizzyingly powerful connection.

As quickly as he'd taken her, he stood and set her on her feet. "They're waiting on us." Daniel collected the items of the first-aid kit, threw them in the box, closed it and left the bathroom in record time.

Disappointment fused with raging desire. Shelby wanted to stand in Daniel's way and demand he stay and face up to what they were feeling. The stony expression on his face made her step aside and allow him to pass.

"Get dressed and meet us in the kitchen in five minutes." He didn't ask, he *demanded*.

Shelby bristled, but clamped her teeth down on her tongue as Daniel crossed her bedroom and passed through the connecting door to his own. Once the door was shut behind him, she was tempted to rip it back open. He couldn't lock it because the door frame was splintered. Instead, she marched to the bed, lifted a pillow and cocked her arm to throw it.

The door opened and Daniel poked his head through and he pointed at the pillow. "Don't do it."

Shelby launched the pillow and it hit the door as he closed it quickly.

Throwing the pillow didn't fix the fact that the man was exasperating, but it made her feel better.

"Five minutes," he reminded her through the closed door.

Part of her wanted to drag her feet and arrive in the kitchen in ten minutes just to spite him. How could he kiss her like that and then practically dump her off his lap and go about business as usual?

She dressed in her jeans and one of her better pull-over blouses. The outfit was not nearly as nice as the slacks and cashmere sweater Kate had given her to wear, but they felt more like her and she felt more normal in them. Running a brush through her hair, she washed her face and applied a little blush to her pale cheeks and a bit of mascara to her eyes. Not that she wanted to look better for anyone but herself.

Slipping into her favorite sandals, she let herself out of her room, betting Mr. Bossypants was already in kitchen making plans for her without her input. She hurried down the stairs and found the kitchen by following the sound of voices.

"Well, the fact is she's not safe in Raleigh."

"The house is wired for security and the gate should help keep people out."

"How does that explain someone being in her room last night?"

"We don't know that for sure." Shelby stepped into the room. "I could have been imagining things."

"There have been too many attempts already. I'm afraid you're not safe here," Daniel said.

"Then I can go home?" she asked with a bright smile.

"No!" Kate and her grandfather both said at once.

They smiled at each other, and then her grandfather faced her. "It's not safe at the bar."

"I had no problems there last night."

"But you had problems yesterday afternoon and this morning," Daniel pointed out.

Shelby glared at Daniel, sitting quietly in a chair across the table, drinking coffee. "So I made a bad choice in going out without my watchdog. I won't do that again."

"And what about school?" Kate asked.

Daniel's jaw tightened. "She's not going."

"The hell I'm not."

"You got your assignments, you can work on them and turn them in when we get this thing resolved. Your instructors will work with you."

"Maybe and maybe not." Shelby crossed her arms over her chest. "Did anyone even bother to ask what I want to do?"

Her grandfather reached for her hand. "Honey, you need to listen to what these people are saying."

"I can't live like this. I'm just as much a prisoner in this house as I was in that basement."

Daniel stood and waved his hand toward the door. "If you don't like it, go."

Her back straightened. "I just might."

"No, either you will or you won't, but stop straddling the fence." He pinned her with his stare.

No one else said a word, each waiting expectantly for her response. "It's my life."

"Yes, it is. And if you step out of this house, off this property by yourself, you'll end up in the hellhole you were in before, and maybe for longer than two weeks this time. And they might not be as nice to you. You might not even get bologna sandwiches. They could decide it would be fun to assault and torture you."

The blood rushed from Shelby's face and a cold shiver shook her. Her grandfather's face paled and he shook his head, his eyes pleading with her.

"Daniel," Kate warned.

"No, Kate. If she wants to go out on her own, she needs to know the truth. No sugarcoating." Daniel stepped up to her. "If you leave, you might die this time."

Shelby sucked in a breath, finding it harder to breathe than moments before, her hands growing clammy. She rubbed her palms on her jeans and stared down at the scabs just beginning to heal.

"Is that what you want?" Daniel asked softly.

She shook her head, her eyes blurring. "No."

Kate stood and came to her side, laying a hand on her arm. "Then let us protect you. Let Daniel keep you safe until we can figure this out."

"How to your propose to keep her safe if she's not even safe in this house?" Thad asked.

"I could assign another agent to the detail," Jed offered.

"Thank you, Jed," Kate patted his hand. "I appreciate the offer, but after D'Angelis proved to be a traitor and his death took place in a public facility surrounded by law enforcement officers, I don't know who to trust except my children and Daniel."

"I would be willing to offer my own services," Kincannon said.

Kate frowned. "You're the director. You have another job to do. Finding who's doing this to my family is as important as protecting my granddaughter."

Thad leaned forward. "We could hire an independent bodyguard."

Kate shook her head. "That goes back to my original point. I don't trust anyone but my family and Daniel."

Thad tapped his fingers on the table, his eyebrows dipping low. "I'm leading the investigation from the local law enforcement side. Though I wish I could be here, if we want to catch the person responsible, I can't do both."

Kate nodded. "I know you can't and I won't ask it of you. Which leaves us only one option." She faced Daniel.

Shelby inched closer to him, despite his effort to frighten her.

"What choice is that?" Daniel asked.

"You have to get Shelby out of here."

"And where do you want me to take her?"

"Away." Kate waved her hand in the air. "Someplace no will think to look for her."

Chapter 12

Daniel frowned. "Far enough away she won't be found? That would be the moon."

"We would be the only ones who know where she's going. If the media and everyone else is in the dark about her location, whoever is determined to take her will not be privy to that information."

"I don't know, Mom. If she's far away, Daniel will have no backup in case they get in trouble."

An idea began forming in Daniel's mind. Kate might be on to a plan that held merit. "I know of a place."

Shelby looked at him, her eyes widening. "I can't leave. I have school."

"Like I said, you can bring your work with you and turn it in later when we resolve this case."

"I'm glad you're able to speak for my instructors."

"It's stay here and risk your life or go with Daniel and be safe." Her grandfather reached for her hand. "Please, Shelby. Be reasonable. I love you and I want to be around for great-grandchildren someday."

"Granddad!"

"I'm serious, Shelby. I'm not going to be around forever."

"Don't go pulling the age card on me. You're in better shape than I am and will probably outlive me when I die of natural causes."

"Enough talk about dying." Patrick O'Hara straightened to his full, intimidating height. "You'll go with Daniel, or else."

Shelby laughed out loud. "Granddad, your blustery bull didn't scare me when I was a child and it surely isn't scaring me now. But since you feel so strongly, and I have no desire to spend more time in a dark basement, I'll consider going with Daniel."

Kate let out a heartfelt sigh. "Thank goodness. I really didn't want to order him to kidnap you to keep you safe." Kate smiled.

"It's okay, I'll go peacefully." Shelby turned to Daniel. "And where, pray tell, are we going?"

He smiled. "Maine."

She nodded. "That's pretty far. And do you have a specific place in Maine in mind?"

His grin broadened, the idea solidifying and taking root. "I do."

She waited for him to continue.

His decision made, he stated, "My folks' house."

Shelby backed away. "I can't stay at your parents' house. I don't know them. Can't we hole up in a hotel?"

"That would be too public. If we stay with my family, I'll have built-in backup. My brothers are police officers in the small town where I'm from. One of them lives with my folks, the other comes by often. No one but the people sitting at this table will know where you are."

"Maine?" Shelby shivered. "Isn't it cold up there?"

"Not during the day at this time of year. The nights get chilly. My parents live along the coast in a small fishing town."

"Sounds perfect," Kate said. "How soon can you leave?"

Shelby shot a glance at her grandmother. Did she *want* to get rid of her?

Kate gave her soft smile. "I'd love to keep you here and get to know you better, but as long as you're threatened, I'd rather have you safe."

Daniel nodded. "I can be out of here as soon as we can rent a decoy car and get out of town." He glanced down at Shelby. "Can you be packed in five minutes?"

"I can do better than that," she said. "I can be ready in three minutes."

Patrick pulled Shelby into his arms and stroked her hair. "I just got you back and I'm going to lose you again."

"This time you'll know where I am, Granddad." Shelby kissed his cheek. "And Daniel will keep me safe."

"I know. He's a good man." Patrick stepped back and offered Daniel his hand.

Daniel shook it, feeling like a fraud, knowing he'd betrayed this man's trust by bedding his granddaughter. "I'll take care of her, sir." He owed them all his promise to keep her safe. Her life was his responsibility.

"I'll be back in two shakes." Shelby hurried toward the stairs.

Daniel's gaze followed her.

Kate touched his arm. "You can't let anyone else know where she is."

"I know that." He fished his cell phone out of his pocket and handed it to Kate. "I don't want to take anything that could be tracked. Keep this. If I need to reach you, I'll call from a public phone. For the most part, I'll keep communication to a minimum."

Kate took the phone. "Understood."

"If anything happens, or you suspect you've been discovered, bring her back here," Patrick said. "I don't like having my girl so far away, especially when she's in trouble."

"Yes, sir." Daniel backed away. "If you'll excuse me, I'll get my things."

He took the stairs two at a time and hurried down the hallway, past the room where he and Shelby had made love. Soon, they'd be alone on the road. He prayed he wasn't making a mistake. What if the men trying to take her found her in Maine? They didn't have a handy informant to question about her whereabouts. D'Angelis was inconveniently dead.

Daniel jammed his things into a duffel, checked his weapon, ensuring the clip was fully loaded, and knocked on the connecting door.

"Why bother knocking? The lock's broken," she called out.

He pushed through the door and entered her room.

She had her duffel bag slung over her shoulder. "I'm ready when you are."

"Then let's hit the road."

She nodded. "Do you think this will work?"

"I hope so."

Shelby glanced around the room. "I've never been so far away from home."

"My family is pretty welcoming. They'll do their best to make you feel at home."

"I worry about my grandfather."

"He's on board with this and ready to do anything to keep you safe."

"I'd feel better if I knew someone was looking out for *him*."

"I'll leave word for someone to keep tabs on him."

She glanced up with a small smile, her eyes suspiciously moist. "Then I guess there's nothing else. Let's get going."

Daniel's heart pinched in his chest. He dropped his duffel and held open his arms.

Shelby walked into them. "Why is all this happening to me?"

"You know why."

"I know. But it doesn't make sense. I'm nobody."

"Not to a lot of people, including your grandmother," he said softly. Crooking his finger, he angled her chin up so that he could stare down into blue eyes awash with tears. "It's going to be okay."

"Promise?" she whispered.

He bent to brush a soft kiss across her mouth.

Shelby dropped her duffel, leaned up on her toes and deepened the kiss.

Daniel couldn't back away and didn't want to.

She was like an addiction he was having a difficult time shaking. He crushed her against him, his fingers threading through her silky brown hair. If he could, he'd hold her like this forever.

He broke the kiss and he stepped back to keep from doing it again. "We need to go."

"I suppose."

When she reached for her bag, he got there first. Carrying both bags, he waved her forward.

Shelby descended the stairs first and ran to her grandfather.

He hugged her and kissed her forehead. "Be safe, Shelby. I kinda like having your around." His eyes glistened.

"I'll miss you." She hugged him tight and then stood back.

Kate Winston stepped forward and took Shelby's hands. "I know we haven't had a chance to get to know each other yet, but if you're anything like your grandfather, you're smart and pretty tough. Between you two—" she nodded toward Daniel "—you'll be okay." The older woman leaned forward and kissed Shelby's cheek. "I look forward to spending more time with you in the near future. If you'll let me." Her smile was shaky when she let go of Shelby's hands.

One of Kate's cars had been brought around for them to take. Daniel threw their bags in the backseat and held the door for Shelby.

She slipped in and turned to wave as he shut the door.

Once they left the security of the Winston Estate, Daniel zigzagged through neighborhoods and out onto the main road toward the airport. He parked the car at one of the car rental places, grabbed his bag and Shelby's and walked with her to the neighboring rental lot.

"Why didn't we rent a car at the last one?" Shelby asked.

"If the car we drove was bugged with GPS, they could then find record of our rental there."

"Oh." She waited while Daniel secured a vehicle and then quietly climbed into the four-wheel-drive SUV he'd rented without saying a word.

Once they were on the road headed north, Shelby fell asleep leaning against the window, her dark eyelashes fanned across her cheeks. Daniel had to continually remind himself to keep his focus on what was ahead of him and what might be behind him. But he couldn't help glancing over at her. She looked like a dark angel sent to Earth to torment him and make him question his dedication to the job.

When they found out who was trying to kidnap her and why, Daniel would ask to be assigned somewhere far, far away from the temptation that was Shelby. A career Secret Service agent didn't have time for family or relationships.

Then why the hell couldn't he get her out of his mind?

Shelby didn't wake until the vehicle slowed. When she opened her eyes, it was to a congested six-lane expressway.

"Where are we?"

"Washington, D.C."

"That means we only have nine more hours on the road."

"Roughly."

"Do you want me to drive so that you can stretch?"

"I'm doing okay for now."

"Good, because I'm not good driving in traffic, but I could use a bathroom break when you get past all this."

Once they got past the heaviest of traffic, Daniel pulled into a gas station and topped off the gas tank while Shelby went inside to find a bathroom. The door was locked and there were two women in line to use the facilities.

Shelby roamed the aisles, watching the door to the bathroom, waiting for her turn.

A man in the row with all the snack foods, one over from her, stared, his eyes narrowing so slightly, she wasn't sure if she'd imagined it.

Shelby moved the opposite direction, glancing back over her shoulder.

The man was still watching her, his brows narrowing.

A cold tingle slithered down her spine. The last woman in line at the bathroom exited and Shelby made a dash for it.

Once inside, she took care of her needs and washed her hands. When she came out of the bathroom, she looked down the hallway toward the front of the store, wondering if Daniel had finished filling the tank.

The shuffle of feet behind her made her jump.

"Good, I was getting worried about you."

Daniel moved in front of her, his brow furrowed.

Shelby slipped her hand in his. "Sorry. There was a line."

Daniel curled an arm around her waist and guided her toward the door.

Shelby glanced back at the hallway to the bathrooms. A man turned his back to her and lifted a case of soft drinks. If Shelby wasn't mistaken, it was the same man who'd been staring at her earlier. He glanced over his shoulder, his gaze following her yet again.

A shiver rippled across her skin. Reasoning with herself, she figured the man worked there stocking shelves, and she was getting too paranoid for her own good.

Shelby didn't say anything to Daniel, not sure what she'd actually say if she did. She settled back against the leather seat and tried to let it go. For the next hour, she looked behind them every five minutes for someone following their vehicle, a creepy feeling following her.

By the time they reached the outskirts of New York City, Shelby was ready to be there. Daniel hadn't said much and he hadn't made a move to touch or reassure her in any way.

"Do you want me to drive the rest of the way?" she asked.

"I'm used to making this trip. Why don't you find something on the radio?"

She settled on an old Beach Boys song that reminded her of home, her father and the beaches she grew up on. After a minute of that, she was so homesick she switched the radio off.

"Why'd you do that? I like The Beach Boys. They remind me of home."

"Same here," she said.

He glanced at her and nodded. "I know you miss your home and grandfather, but you'll be back soon enough."

"Are you sure?" She stared out the window, wondering when this nightmare would ever end. When he didn't respond, she glanced his way. "What if whoever is trying to grab me follows me to Maine? Won't we be placing your family in danger?"

"No one will know where you are. And if they do happen to find us, the members of my family can take care of themselves."

"I would hate to bring trouble to your hometown. What if someone is hurt? I'd never forgive myself."

"As my mother would say, 'Don't borrow trouble.'"

Shelby's mouth twisted into a wry grin. "And as my father would say, 'Go with your gut.'"

"And what is your gut telling you?"

"There's a storm rising out to sea, and things will get worse before they get better."

Daniel pulled into the driveway of the house his parents owned on the beach in Bar Harbor, Maine. The sun had set and the stars and streetlights were shining brightly.

No sooner had he parked the SUV than the front door opened and his mother and father stood framed in the doorway, squinting at the strange car parked in their driveway.

Daniel stepped out of the vehicle and walked around to the front of it. "Mom, Dad, it's me, Daniel."

"Daniel!" His mother exclaimed, flying down the steps. "It's Daniel, James."

"I can see that." His father chuckled, following his wife at a more sedate pace.

Daniel smiled. "I hope you don't mind company on short notice."

His mother reached him and enveloped him in a

warm hug. "Oh, honey, you know you're always welcome here. This is your home."

Daniel hugged her back and then pulled back to face her. "Mom, I'm not alone." He walked back to the car, pulled open the passenger door and held out his hand. "This is Shelby O'Hara."

Shelby took his hand and let him help her to her feet. She smiled tentatively at his parents. "Mr. and Mrs. Henderson, we're sorry to be arriving so late and without warning."

Daniel cringed at the way his mother's face lit up. She'd think he and Shelby were together. Nothing would make his mother happier than to see all her sons settled with wives and a couple of kids she could spoil.

"Oh, honey, we're *delighted* to see Daniel. We came down to be with him when he was in the hospital after the shooting, but having him home is so much better." She turned to her husband. "What's it been, almost a year since he's been back to visit?"

Daniel's father nodded. "Thereabout."

Daniel's mother hugged Shelby as though she was a long-lost family member, then turned back to her husband. "Please, call me Lea, and this is James."

Daniel's father reached a hand out to Shelby. When she took it, he pulled her into a hug. "Any friend of Daniel's is welcome."

Her cheeks blushing pink, Shelby hugged James Henderson. "Thank you."

"You know we had the extra bedroom converted into an office. Which leaves Daniel's old bedroom. One of you is welcome to sleep on the couch…." His mother gave them a knowing look. "Unless, of course, you're…together."

"Lea," his dad warned.

"We might be older, but we know what happens between young folk." She leaned close to Shelby and whispered conspiratorially, "We weren't married when Daniel was conceived."

"Now is not the time to confess." Daniel hugged his mother and father. "Shelby can have my room, I'll sleep on the couch." He grabbed their bags out of the backseat to avoid further questioning, but his mother wasn't quite done.

"But since you two are together, that shouldn't matter right?"

Daniel enjoyed the way Shelby squirmed. "We're not…together. We've only known each other a couple of days."

His mother waved a hand. "It only takes a moment to know someone's the one. I fell in love with Daniel's father the day I met him." She took Shelby's hand. "Come inside. I have some leftover clam chowder I can heat up. Do you like hot tea or the iced tea they love so much in the South?"

"I'd love some hot tea. But I don't want to be a bother."

"Be a bother," Daniel said. "My mother loves to bother."

"Mothers *like* to bother." His mother squeezed her arm. "Don't they, Shelby?"

Shelby stiffened.

"Mom, Shelby's mother passed away when she was a little girl."

"Oh, honey, I'm so sorry. How awful to grow up without her."

"My grandfather raised me." Shelby glanced at Daniel. "I think he did a good job."

"I'm sure he did." Daniel's mother patted her arm and led her to the kitchen. "Now, you sit down there while I fix that cup of tea."

"If you don't mind, I'd like to find a bathroom."

"Of course. Let me show you."

Daniel's father touched his wife's arm. "Let Daniel. You and I can fix the tea. Personally, I'd rather have a cup of coffee."

"You know you shouldn't drink coffee at night. It keeps you awake."

"If I want a cup of coffee, I'll have coffee."

"Don't you take that tone with me, James. I have to sleep with you."

Daniel tipped his head to the side and Shelby preceded him from the room, glancing back over her shoulder.

"Are they mad at each other?" she asked when they were halfway down the hall.

The sound of his parents arguing carried into the hallway. "No. That's just the way they are. Mom takes care of Dad and he takes care of her."

Her brow furrowed. "Kind of like me and my grandfather." She sighed. "Good. I didn't want to be the cause of a fight."

"No, you're not the cause of a fight. They love each other very much. Mom needs someone to need her, and my father lets her fuss over him."

Daniel opened a door off the hall. "This is my old bedroom." He entered and dropped her bag on the bed. "The bathroom is right across the hall." He stepped back out into the hallway. "Make yourself at home, and if you need anything just ask. I'll be in the kitchen." He left her standing in the hallway to avoid the temptation of kissing her again. The last thing he needed was to get his mother's hopes up. Being with Shelby was temporary.

He hurried away. He couldn't keep Shelby's situation to himself. His parents had to know what they were up against, should someone find Shelby here.

When he entered the kitchen his mother turned from the stove where a kettle of water had just worked up a steam. "Shelby seems very nice. How did you two meet?"

"Lea, that's none of our business."

"I'm his mother. I have every right to pry." She raised her brows and directed a questioning look toward Daniel.

"I'm on assignment to protect her."

His mother's brows dipped. "Protect her from what?"

"She's already been kidnapped and held captive once, and there have been other attempts made."

"Oh, dear." His mother set the kettle on a cool burner and turned. "Why?"

Daniel smiled. "She's the granddaughter of Kate Winston."

"*The* Kate Winston? The former vice president?" his father asked.

Daniel nodded.

"Oh, dear." His mother pressed her hand to her chest. "Practically a celebrity."

"Is there anything we can do to help?" Daniel's father asked, slipping his arm around his wife's waist.

"Help me keep an eye out for anything suspicious."

"Like what?" His mother leaned into his father's embrace.

"Strange cars driving by on the street, strangers hanging around. If anyone calls to ask for Shelby, you don't have any idea who she is. Let me know if anything is out of the ordinary."

"We can do that."

"And if at any time you feel unsafe or uncomfortable with us being here, let me know. We'll leave. Shelby and I don't want anything bad to happen to you two."

Shelby entered the room at that time. "Seriously, I don't want to be here if it's going to put you in danger."

"Don't be absurd." His mother opened the cabinet and retrieved four ceramic cups. "We're a family of law enforcement officers. James just retired after thirty years as a police officer and police chief. Daniel's brothers are both on the Bar Harbor police force."

James nodded. "We'll look out for you."

"Thank you," Shelby said.

Daniel's chest swelled. He'd known he could count on his family to help him keep Shelby safe. He just hoped and prayed they wouldn't need the help.

Chapter 13

Shelby sat at the table while Lea bustled around the kitchen scooping chowder into bowls and warming them in the microwave. Playful banter and shared stories about life on the police force filled the air and gave her the impression of the warmth between them and the love for their son.

When the front door opened and slammed shut, she jumped.

"That will be Daniel's brother," Lea reassured her. "He just got off his shift." She filled another bowl full of chowder and popped it into the microwave. "You two will have to fill him in on what's going on."

Daniel stood.

"Whose car is that?" A man looking a lot like Daniel entered the room and grinned, then pulled Daniel into a bear hug. "Well, you ol' son of a—"

"Robert." Daniel's mother nodded toward Shelby. "Keep it clean. We have company."

Robert's grin broadened. "As I was saying, you ol' son of a—"

"Robert!" Lea Henderson glared at her son. "Be nice and say hello to Shelby."

Shelby stood and held out our hand. "Nice to meet you."

"Well, hello." He gripped her hand, and his green-eyed gaze, so much like his brother's, roved her from head to toe. "The pleasure is all mine."

Daniel stepped forward. "Back off, Rob."

"Don't tell me, you're with him?" Robert rolled his eyes toward Daniel. "I don't know what you did to deserve her, but if she's got a sister, I got dibs." Robert winked. "Seriously, what do you see in that broken-down secret agent?"

Shelby didn't know how to answer that, so she kept her comments to herself.

Daniel's father saved her from answering. "Quit harassing your brother, son, and sit." He pulled out a chair and pointed. "We have serious matters to discuss."

At the tone of his father's voice, Robert sat, wiping the smile off his face. "What's going on?"

By the time Daniel filled him in, it was getting late and the stress of the past couple of weeks weighed heavily on Shelby's eyelids.

Robert shook his head. "Damn, Shelby, who'd you make mad?"

"I don't know." She covered her mouth as she yawned.

"Oh, honey, you need to get some rest." Mrs. Henderson slipped an arm around her and led her out of the kitchen. "We get up early around here, but don't feel like you have to, as well. Sleep as long as you need to."

"I'm okay, just tired."

His mother patted her arm. "Don't you worry. My men will make sure you're well protected."

"I don't want to be a burden," Shelby said.

Mrs. Henderson stopped in front of Daniel's bedroom door. "Honey, you're not a burden. I'm just sorry this is happening to you. I can't imagine how terrified you must have been." Her eyes misted and she pulled Shelby into a tight hug. "Two weeks held captive is awful. Your grandfather must have been beside himself."

Shelby's own eyes filled with tears. The warmth of Mrs. Henderson's hug reminded her of her grandfather. It made her feel homesick and wish everything could go back to the way it used to be. Before she'd been kidnapped. Before she'd learned who her grandmother was. But if she'd never been kidnapped, and if she wasn't Kate Winston's granddaughter, she'd never have met Daniel.

Lea held Shelby at arm's length and forced a watery smile. "Now, you get some rest and don't worry. We'll take good care of you." She cupped her face. "Such a pretty girl and so brave. Daniel would be smart not to let you slip through his fingers." She winked. "Speaking of Daniel, I'd better get him a blanket." Mrs. Henderson kissed Shelby's cheek. "Good night, dear."

Shelby entered Daniel's bedroom and closed the door behind her at the same time she flipped the light switch on.

The room was decorated in black, gold and white. Mrs. Henderson must have upgraded the decorations since her son had left the nest. The comforter, curtains and matching area rug looked new. But it was the photographs on the wall that drew Shelby.

Some of the pictures were of a miniature Daniel with laughter in his eyes and a smile on his face. Others were of the grown-up Daniel, hanging with his brothers or standing on the beach, looking out over the ocean. All of the pictures had been enlarged and printed in black-and-white to match the decor. Tastefully done, the photos personalized the room without making it a child's room. Obviously, the Hendersons loved their sons.

Having grown up an only child with one parental figure, Shelby had known a different life. There had been times, when she'd been at a sleepover with friends, that she'd observed families with a mom, dad and siblings and had wondered what it would be like growing up in the chaos.

Since she was a little girl, she'd sworn she'd have at least two kids so they'd never be lonely. They'd always have each other to play with.

Shelby roamed around the bedroom, feeling as if she was getting a glimpse into the boy who'd become Daniel. What a happy childhood he must have had. Not that hers had been unhappy. She paused at the French doors looking out over the ocean. The moon was full, shining brightly on the water and the silvery sands of the beach. After being cooped up in the car for the past thirteen hours, she needed to stretch her legs.

Pushing aside her exhaustion, she opened the door and stepped out onto the porch, inhaling the salty tang in the air, so much like home. A light, cool breeze lifted her hair off her face. She crossed the wooden planks and kicked off her shoes, then hurried down the steps, the sea calling to her.

Once her feet hit the sand, she couldn't stop. She walked out to where the tide slipped in and out, wetting the sand, packing it firmly.

With the moonlight lighting her way, Shelby set off, walking down the beach, her face to the wind, beach houses on one side, the ocean on the other. For the first time in weeks, she felt free. Free of captivity, free of confining walls and fences, free from potential exposure to the public as the granddaughter of a wealthy and politically connected woman.

On the beach, Shelby could be who she was. A child born and raised by a selfless grandfather who'd done the best he could with a little girl.

Caught up in the beauty and the feeling she'd come home, Shelby didn't hear the footsteps slapping against the sand behind her until they were almost upon her. Startled, she spun around to see a dark figure hell-bent on catching her.

Her heart slamming into her ribs, she took off running.

"Shelby!" A familiar voice called out. "Shelby, wait. It's me, Daniel."

She stopped at once and looked back at him as he raced to catch up with her.

Even in the dark, she could tell he favored his left leg. When he ground to a halt, he bent over, catching his breath while rubbing his leg. When he had his breathing under control, he straightened and glared at her. "Where the hell do you think you're going?"

"For a walk." She stared at his leg. "Is that where you were shot?"

"One of the places," he said. "You can't just go walking off without telling me. What if someone had attacked you? What if those jerks who'd taken you the first time somehow found out where you were and were waiting for you to take one step alone?"

Shelby touched a finger to his lips. "What if you would be quiet, take a deep breath of the salty air and enjoy the moonlight? Hmm? Think you can do that?" She crossed her legs and sank to the sand, catching his hand as she went down. "Come on, give that leg a break."

"It's fine."

"No, it's not." She pointed at the sand beside her. "Sit." With a smile, she added, "Please."

"I don't even have my gun on me."

"Good. Hopefully, we'll have this one night without bad guys and without guns to remind us there are bad guys. We can enjoy a beautiful night brought to you by a delightful moon." She held on to his hand until he sighed and lowered himself to the ground, stretching his sore leg out in front of him.

"See? That wasn't so hard, was it?" She lay back on the sand, crossing her arms behind her head. "Whenever school, friends, boyfriends or Granddad got me down, I'd sneak out at night and walk along the shore. The sound of the surf and the smell of salt in the air grounded me, reminding me that no matter how bad things were, the beach was only a few yards away."

Daniel lay down beside her, his hand behind his head. "Until you were kidnapped?"

"Yeah." Then she hadn't had the luxury of thinking the beach was only a few yards away. She'd been trapped in a dark, dingy place with no access to a beach or a window to look out on her beloved shoreline. Though it was dark out, the moonlight gave her hope, dispelling some of the blackness she'd experienced in that basement.

Daniel leaned up on one elbow and stared down at her. "You're safe now."

"I know." Her stomach fluttered and her pulse raced. Suddenly, she didn't feel so safe. From the bad guys, maybe. But from Daniel? Not so much. She realized she was in danger of falling for this man who'd told her more than once he wasn't in it for the long haul.

He smoothed his hand through her hair, brushing it back from her cheek. "Did you know that your hair looks like blue-black ink in the moonlight?"

"Did you know you could kiss me and I wouldn't object?" she whispered. She reached up and curled her fingers around the back of his neck. "Need a little help with that decision?"

"My head is telling me not to go there…but for some reason, I can't resist." He swept low, taking her lips in a crushing kiss, his tongue lancing out to caress hers in long slow thrusts.

Her core ached and her belly tightened with a need to be lying naked with this man or running into the waves, making love with him. When he let her up for air, she asked, "How cold is the water here?"

He kissed her forehead and the tip of her nose. "Around sixty degrees. Why?"

She laughed. "I've always wanted to go skinny-dipping, but never mind."

He pushed to his feet and reached toward her. "Come on." He captured her hand, dragging her up with him and started walking back toward the house.

Disappointment made her lag behind him. Why had she opened her big mouth? Maybe he didn't want to get naked in the water with her. Maybe he'd kissed her and had second thoughts.

She should have just gone to bed instead of venturing out on the beach and filling her head with sexy ideas about things she wanted to do to his body.

They mounted the porch steps, entered through the open French doors into his room and closed the door behind them. When Shelby thought he'd let go of her hand and leave her alone, she was wrong.

Daniel held on to her hand and continued through the bedroom to the door leading out into the hallway. It was dark and quiet, and the bathroom door stood open, the light off. Without pausing, Daniel crossed the hall, pulling her into the bathroom behind him. Not until he shut the door and twisted the lock did he turn and face her. Then he was kissing her, pressing her back against the wooden door.

She'd barely had time to catch her breath when he cupped her bottom and lifted. She wrapped her legs around his waist, feeling the hard ridge of him beneath his jeans pressing against her center.

"The ocean is too cold for skinny-dipping, but in case you didn't notice, there is a bathtub big enough for two."

Shelby glanced at the tub as Daniel trailed kisses along the side of her neck and down to where the pulse beat at the base of her throat. "Why would your parents install a tub this size in the guest bathroom?"

"You're looking a gift horse in the mouth?"

"No, no. I'm glad they did." She reached for the buttons on her shirt. "Is it hot in here?"

"Extremely." He set her on the floor, pushed her fingers aside and finished unbuttoning her shirt, then slid it off her shoulders, exposing her lacy bra. He bent to bite her nipple through the fabric.

Shelby yanked his T-shirt from his waistband, shoved it up over his head and tossed it to the floor. "Won't your parents hear us...you know...making noise?"

"Probably." He reached behind him and turned the handle on the bathtub faucet, adjusting it to the right temperature before returning his focus to her.

With her hands on the button of his jeans, she paused. "We really shouldn't."

"You're right. We shouldn't." He covered her hands with his and ripped open his jeans. "But we are."

She took over, dragging his zipper down. "Just say the word and I'll stop."

"Don't tease." He unclipped her bra in the back and flung it to the side.

"I feel guilty, doing this in your parents' hou—"

Daniel pressed his mouth to hers. "Anyone tell you that you talk too much?" He bit her bottom lip and tugged on it, then let go.

Shelby ran her tongue across the lip. "Just you."

"Then stop talking and get in the water." He quickly unbuttoned and unzipped her jeans and dragged them down over her legs. She stepped out of them and climbed into the tub, the water rising up to her ankles.

Moonlight shone through the glass-brick window over the tub, turning Daniel's body dark blue and silvery.

Shelby's breath caught and held as he stepped into the tub with her.

"Ever been skinny-dipping in a bathtub?" He eased into the water and pulled her down to lay across him, the displaced water rising around them.

"Not until now." She lay against the side of his chest, her hands smoothing over taut muscles, sliding lower, across rock-solid abs to the jutting evidence of his desire.

When her fingers curled around him, he thrust upward, sliding through her wet grip.

"You make me crazy," he whispered.

"Good." She moved over him, bracing her knees on either side of his hips, her entrance poised to receive him. "That makes two of us." It took every ounce of restraint to keep from taking him into her.

He cupped her cheek, brushing his thumb over her lip. "What are we going to do about it?"

Shelby kissed his thumb. "We're going to start with protection." She leaned over the side of the tub and reached for his jeans.

He caressed her bottom, his hand gliding across her skin, his fingers curving around to tickle the inside of her thigh.

She tensed, her search for his wallet focused, almost desperate. When she found it, she almost cried out in relief. "Please tell me you have one."

"And if I don't?" He chuckled, his finger finding her center and sliding into her channel.

Shelby gasped and breathed, "Then this night would be over. When I'm ready to have a baby, I'll forgo contraception." She flipped open the wallet and fished inside for the foil packet she'd known would be there. "You must have made top scores in agent school for being prepared." She held up the condom in triumph and tore it open. Scooting back, she rolled it down over him.

"I learned something else in agent school." He gripped her hips and held her up over him, nudging her, teasing her.

"Oh, yeah? Are you like James Bond and you kiss every girl involved in your case?"

"That's a good idea." He leaned up and kissed her lips. "But no. I learned that for every action, there's a reaction." He eased her down.

"I'm beginning to see your point," she said, her channel sliding around his shaft. "Perhaps you can drive it home?"

"Impatient?" He slowed her descent, guiding her down, one agonizing inch at a time.

"I'm a quick learner, are you a quick teacher?" She tried to speed up the process, but he held her at bay.

"Some things take a more delicate approach."

"Damn the delicate approach, I want you." She leaned down and took his lips as he started thrusting up into her, hard and fast.

"That's more like it," she said against his lips. She pushed against his chest, her back arching as she rode him, water splashing up around them.

All too soon, Daniel thrust hard and held her hips as his member throbbed inside her. He gave it a minute, then stood her on her feet and rose, water running down over his torso.

He soaped her body, she soaped his and together, they splashed each other free of suds. Then Daniel scooped her up and stepped out of the tub, setting her on the bath mat then grabbing two towels.

Shelby worked on drying him off, memorizing every inch of him as she worked over his body.

When she was done, Daniel dried her. He dropped to his knees and started at her feet, sliding the soft terry cloth up her calves and over her thighs, spreading her legs as he went. He dried the mound of hair at the apex of her thighs, then parted her folds and bent to touch that sliver of flesh nestled between with his tongue.

Shelby moaned and threaded her fingers through his short hair, urging him to give her more. "Please."

"Like that?" He tongued her again, sliding across her in a smooth, wet stroke.

She came up on her toes, her fingers digging into his scalp, aching to her very core. "Oh, yes!"

"Well, there might be more of that later." He rose and dried her bottom, her waist and upward to her breasts. There he paused to taste a nipple, sucking it into his mouth, rolling the bud between his teeth.

Shelby's body was on fire, craving anything and everything he could do to her. She cupped the back of his head and pressed her breast deeper into his mouth, her other hand sliding down his back to caress his tight ass.

When she thought she couldn't stand another moment of excruciating pleasure, he swept her into his arms, kicked open the bathroom door and strode across the hall.

Shelby clung to him, trying to cover her nakedness in case his family happened to be roaming the house and caught them on display.

A door opened at the other end of the hallway just as Daniel stepped across the threshold into his old bedroom. He kicked the door shut behind them.

"Are you insane? What if your mother or father had witnessed that?"

"I'm pretty sure I've seen them do something similar before. I didn't learn *everything* in agent school." He kissed her and tossed her on the bed.

Shelby liked it when he played rough and disregarded the rules. But in his parents' house?

Then he climbed over her, leaning up on his arms. "I didn't sign on to this job to make love to you."

She caressed his face, smiling up at him. "Consider it a perk."

"What happens when this is case is cleared?"

"I guess it's up to us."

"I'm an agent—"

She pressed a finger to his lips. "I know. Relationships aren't in the job description. So we take what we can get and part ways when you move on to your next assignment."

He frowned down at her. "You're okay with that?"

No, she wasn't, but she didn't have any other choice. Shelby forced a smile. "I'd rather have you for a little while than not at all." She slid her calf up the side of his thigh. "Now, are we going talk all night or are we going to make good use of the time we have together?" She cupped the back of his neck and brought his face close to hers. "Because I can think of a lot better things to do than talk."

"You know, I don't know what I did without you."

"Yeah, well, you'll find out soon enough. Now shut up and kiss me."

Daniel complied, kissing her deeply, taking her breath away with his tender caresses.

If she wished they could be together for longer than

the night, for a lifetime, she pushed the thought to the back of her mind and focused on what they had in that moment. Tomorrow the case might be solved, Daniel might move on and she'd be left to forget about him. Then again, tomorrow might never come and tonight might be all they had together.

Chapter 14

Daniel woke to the sun shining in through a window and the sound of voices coming from another room. When he tried to move, his arm was weighted down and something warm and soft snuggled up against his side.

Shelby's hand rested across his belly and her head lay in the crook of his shoulder, her cheek pressed against his chest. Her warm breath feathered across his skin, stirring him to back to life.

Part of him didn't want to wake her. He wanted to drink his fill, memorizing every contour of her face, her shoulder, breasts and hips to store the images in his mind for when she was no longer part of his life.

She stirred, her hand drifting lower until her knuckles bumped against his rapidly growing erection. He wanted her, but figured she needed her sleep after being up all night.

If he was a gentleman and very careful, he could slip out from under her, dress, go to the kitchen and let her sleep.

When her fingers curled around his shaft, all gentlemanly thoughts flew out the window and he thrust upward.

Shelby's eyes remained closed, but her breathing grew faster and her hand moved up and down, pumping him as he rocked his hips.

Within a few seconds, he rocketed over the edge, sensations exploding inside. Her movement continued until he captured her wrist and held it. "I take it you're awake."

"No," she said, her eyes still closed.

"Perhaps you need someone to wake you?"

"Perhaps," she whispered.

He leaned up on his elbow and touched a finger to her mouth, following it with his lips.

She was beautiful, her face kissed by sleep, her body perfectly proportioned and her skin as smooth to the touch as the finest silk.

Moving to her neck, he traced a path with his finger that his lips followed. As he worked his way downward, he tweaked a nipple until it budded into a tight little bead, then captured it with his lips, sucking it into his mouth.

Shelby's back arched and she moaned, her eyes still closed, a smile curling the corners of her lips.

His fingers slipped over her ribs and into her belly button, lower still to the puff of curls at the apex of her thighs.

She eased her legs apart, offering herself to his ministrations.

He accepted, parting her folds to stroke a finger across that narrow strip of flesh between.

Her breath caught and her eyes opened, their blue depths dark with desire.

His gaze captured hers, and he stroked again, sliding deeper to her slick entrance, damp with the dew of her arousal.

Daniel's member throbbed at the remembered feel of her tight, drenched channel encasing him in her heat.

Wanting her to experience that sense of utter ecstasy, he slipped down her body and lay between her legs, draping her thighs over his shoulders. He kissed the tender inner flesh and trailed his tongue and lips toward her center.

He hovered, blowing a warm stream of air over her dampness, then he flicked her nubbin with the tip of his tongue.

"There," she said. Digging her heels into the mattress, she lifted her hips up.

He tasted her again, licking, tweaking and flicking her until she twisted her fingers in his hair and gasped. "Stop."

"Am I hurting you?" he asked, concerned.

"Yes. No. In the most wonderful way." She remained tight, tense, her hips rocking even though he wasn't touching her at this point. A few moments later, she lowered herself to rest on the mattress, her arm flung over her head, her breathing slowing. "Wow."

Daniel grinned, smacked her thigh and rose to his feet.

"Wait." She grabbed his hand. "Where are you going? You're not done yet. I want you inside me."

"It'll have to wait. I'm out of condoms." He winked

and bent over her, kissing her lips. "Besides, my mother will be knocking on the door any min—"

A soft tapping sound interrupted him.

Shelby yanked the sheet up over her body, her eyes round, her cheeks flushed a bright pink.

"Good morning, Shelby. I hope that rowdy son of mine let you sleep. How do you like your eggs?" Mrs. Henderson asked from the other side of the door.

"Uh…scrambled, please."

"Do you two need the clothes you left in the bathroom? Or can I run them through the wash for you?"

Daniel laughed out loud while Shelby glared at him.

"Wash them, if you don't mind," Daniel responded.

"In the meantime, I have your duffel bag. I'll leave it here by the door. Breakfast will be ready in five minutes."

"Thank you, Mrs. Henderson."

Footsteps led away from the door.

Daniel opened it, grabbed the duffel and closed it again and was promptly hit by a flying pillow.

"I've never been so embarrassed in my life." Shelby threw the sheet back and stood, naked, angry and more beautiful than any woman he'd ever been with. Her blue eyes flashing, she advanced on him. "Why didn't you warn me sooner?"

He pulled her into his arms. "I didn't want to spoil the moment." With her naked body pressed to his, he wanted nothing more than to go back to bed and take her with him. "Why don't we skip breakfast?"

She leaned into him, her pelvis nudging his member. For a moment, she hesitated, then she leaned back. "We'd better get going. I refuse to show up to breakfast naked or give your mother the opportunity to come storming in to demand we make an appearance."

He kissed her. "Mom doesn't storm." He kissed her again. "Not much, anyway."

Three loud knocks pounded on the door.

"Hey, you two, break it up in there. Mom's got breakfast waiting. Humph! Not together, my royal hind end."

"Beat it, Robert!" Daniel yelled over his shoulder. "I guess we'd better show up."

Shelby dressed then crossed the hall to the bathroom.

Daniel slipped on his jeans and joined her to splash water over his face, then he ran a comb through his hair. Standing beside her at the sink felt natural and good. He could imagine what it would be like to live with her on a permanent basis.

The thought caught him by surprise, and he nearly bolted for the door. "I'll see you in the kitchen. Take your time."

She ran the brush through her hair one last time and smiled. "I'm ready." No makeup, her hair falling straight and shiny to her shoulders, she was everything a man could ask for.

A man who wasn't an agent, disappearing for weeks at a time on assignment.

If he wasn't careful, he'd fall for Shelby, and what would that accomplish? Nothing but heartache.

Keep it simple. This is only a fling, he tried to remind himself.

Shelby entered the kitchen behind Daniel, her face burning and almost afraid to face Daniel's parents.

"Shelby, you look refreshed, I hope you slept well. Sit." Mrs. Henderson smiled and waved a spatula toward the table. "Robert beat you to the scrambled eggs, but I'll have yours ready in just a minute. "Daniel, get the juice from the refrigerator and pour your guest a glass."

Daniel leaned close to Shelby and said in a loud whisper, "Our mother doesn't ask, she orders and we obey."

"Damn right we do," Robert said, taking a deep bite out of a piece of toast slathered in jelly. "Do as she says or miss out on her great cooking."

Shelby sat the table, enjoying the teasing between the brothers.

"All I have to say is, yes, ma'am!" Daniel yanked open the refrigerator and grabbed the jug of orange juice. "Where's Dad?"

"He's down at the marina, buying up enough lobster for a lobster bake this afternoon."

"Is there a festival or something?"

"No, but we had invited a few friends over before we knew you two were coming." Mrs. Henderson frowned. "We can cancel if want us to."

"No, no. We're the ones intruding on your plans," Shelby said. "Besides, I have to admit, though I've lived on the beach all my life, I've never been to a lobster bake."

"Then you're in for a real treat." Robert grinned. "I'm in charge of setting up the pit."

"You?" Daniel's brow wrinkled. "I remember you almost burned down a tent the last time you were in charge of the pit."

"That was eight years ago. I've had more success since then."

"Since he joined the police department, he's become a model citizen." Mrs. Henderson's chest swelled. "I'm so proud of my boys."

"Speaking of boys, where's Marcus?" Daniel asked.

"He and Stacey will join us this afternoon." Mrs. Henderson laid a plate full of fluffy yellow eggs in front of Shelby, along with a smaller plate of toast and bacon. "Eat up. I need you two to pick up some extra tablecloths at the store in town. It's not very far and you can show Shelby around. Take her down on Main to the yogurt shop."

"Mom, we're not here on vacation."

"Good grief, son, you can't hold her prisoner. Get out and show her a good time." Lea winked at Shelby. "Daniel can be too serious sometimes."

"I've noticed," Shelby said.

"All right, then, a day in Bar Harbor it is." He dug into his scrambled eggs. "If we don't, my mother will nag me until I do something to entertain our guest."

"He's got that right," Lea said.

Shelby felt more at home in the Henderson house than she'd ever thought she would. She genuinely liked Daniel's parents and even though his brother teased him, she could tell they loved each other.

Ten minutes later, she and Daniel were on their way to Bar Harbor in his father's truck.

"Don't be late. The party starts at five!" his mother called out as the truck pulled out of the driveway.

Once they were out of sight of his home, Daniel glanced her way. "Sorry, my mother loves to organize our lives."

Shelby smiled. "I think she's sweet."

"My father puts up with her. She has to have a project or *he* becomes her project."

Shelby's smile lasted all the way into town. She liked his parents and the way he and his brother acted together. If she ever had a family, she wanted a husband who cared and definitely more than one child. As an only child, she hadn't known what she was missing. Her grandfather had tried to fill all the gaps by being her father, mother and best friend when she needed a shoulder to cry on. It wasn't the same as having siblings, but she wouldn't trade her grandfather for anything. He'd been the center of her universe for so long.

Daniel parked just off Main Street and they walked along the sidewalks, window-shopping. Daniel held her hand and she pretended they were a couple, there to relax and enjoy the small tourist town.

What did it hurt to imagine? She knew this wasn't real. As directed, they stopped at the yogurt shop and got a double-dip waffle cone that melted as they stood outside the store, licking as fast as they could. Shelby caught a glimpse of them reflected in the window and a lump formed in her throat.

They looked like a couple. As if they belonged together. Her heart fluttered and her gut knotted. If only...

Another reflection caught her attention. A man passed behind them, his dark head down, his gaze shooting to the side, capturing hers for a brief second.

Maybe her imagination was overactive, but she could swear it was the same man she'd seen on the trip up from North Carolina. The one who'd been in the convenience store when she'd come out of the bathroom.

Shelby's head whipped around. "I swear I've seen that man before, in North Carolina."

"What man?"

A crowd of teenagers chose that moment to walk by, crowding the sidewalk, jostling each other and bumping into her and Daniel.

She craned her neck and stood on her toes. "I don't see him now." With a shrug, she dropped down on her feet. "I'm probably just paranoid."

"You're dripping." Daniel handed her a napkin.

Shelby had been searching for the stranger so long, her frozen yogurt had leaked through the hole in the bottom of the cone. She quickly licked the drips and sucked on the tip. When she'd eaten all she could, she tossed the rest into a nearby trash can and wiped her hands and mouth with the tattered napkin.

Daniel stuffed the last bite into his mouth and licked his lips. "Nothing better than frozen yogurt on a sunny day."

"Missed a spot."

"Where?" He tipped his face from side to side.

Shelby caught his cheeks between her palms and bent his head toward her. "Here." She kissed the tip of his nose and then took his lips in a sweet, creamy kiss.

When she stepped back, he grabbed her around the middle and pulled her against him. "You missed a spot, too." His mouth brushed across hers, then his tongue swept along her lips and pushed between her teeth. When he came up, he grinned. "I think I got it." He grabbed her hand. "Come on, there's something I want to show you. We can get there and back if we hurry."

"Where?"

"You'll see."

He led her back to the truck and drove around the point to park along the side of the road next to other vehicles.

Daniel got out and helped Shelby down. Then he grabbed her hand. "We'll have to hurry."

"Why?"

"We have to beat the tide."

Not sure what he was talking about, she half ran and half walked down a road toward the water.

When she reached the end of the road, it turned into a gravel sandbar that led across the bay to an island.

"That's Bar Island. While the tide is out, you can get there and back on foot. Come on." He hustled her across the long bar to the small island with lush green trees and giant boulders peppering the shore.

By the time they reached the island, Shelby was panting.

"Now you can have the best view of Bar Harbor. Turn around."

She turned and stared back at the point where the grand hotels lined the shores and a huge sailing ship with four tall masts lay anchored off the shore. Sailboats and yachts skimmed through the water around them.

A few other hikers were walking back across the land bridge to Bar Harbor, leaving Daniel and Shelby alone on the island.

Shelby could almost imagine how it would be if she and Daniel were marooned on a deserted island. After all the drama of the past few days, it sounded like heaven.

Daniel slipped an arm around her waist and hugged

her close against him. "I almost wish we didn't have to go back."

Her stomach fluttered. It was as if he'd read her mind.

"We have a date with some lobster tonight and it gets pretty cold out here, otherwise I'd say to hell with it." He carried her hand to his lips and kissed her palm. "We'd better get back. The tide is coming in. If we don't hurry, we'll be stranded."

She sighed and held tightly to Daniel's hand as they hurried back across the land bridge, the water rapidly inching up the sides. At one point, they had to leap to get over a spot where the water completely covered the sandbar. They ran the rest of the way, the water rising to cover their feet as they reached shore.

Shelby ran up the bank and turned, looking back, her heart hammering against her ribs. The land bridge had completely disappeared and only water stretched between the mainland and Bar Island.

Shelby laughed and leaned into Daniel. "That was amazing."

"Bar Harbor has its attractions. My brothers and I got caught on the island more than once. Mom and Dad grounded us from going there until we could prove we had enough sense to get off before the tide came in."

"You and your brothers sound as if you have given your parents many a gray hair."

He turned and started up the road toward the street where they'd parked the truck. "My parents were both gifted with healthy heads of hair that haven't turned gray even as they entered their fifties. I hope to inherit that particular trait from them."

Shelby tilted her head. "I hadn't pegged you for a vain man."

"Isn't it always said that to be successful in life, you have to keep a full head of hair and stand over six feet tall?" He stood straighter, far exceeding the height limit for success. "So far, I meet the criteria."

"Success is relative. There's the extremely rich, like my grandmother, who have enough money to own a car in a color to match every outfit." Shelby looked ahead at the passing cars, picturing her grandfather waiting on customers, a smile on his face. "And there's the small-business owner just trying to make a living. I consider my grandfather successful. When he took over the bar from his father, he brought it back to life. It doesn't make a ton of money, but it employs a number of people, provides decent food and drinks and generates enough profit that I was able to go to college."

"He is a successful man. And his greatest success of all was raising you to be an amazing woman."

She shrugged. "I'm not that amazing yet. But I hope to be. My grandfather gave up a lot to raise my mother and then me. He deserves an easier life."

They arrived at the street and turned toward the truck. "Do you think your grandfather would want an easier life?"

Shelby snorted. "No. Sitting around watching television would drive him nuts. He thrives on being with people."

Daniel held the door to the truck open for Shelby and helped her up into it. "Your grandfather is a special man."

Her heart squeezing in her chest, her gaze met his. "He is, and I miss him already."

Daniel leaned in and kissed her lips. "We'll get you home soon."

"I hope so."

After closing her door, Daniel rounded the front of the truck and stepped out into the street to open his own door.

Shelby's gaze followed him, admiring how tall and straight he stood, like a man with military training— strong, proud and determined to do what was right.

She glanced over her shoulder, gauging the traffic flow as Daniel opened his door.

A dark SUV barreled toward the truck, faster than the posted speed limit.

Daniel had his hand on the steering wheel and was about to step up into the truck.

Shelby reached across the seat, grabbed his hand and pulled as hard as she could. "Get in!"

Daniel sprawled across the seat and pulled his feet into the truck's cab right before the SUV slammed into the open door of the truck, ripping it right off its hinges and sending it flying across the pavement into oncoming traffic. The truck rocked violently, skidded forward and slid to a stop.

A car coming from the other direction swerved out of the SUV's way and ran up on the opposite sidewalk, scattering pedestrians.

The SUV never slowed as it continued down the street, burning a layer of rubber off the tires as it accelerated.

Daniel jumped out of the truck and raced after the speeding vehicle. He ground to a halt and turned back, asking a man on the side of the road, "Did you see a license plate?"

The man shook his head.

When Daniel reached the truck, he leaned in. "You okay?"

Shelby nodded. "I should be asking you that. It was your side that was hit."

"I am now. Stay put while I clean up the mess."

"But I can help."

"I'd feel better if you stayed where you are. Please." He reached in and squeezed her hand and then circled the truck to check the damage.

A couple stopped to ask if he was okay or needed help.

Shelby debated getting out, but figured she'd cause him less worry by staying where she was.

Daniel retrieved the damaged door from the middle of the road and tossed it into the truck bed. Then he climbed into the doorless side of the pickup and buckled his seat belt. "I don't like it."

"You think it was just an accident?"

He shook his head. "I hope the hell it wasn't something to do with you."

Shelby's gut was knotted, her hands shaking. Daniel had almost been hit. "It looked as if he was aiming for you."

Daniel turned the key in the ignition and the engine fired up. "You sure it wasn't some kid texting?"

"I didn't see the driver."

He rested his hand on the gearshift. "Did you happen to catch a license plate number?"

Shelby shook her head. "It all happened too fast."

Daniel shifted into Drive and pulled out onto the street. "When we get to my parent's home, I'll call my brother on the police force and have him submit the hit-and-run as an anonymous report. They can be on the lookout for the SUV."

Shelby shivered. "That man nearly killed you."

"But he didn't. Let's get back to the house. I have to break it to my father that I wrecked his favorite truck." Daniel's mouth twisted. "I haven't had to do that for over ten years."

Shelby sat in the seat beside him, her hands clasped together to keep them from shaking. She'd almost lost Daniel and she was shocked at how much she cared.

Chapter 15

When Daniel pulled into his parents' driveway, the street was lined with cars. People he vaguely remembered were climbing out, carrying beach blankets and tote bags, and wearing large beach hats.

"We're just in time for the party."

"I don't feel much like partying," Shelby said.

"Look, we can't dwell on what happened. It'll solve nothing. Dad's insurance will cover the damage and fix up the truck like new." He unbuckled his seat belt and slipped out of his side of the truck.

"I could care less about the truck. It's *you* I worry about."

"I'm okay." He helped her out of the truck. "Put it all behind you. We're here and my parents have planned an epic lobster bake that my brother is cooking." He held out a hand for her and she placed her more delicate one in it. "All we have to do is play on the beach, maybe take the WaveRunners out and enjoy this beautiful, sunny day." He grinned and slipped an arm around her waist. "See? I'm fine, you're fine. We're gonna have a good time."

Shelby stepped down from the truck, still holding on after she was safely on the ground.

He wished he felt as confident as he was pretending to be. The earlier wreck had shaken him almost as much as it had Shelby. Especially since he'd only recently returned to duty after being in the hospital for gunshot wounds.

"You go inside, find your skimpiest bikini and get ready for a party."

"How do you know I have a skimpy bikini?"

He raised his hand. "I admit, I noticed your tan line last night. You, my dear, have a teeny-weeny bikini that I'm betting will make all the other girls green with envy."

"Fine. I'll get changed, but don't disappear for long." She walked ahead of him into the house.

"I'll be there in a minute. I need to report the accident and then find my father and pull him aside to break the news."

"You want me to be with you?"

"No, thanks, I've got this."

He sent Shelby down the hallway and he ducked into the kitchen where he found his mother at the center island butcher block chopping lettuce and tomatoes for a salad.

"Where's Dad?"

She glanced up, her keen-eyed gaze piercing through him. "Something wrong?"

He never could lie to his mother, she saw through him and his brothers every time. "Yeah, but I need to tell him."

She wiped her hands on her apron and turned to peer out the back window over the kitchen sink. "He's out on the porch talking with the neighbor."

"Daniel!" Marcus, the youngest of the Henderson boys entered the kitchen, a pretty blonde holding on to his arm wearing a bright red bikini and a sheer wrap over the revealing scraps of material. "Stacey, this is my oldest brother, Daniel. Daniel, this is Stacey."

"Nice to meet you." He shook Stacey's hand, then enveloped his baby brother in a bear hug. "How are you?"

"Good. I'm working the graveyard shift for the next two weeks, but other than my nights and days being confused, I'm fine."

"I might need your assistance in a minute. First, I need to find Dad."

"I'll help your mother. You go on." Stacey smiled and gave Marcus a shove toward the door.

Daniel pushed through the back door and stepped out onto the porch.

James Henderson stood on the porch with a group of men, talking as he looked out over the expanse of beach a hundred feet from his yard.

"Dad," Daniel said. "I need you for a few minutes."

Just then, Robert climbed the porch steps. "The coals are getting hot. We'll be ready for the lobster and fixings soon."

"Your brother needs my attention." Daniel's father said. "I'll be right back."

Daniel nodded to Robert. "If you've got a minute, I could use your advice, as well."

"Sounds serious." Robert wiped his hands on the apron he had tied around his neck.

Daniel led the way around to the other side of the house and out to the damaged pickup.

"Wow, Daniel!" Marcus stood back, his eyes wide. "I put a dent in Dad's old truck back in the day, but never ripped a door off."

"I didn't rip it off. Someone sideswiped me on one of the main roads. From what Shelby witnessed, it appeared he was aiming straight for me."

His father ran his hand over the ragged edges of the hinges. "Damn." He looked up. "You sure you're okay? That SUV hit hard enough to rip the door clean off the hinges. If it had hit you… Damn. Don't tell your mother. Let her think it happened while you were clear of the vehicle."

"Tell me what?" His mother walked out of the house, wiping her hands on her apron.

"Nothing, dear."

"Oh, dear lord, what happened to your truck?"

"An accident. The insurance will cover it. We have a lobster bake about to kick off—we don't have time to worry about a dumb old truck." Daniel's father wrapped his arm around his wife and guided her back in the house.

"Do you think this had anything to do with Shelby's situation?" his mother asked.

"I don't know, but I could use some extra eyes watching out for her at the lobster bake."

"You got it."

Daniel entered the house and went in search of

Shelby. When he opened the door to his bedroom, he stopped, his breath stolen away by the beauty standing in front of him.

"Too much?" Shelby turned left then right, displaying a lot of her beautiful skin in a tiny powder-blue bikini that matched her eyes perfectly.

"Too little."

"I thought you liked tiny bikinis."

"I do, but in private. Every male eye will be on you at the lobster bake."

"I doubt that."

"Really?" He turned her to look into the mirror over the dresser. "Look at yourself. You're amazing." His hands rested on her hips, and he pulled her back against him, nuzzling her neck.

"I believe we're expected."

"Let them all wait."

"Daniel!" His mother called out. "Could you help Marcus get the WaveRunners started?"

Daniel drew in a deep breath and let it out slowly. "Duty calls. And you're coming with me." He glanced down. "Do you have a T-shirt or some kind of cover-up?"

"I thought you wanted me in a bikini."

"Oh, you'll need the bikini where we're going."

"I thought you said the ocean temp was around sixty degrees."

"It is, but the idea is not to stay in it for long." He nodded toward her duffel. "Get that T-shirt and I'll grab some towels."

Daniel found the beach towels in the hall closet.

Shelby emerged from the bedroom wearing a Hawaiian patterned skirt over her bikini bottoms.

He groaned. The cover-up did little to detract from her shapely curves, if not enhancing them exponentially. He'd be fighting off the local guys before the end of the evening.

He hurried out to the beach where Robert had dug a pit in the gravelly sand, and the smell of roasting lobster filled the air.

Marcus waved to him from the water's edge where two WaveRunners stood.

Shelby followed Daniel to his brother. Marcus had the engine compartment open and he fiddled with the wires inside.

He glanced up, his gaze traveling over Shelby's exquisite body and the blue bikini. Marcus gave a slow, sexy wolf whistle and got punched in the shoulder by his older brother for it.

"Keep your tongue in your head, little brother. You have a girlfriend."

"So I have a girlfriend. Does it hurt to recognize beauty when you see it?"

"I don't know. You tell me." Daniel punched his brother's arm again.

Marcus rubbed the shoulder, frowning. "I guess it does." Then he looked down at the WaveRunner. "I've tried all the easy solutions."

Daniel looked at the engine, spotted the problem and had it running in less than five minutes. He turned to Shelby. "This is why you needed the bikini."

"We're going to ride those?" Her blue eyes lit up and she grinned, stripping her skirt down over her legs. "I've only ridden something like this twice, so I'll need a little instruction."

"You can ride with me, and Marcus will take the other."

"Good." She gripped the handles and, with Daniel's help, pushed the machine out into deeper water. He helped her mount the WaveRunner, then he climbed up behind her, straddling her hips.

With a few short instructions, he guided her in how to start, give it gas and stop. "It really is simple. And don't be afraid of speed. Going too slow makes it unstable."

"Ready?" she asked, her fingers curled tightly around the handgrips.

"Ready."

She gave it the gas and the WaveRunner shot forward, almost unseating him.

He grabbed her around the waist and held on as she plowed through the waves closest to shore, riding up then sinking down. Once she'd cleared the waves, she gave it all it would take, zooming across the bay, her hair flying out behind her.

Shelby let out an excited whoop and turned sharply, the tail end of the machine swinging out behind them. The centrifugal force nearly threw Daniel off on the next turn. He braced his feet on the running boards and held on tightly.

After a moment, she slowed to a halt. "Are you okay back there?"

"Doing fine," he said, enjoying the look of rapture on her face. "Are you sure you've only driven one of these two times?"

She shrugged. "Only two," she confirmed.

Marcus blew past them, headed along the shoreline toward the point.

"Hold on!" Shelby shouted and gunned the throttle, shooting forward.

Daniel's feet left the running boards. He held on tightly around Shelby's waist as she raced after Marcus. Marcus pulled sharply around and headed back in the opposite direction.

Not to be outdone, Shelby followed suit.

As Shelby made a sweeping turn, Daniel held on to her.

Before she got all the way around, a motorboat came out of nowhere, aimed straight for her.

"Turn!" Daniel shouted.

Shelby jerked the handlebar to the right and gunned it.

Daniel clung to her waist, gripping the seat of the WaveRunner with his thighs.

At first, he thought the driver of the boat wasn't paying attention. Daniel looked over his shoulder. The boat turned around and headed straight for them again.

"He's coming back!" he yelled.

"What should I do?" Shelby cried.

"Go straight until I tell you to turn." Daniel prayed he could judge the speed of both watercraft.

The boat sped toward them, full-on, as fast as it could go.

Shelby gave the little WaveRunner all it had.

"Slow down."

"What?"

"You heard me, slow down," he insisted.

The boat was almost on them when Daniel yelled, "Turn right!" He reached around her and laid his hands over hers, yanking the handlebar to the right at the same time as he gunned the throttle. He could feel the blast of air and spray from the wake churned up by the motor.

When the boat turned and aimed for them yet again, Marcus raced in front of them, kicking up a rooster tail that splashed into the driver's face. The craft slowed, then sped up again.

Daniel aimed for the shore, giving the WaveRunner all it had. They couldn't keep up the fight with the motorboat; their best chance was to run ashore and get out of the water altogether.

His focus on the shore, Daniel steered to one side of where the people who had gathered for the lobster bake were now crowded, witnessing their fight for survival.

When they realized he was heading straight for them, the mass of people dodged to the side. Daniel ran the WaveRunner all the way up on dry land before he killed the engine, jumped off and pulled Shelby into his arms.

Robert stood on the shore, his weapon pointed at the boat behind them.

At the last minute, the motorboat whipped to the left and raced away, speeding across the water and around the point, out of sight.

Marcus brought his WaveRunner ashore and jumped off. "What the hell was that all about?"

With Shelby tucked in the crook of his arm, her body shaking and her face pale, Daniel had reached his boiling point. "Let's take this discussion inside."

Shelby was thankful for Daniel's support as she walked up the beach to the house. The fear of being chased by a motorboat full of thugs ranked right up there with being kidnapped and held hostage.

She and Daniel had come very close to being killed or drowning in the wake of their attacker's boat.

Mrs. Henderson came into the kitchen from another part of the house, took one look at her sons and Shelby and asked, "What happened?"

Daniel filled her and his father in on the attack and his mother's face blanched.

"Oh, my dear, sweet child." She wrapped Shelby in a tight hug and patted her hair, treating her as if she were a frightened little girl.

Tears welled in Shelby's eyes at the care and concern from a woman who'd only known her a day.

Daniel's father patted her back. "Are you okay?"

Shelby nodded, unable to speak around the tight knot constricting her vocal cords.

Robert was on his cell phone, giving details of the attack to what sounded like the police station where he worked.

Mrs. Henderson set her at arm's length and guided her to a chair. "Sit down before you collapse."

Grateful for the chair, Shelby sank onto the seat before her wobbly legs buckled.

A moment later, Mrs. Henderson planted a hot mug of tea in front of her. "Drink that. You're shaking like a leaf."

Shelby wrapped her hands around the warm mug, thankful for something to keep them from trembling.

Marcus charged into the room. "Holy smokes! That was insane. I didn't think you two were going to make it."

Mrs. Henderson frowned at her youngest son. "Marcus."

"Well, it's true. I thought that boat would run them right over."

Shelby forced a laugh she didn't feel. "You and me both."

Robert clicked the off button and turned toward Daniel and Shelby. "The station put out a report to the Maine marine patrol and the state police."

"Should we send everyone home?" Mrs. Henderson asked. "I'd hate for anyone else to get hurt."

"Not on my account." Shelby pushed to her feet, thankful her knees held. "I should leave. It was a bad idea to come here. The people after me seem to know where I'm going almost before I do."

"You're not going anywhere." Lea slipped an arm around her waist. "You're staying with us until we can figure this out."

She shook her head. "I can't get you all involved. It's too dangerous."

"We're not going anywhere until I check in with Kate and my boss," Daniel said.

"In the meantime, we have lobster for dinner." Mr. Henderson nodded toward Robert. "Or are they burning?"

"I'm on it." Robert spun and headed out the door at a jog.

"I'm keeping you all from your guests." Shelby smiled at the Hendersons. "I was really looking forward to the lobster bake."

"The guests know the routine. Sit on the beach, play music and eat lobster. We don't have to entertain them. And if you're surrounded by my big, strapping sons, there's no reason you still can't participate."

Daniel frowned. "It'll be dark outside soon."

"If we're all there," Marcus pointed out, "whoever is after her won't be able to get to her." He hooked Shelby's elbow. "What do you say, sister?" He followed with a playful wink.

"I'm game. Isn't Maine known for its lobster? It would be a crime to leave without trying some." She glanced at Daniel.

His face was set in stone, his brows dipped low. "I don't know if this is such a good idea."

"We won't go out on the water."

"What if they start shooting at you?"

"Then they could get me on the porch as easily as on the beach. And if I wear a hoodie, maybe they won't pick me out of the crowd."

"She has a point, dear." Daniel's mother touched his arm. "Let the girl enjoy her first lobster bake. We'll stay with her while she's outside. Won't we?" She glanced around at her two sons and her husband.

Daniel's frown eased slightly. "Okay, but we're not staying out all night."

"Agreed," Marcus said. He tugged on Shelby's arm. "Come on, the lobster won't last long with this hungry bunch. And I'd like to show up out there with the prettiest girl in a bikini."

Shelby glanced back at Daniel, hesitant to leave the house without him by her side.

"Beat it, Marcus." Daniel grabbed Shelby's arm from the other side. "You have your own date."

"Darn, I've always wanted to have two women to myself." Marcus winked.

"And how would Stacey feel about that?"

"Surely she'd understand. Most women would, right?"

"Marcus Henderson," his mother chastised. "Quit before you dig yourself into a hole."

"Yes, ma'am."

"Marcus?" Stacey entered through the back door. "Marcus? Are you in here?"

"There's my cue." Marcus hurried forward to take Stacey in his arms. "There you are. I've been searching all over for you."

Her brows wrinkled. "I was getting my things out of your car. Seems I missed all the excitement. What happened?"

He took her hand and led her out the back door. "Just a little fun and games on the WaveRunner, courtesy of my brother and his girlfriend."

Shelby opened her mouth to straighten them out about the girlfriend label. She wasn't Daniel's girlfriend. Lover, maybe, but girlfriend implied a level of commitment he wasn't willing to give.

But after running from a crazed motorboat driver, she didn't think it was worth the trouble to argue over something as minuscule as being called Daniel's girlfriend.

Instead of guiding her out the back door, he led her to his bedroom.

"I thought we were having lobster."

He rifled through his dresser and unearthed an old U2 T-shirt and held it open. "Much as I love you in that bikini, it's a moving target. Wear this." She took the shirt from him and put it on. The hem fell over her hips and halfway down her thighs, covering all her curves. So much for attracting Daniel's attention. He took out an old baseball cap from his closet and handed it to her. "I wore that to the junior varsity championships my freshman year in high school."

She held the hat in her hand, sensing another piece of Daniel's history in the item. He'd had a normal childhood, surrounded by a loving mother, father and siblings to keep him company.

Shelby would have loved being a part of a family like Daniel's. But she had her grandfather, and he was everything to her. The only times she'd missed her mother was at mother–daughter events in grade school and high school.

She pulled the cap over her head and stuffed her hair beneath it. "There. Am I a nondescript blob enough so that no one will suspect it's Shelby O'Hara beneath the brim?"

Daniel stood back, his eyes narrowing, the green so deep it reminded her of an evergreen forest at dusk, deep, mysterious and unfathomable. "I wouldn't say you were a blob. Even your legs are sexy sticking out from the hem of the T-shirt." He dragged her into his arms and held her close. "We don't have to go out if you don't want to."

"Your parents went to all the trouble of a lobster bake, we might as well make a showing. Besides, I wasn't kidding about the Maine lobster. I want the real thing, not some farm-raised lobsters."

Daniel kissed the tip of her nose, took her hand and walked to the door. "Come on. I have a lobster with your name on it."

With her hand in his, Shelby felt as if she could conquer the world, bad guys be damned.

She pushed to the back of her mind the reality that he would someday soon leave her. She'd gotten used to having him around. And the more she learned about him, the more there was to love.

She stumbled, her heart beating more wildly in her chest than when she'd been kidnapped or chased by a killer boat.

Could it be that she'd committed the ultimate mistake? Was she falling in love with Daniel?

If so, she was in for a whole lot of heartbreak.

Chapter 16

Daniel stayed attached to Shelby's side as family and friends gathered around the fire pit with plates of steaming lobster, corn on the cob and clams. If he wasn't so scared of someone taking a potshot at her, he'd relax and enjoy watching her experience her first lobster bake.

But every loud noise and every engine rev made him jump. With the sun beneath the horizon for the night, the air had chilled. He'd stuck his pistol in the pocket of his jacket and kept one hand on it at all times, the other arm around Shelby. Not only did he like holding Shelby, but it also kept her close and secure against his side.

Shelby dug into the lobster like a pro, her face covered in juice, her lips dripping with butter sauce.

Daniel couldn't resist. He leaned over and captured

a drop of butter, sucking her bottom lip into his mouth. "Mmm. Tasty."

"The butter?"

"No, you."

She leaned into him, staring at the fire. "I could stay like this forever."

"Not me."

She sat up straight. "I'm sorry. Was I making you uncomfortable?"

"Yes," he said. "In the best, worst way." He shifted, tugging his jeans to a looser position.

She smiled, her blue eyes shining. "In that case..." Leaning back against him, she took another piece of lobster, dipped it in a cup of butter, popped it into her mouth, chewed and swallowed.

Every movement she made looked incredibly sexy. She even made butter look desirable. When she started licking her fingers, he grabbed her hand, raised it to his lips and sucked her finger into his mouth. "Mmm. You're delicious."

She laughed. "Not me, the butter."

He sucked her finger into his mouth again. "No, it's you."

Shelby pulled her finger from his mouth and kissed his lips. "Do you kiss all your jobs like this?"

"Mostly when I'm undercover. You and Kate Winston are my only bodyguard gigs so far in the Secret Service."

"Really?" She stared at him for a moment. "You haven't kissed Kate, have you?" Her brows furrowed. "I mean that would be really weird, kissing my grand-mother and all."

Daniel laughed. "No, I haven't kissed Kate. You are my only lapse in professionalism."

Her furrows deepened. "That doesn't sound romantic at all."

"It wasn't supposed to."

She clucked her tongue. "Here we are, on a beach with a fire warming our faces, the sound of the surf to give the place ambience and you ruin it by calling me a lapse in professionalism."

"It's a lapse I can't seem to shake."

"Then stop trying." She stood, held out her hand, looking a lot younger than her twenty-three years wearing the extralong T-shirt. She turned to his mother and father. "This was lovely. Thank you for including me."

His father and brothers stood. "Do you want us to follow you two to the house?"

Shelby glanced at Daniel. "I think we'll be okay."

Daniel took her hand and let her tug him to his feet. "Are you ready to go inside?" He glanced around, carefully searching the shadows for anyone lurking, waiting to pounce.

"Yes, I'm ready." Her lips quirked at the corners as they moved away from the people sprawled on the beach, finishing up the last of the clams and lobster. "I'm ready to show you that I'm not a lapse in professionalism." She tilted her head, a lift to her step. "I'm more of a rebellious streak you'll soon grow out of." She left him standing in the sand and ran up the path to the house.

Daniel's pulse kicked up and he ran after her. Catching her by the waist, he swung her around and set her on her feet. "A rebellious streak, huh?" Taking her hand, he climbed the steps slowly enough for her to keep up, when he'd rather be running through the door and down the hallway to his bedroom.

She paused on the porch and looked out over the bay where the moonlight glistened like diamonds on the water. "You grew up in a beautiful place."

He wrapped his arms around her waist and pulled her back against him, nibbling at her neck. "You wouldn't think so in the winter. It's brutally cold."

"I'm sure you find ways to keep warm." Shelby leaned her head to the side, allowing him better access to her neck.

He pulled her hat off, letting her hair down around her shoulders, loving the way it fell into place no matter how disturbed by a hat, wind or rain. Perfect in every way, and he was so very wrong for her.

She deserved a man who'd stick around, be there for her when she needed him. A man who'd share diaper duty when kids came along, who'd go to all the soccer games and T-ball practice. Not a man who'd be on assignment, away from home, out of contact for weeks at a time.

Shelby needed someone else. Not him. He stiffened and was about to pull away when her hands curled around his and brought them up beneath the T-shirt to cup her bikini-clad breasts.

"I can tell when you start thinking too much." She reached behind her and loosened the clasp on the bikini top, giving his hands free access to her. "Stop thinking and live in the moment. I don't expect anything from you past today."

He couldn't stop himself. Not now that she'd invited him to play. With his palms cupping her, he couldn't focus past the way her nipples tightened into little buds. He closed his fingers around the knobby tips and pinched, pulling softly.

Her back arched and her hands cupped his, encouraging him to continue. While one hand stayed firmly over one breast, she dragged the other downward and slipped it beneath the elastic of her bikini bottom.

As they stood on the porch in the moonlight, his fingers curled around her sex, one sliding up inside her.

She leaned into him, rubbing her bottom against the ridge beneath his shorts, letting her head drop back against his shoulder.

"Shouldn't we take this inside?" he whispered against her earlobe.

"I thought I was your rebellious streak. Are you telling me you're a lot tamer than that?"

His blood coursed through his veins. "I think I had you all wrong."

"How's that?" Her hand curved over the one in her bottoms, pressing another finger into her channel.

"You're not a goody-goody at all."

"I never claimed to be. However, I was a little more conservative until I met a Secret Service agent who lured me over to the dark side." She led his finger to her sweet spot, parting her folds for him to concentrate on the center. "You make me want to be bad."

"And you make me want to forget all the rules."

"Rules?" She snorted. "What rules?"

He flicked her nubbin and her body went rigid against him. "Like that?"

"Please, do it again," she said through gritted teeth.

He nipped her exposed throat and rubbed her with his thumb while thrusting two fingers into her slick entrance.

She dragged in a deep breath, which pushed her breasts out, the one in his hand swelling against his palm.

His shaft hardened to steel and he couldn't hold back any longer. He scooped her up in his arms, carried her to the French doors to his bedroom, flung them open and strode in. After he set her on her feet, he ripped the T-shirt up over her head and threw it across the room. Her bikini top hung by the strap around her neck, her breasts bobbing free of the fabric.

Daniel tugged the bow at the back and the top fell to the floor at his feet. She stood in the blue bikini bottoms, her back straight, her breasts perfect, her narrow waist flaring down to the gentle swell of her hips.

Her gaze locked with his as she slipped the bikini bottoms down her legs and stood naked in front of him. She held out her hand.

He took it and she walked backward, leading him toward the bed. Once there, she slid his polo shirt up and over his head, then hooked her hands in the elastic waistband of his swim trunks and slid them down over his hips. Together they climbed up onto the bed and began a slow, sexy exploration of each other's bodies, taking their time. Daniel left kisses all along the length of her torso, tasting her smooth skin with his tongue, nibbling on the turgid peaks of her nipples.

When he couldn't take any more, he reached into the drawer beside the bed and fished for a condom. When he found one, Shelby took it from him and slid it down over him, her hands lingering at the base.

Her expression was sad. "I don't know why, but I feel like this might be our last time together." She reached out, captured his face in her hands and pulled him down for a kiss, a single tear sliding from the corner of one eye.

As much as he wanted to refute her claim, Daniel didn't. He never knew what the next day would bring. If the men who were after her were miraculously caught, he'd be reassigned, maybe back to detective duties or bodyguard work for Kate Winston. In which case, he'd see Shelby, but not as much. Maybe not at all if she went back to her life on the Outer Banks.

"What was it you said? Let's make good use of the time we have together." He'd worry about tomorrow when it came.

Settling between her legs, he nudged her entrance with his thick, hard member, and then bent to claim her lips as he thrust into her in one long, swift push.

She gasped against his lips, her fingers digging into his hips, pushing back, then pulling him forward until he settled into a smooth, steady rhythm.

Shelby dug her heels into the mattress and met his every movement, driving him deeper. When at last he launched off the precipice, he held her close, buried deep inside her, wondering how he'd live without her.

This woman he'd pulled out of a fire had pulled him out of the rut he'd been in and reminded him that there was more to living life than a single-minded focus on his job.

He dropped down to lie beside her, gathered her in his arms and held her for a long time, his mind drifting back over the time they'd been together. Though short, it felt like a lifetime. She was the only woman he felt he really knew and who could touch his heart.

After a while, he slipped out of the bed and dressed.

"Where are you going?" Shelby sat up, the sheet falling around her waist. Moonlight shone in through the window, making her body glow a silvery-blue.

Daniel bent to kiss her.

"Come back to bed," she urged.

"I have to make a phone call."

"Then you'll come back?"

"I promise."

She slipped out of the bed.

"Where are you going?" he asked.

She slipped into a pair of jeans and threw the big T-shirt over her head, pushing her arms through. "The bathroom, to brush my teeth and wash my face."

"I'll go with you." He put his phone in his back pocket.

Shelby held up her hand. "No. Sometimes a girl needs her privacy."

He nodded, walked her to the door and watched as she crossed the hall. When he was certain she was inside and safe, he stepped back into the bedroom, grabbed the portable phone from the nightstand and stepped out through the French doors onto the porch. He punched in the numbers for Kate Winston's personal cell phone.

Debra answered on the first ring. "Good evening, this is Debra, Kate Winston's assistant. How can I help you?"

"Debra, this is Daniel Henderson. Is Kate available?"

"Sorry, Daniel. She's at a fund-raiser dinner. Can I take a message for her?"

He held the phone, thinking through his options. "Yes. Have her call me when she's free."

"Is it an emergency?"

"Yes."

"Should I take her out of the dinner to get her to return that call?"

"No. Have her call me when she'd normally come out."

"Yes, sir." Debra hesitated. "Is her granddaughter all right?"

"Yes. But there have been some incidents."

"Are you safe now?"

"We are, but I'm not certain for how long."

"I'll have her call as soon as she's out."

"Thank you."

Daniel hung up and dialed Jed Kincannon.

"Kincannon speaking."

"Mr. Kincannon, Daniel Henderson here."

"Daniel, what's happening in Maine?"

He filled the director in on the occurrences and finished by saying, "I think whoever is after Shelby has followed us up here. I'm for bringing her back to North Carolina, closer to home and family."

"I agree. Let me get with Kate and see if she feels the same. In the meantime, I'd wait until morning to head out."

"Yes, sir." Daniel hit the end button and was turning around when he heard footsteps on the porch beside him.

He turned to confront whoever it was, but before he knew what was happening, he was hit on the back of the head with something cold and hard.

Pain ripped through his skull and darkness engulfed him.

* * *

Shelby washed her face, finger combed her hair and brushed her teeth, taking longer than necessary to give Daniel time to check in with her grandmother without interrupting his report. When she'd done all she could to waste time, she crossed the hallway and entered the bedroom, closing and locking the door behind her. After the bright lights of the bathroom, the darkness of the bedroom left her blinded while her eyes adjusted.

A movement she caught in her peripheral vision made her turn with a smile on her face. "Well, what did Kate say?"

Two men grabbed her. One clamped his meaty hand over her mouth before she had a chance to scream. She struggled, kicking and bucking, desperate to break free. The second man grabbed for her feet.

Shelby slammed her heel into the nose of the guy holding her feet. He grunted as blood spurted out then he growled, his eyes blazing in the light from the window. He swung his arm and backhanded her in the face.

Her head whipped around and her vision blurred. For a moment she was too dizzy to fight, teetering on the verge of blacking out.

The man holding her from behind spun her around, slapped duct tape over her mouth and used it to bind her wrists and ankles. Then he tossed her over his shoulder.

With the bleeding man leading the way, they exited through the French doors and ran across the porch to the steps, leading out to the road. They clung to the shadows of trees as they hurried parallel to the pavement.

Shelby bounced against the man's back, wiggling

pitifully and fighting back the dark cloud of unconsciousness threatening to overtake her.

When they emerged onto the road, they dumped her in the trunk of a dark sedan and closed the lid.

Her heart racing and her head throbbing, Shelby tried to scream. But no one would hear her, no one could. The nightmare she thought she'd escaped had come back to haunt her, and all she could think about was Daniel. Where was he? Why hadn't he come to her rescue?

Unless they had killed him before taking her.

Overwhelmed by fear, trapped in a small, dark, tight space and dizzy from the blow to her face, Shelby succumbed to the darkness.

Chapter 17

"Daniel!"

Someone was shaking him, and every time they did, he felt as if he was being hit in the head with an electric prod.

Daniel fought back the black fog and emerged into a dull yellow light filled with shadows. He was lying facedown on the wooden planks of the porch, his head throbbing.

"Daniel, where's Shelby?" He focused on the voice, finally identifying it as his mother's.

"Shelby?" he muttered, afraid to worsen the pain splitting the back of his head.

"You know, the woman you were protecting?" his mother said. "James, call 911. We need an ambulance."

Memories of Shelby lying naked in the bed rushed back to Daniel, along with the shadowy movement before the crashing pain in the back of his head. "Shelby." He pushed to a sitting position, swayed and would have fallen if Marcus hadn't caught him.

"Stay down until the ambulance gets here," Marcus said.

"Can't." Daniel tried to get up, but his brother's hand on his shoulder kept him from rising. "Let me go. Where's Shelby?"

"Oh, baby, she's gone," his mother said, tears trickling down her cheeks. "Everyone started leaving the lobster bake and we came up to check on you and Shelby. We found you, but not her."

Daniel cursed and tried again to rise, finally knocking his brother's hand off his shoulder. "We have to find her." When he made it to his feet, he staggered, his shoulder slamming into the wall before he could right himself.

His father looped his arm over his shoulder. "If you're going to be stubborn about this, at least let me help you inside. We can call whomever you need to notify. Robert is already on the phone with local police and he'll put the word out to the state police."

"I failed her, Dad." Daniel squeezed shut his eyes as another stabbing pain ripped through his head.

"You did no such thing. You were overpowered. If anything, we failed her by not being here for you both."

"No, it was my responsibility. My promise to protect her." He straightened, his vision blurring for a moment before it cleared. "I have to find her."

"At least come into the house in the light." His father angled him toward the open French doors and stepped inside. The room didn't look much different, other than the fact that the lamp on the nightstand had been knocked over and the throw rug on the floor was bunched and dark red strains trailed toward the door. Someone had put up a fight, and Shelby was gone, leaving a gaping emptiness in the room and his chest. How could he have been so careless?

"The phone. Where's the phone?" He held out his hand and his mother slapped the portable phone into it. "I found it out on the porch. It's cracked, but it still works."

Daniel blinked to clear his vision and punched the numbers for Kate. He could barely focus as his father walked him into the kitchen and eased him into a chair.

The phone was answered on the first ring. Before Kate's assistant could say a word, Daniel spoke, "Shelby's been kidnapped."

"I'll notify Mrs. Winston at once and have her call you back immediately. I assume she can reach you at this number?"

"Yes."

"She'll be with you momentarily." Debra hung up.

Daniel laid his head on the kitchen table. "Who would have known to follow us here?"

"Everyone has been asking about the woman you brought home, but we gave them a different name," his mother said. "We called her Celia Townsend, like you asked us to."

"No," Daniel moaned, his head hurting so badly he couldn't think straight. "It had to be someone back in North Carolina. Can I get a bottle of painkillers?"

"You need to see a doctor," his mother insisted, but she dug in the medicine cabinet next to the stove and brought out a bottle. "Ibuprofen will have to do." She shook out two pills and handed them to Daniel with a glass of water.

"Who knew Shelby was here, besides you?" Robert asked.

Before he could answer, the phone rang, the sound splitting Daniel's head in half each time it chirped. He hit the talk button and said, "Kate?"

"What happened?" Kate's voice sounded calm but intense.

Daniel told her what he knew and then asked, "Who besides your sons, Patrick and Director Kincannon would have known where I was taking her?"

"No one. Patrick's been with me the entire time, and I'd trust my sons with my life and Shelby's. They wouldn't have given out that information to anyone."

A sinking feeling filled his gut, adding more pain to the ache in his head. "The only other person who knew we were coming up here was my boss, Jed Kincannon."

Kate was silent for a moment. "Do you think he had anything to do with Shelby's disappearance? Are you sure you didn't let it slip to anyone else?"

"Shelby and I didn't tell anyone we were coming here. We went to great lengths to make sure we didn't leave a trail that could be easily followed. Only someone who knew we were going to be here would have gotten men up here that fast."

"Why would the director of the Secret Service take my granddaughter?"

"I don't know, and it doesn't make sense." Daniel tried to shake his head, but the pain intensified with the movement. "I could be wrong. It had to be someone else. Could anyone have listened in? Have you had the house swept for bugs?"

"My security team sweeps every morning. No one could have listened to our conversation," Kate assured him.

"It doesn't change the fact that she's gone." Hopelessness filled him when he considered the vastness of the country. Shelby could be anywhere. "And I have no idea where to begin to look. Our only clue is not much more than a suspicion that the Cartel is involved." His elbow on the table, he rested his forehead against his palm.

"Then we start there. I'm sending my private jet to pick you up. I'll have Debra notify you when it takes off and give you an expected arrival time."

"I can't leave Bar Harbor. What if they're holding her close by?"

"If this is about me, they'll bring her closer to the source. I need you here." Kate paused. "But while you're waiting for the jet, have a doctor check you out for concussion."

"I feel fine," he lied, the pain pulsing in waves through his head.

"I don't care how you feel," she said, her tone clipped, no-nonsense. "Get checked. I don't want you on a plane if you're suffering from a concussion. And you're probably in no condition to drive back down here."

And it would take too long. The thought of the thirteen-hour drive made him cringe. "Okay, I'll have the doc check me out, but I'll be on that plane."

"Good. We need you here to lead the investigation. I want my granddaughter back, unharmed."

"Agreed." He wanted Shelby back, safe and in his arms.

Kate hung up about the time the ambulance showed up, sirens wailing, reigniting the pain in Daniel's head.

His mother stood with her hands on her hips, her diminutive form no less intimidating. "Now, don't you say one word about the ambulance. You're going to the hospital if I have to knock you out to take you."

Daniel grinned, the effort costing him another wave of agony. "Okay. I'll go, but you didn't have to send for the cavalry. You could have taken me in the truck."

"Not in my truck," his dad said. "It's wrecked, as you well know." He stared at Daniel, his eyes narrowing. "I think you got hit harder than you think."

Daniel tenderly felt the egg-size knot at the back of his head. "I remember the truck."

"Good, then let the EMTs check you over." His father nodded to his mother. "Show them in."

Daniel's mother hurried to the door as the bell rang.

"If they say you don't need to ride in the ambulance, I'll take you in my car," Robert offered.

Daniel closed his eyes, the bright lights making his head throb. How long did it take for ibuprofen to work? "I don't care as long as I'm at the airport when the jet gets there."

"We'll get you there, even if we have to give you a police escort," Robert reassured him.

"We can do that?" Marcus asked.

"Shh." Robert shook his head and winked at his brother. "Don't advertise it, but I have connections on the police force."

Marcus shook his head. "I work there, too."

His mother entered the kitchen, followed by two emergency medical technicians, one of whom carried a medical kit.

After taking his blood pressure, checking his pulse, examining the lump on the back of his head and shining a light into his eyes, the technicians asked if he wanted to ride in the ambulance to the hospital for further examination.

"No, thanks. I have to go." Daniel tried to stand.

Robert pressed a hand on his shoulder, keeping him down. "You're not going anywhere until the doctor clears you. You might as well see one before you fly."

"We'll get him there," his mother assured the paramedic and showed him out of the kitchen.

The phone rang as they were headed for the front door. Debra relayed the expected time of arrival of the jet and said that Kate would be at the airport to greet him on his return.

Daniel rode to the hospital with Robert, his mother and father in the backseat with him, Marcus and Stacey choosing to hold down the home front just in case someone called with a ransom demand.

Daniel didn't think it would happen. Not with his parents. They weren't wealthy in any sense of the word. Not like Kate Winston. If a ransom were demanded, it would be Kate's money they'd be after. The sooner he returned to Raleigh the better.

After the doctor on call at the emergency room checked him over and ran a few tests, he gave him some pain meds and told him to take it easy for a few days.

By the time he was done at the hospital, it was almost time for the jet to land at the Bar Harbor Airport.

The ibuprofen had taken the edge off his headache and he was almost feeling normal when he boarded the luxury jet. Once he was inside, a flight attendant served him a drink. He asked her to wake him if there were any communications from Mrs. Winston. Then he reclined in the leather seat and dozed fitfully, thinking about the people who knew of their plans to go to Maine, reviewing the attempts on Kate's life and those on her family members.

When he'd spun the possibilities every which way until his head ached, he thought about Shelby and what she must be going through. His heart broke for her, imagining her terror at being kidnapped for the second time in less than a week.

If it was the last thing he did, he'd free her and make her captors pay for what they'd done.

When the plane landed in Raleigh, the pain had subsided to a dull ache, and Daniel was more in control. The catnap he'd taken refreshed him and he was ready to find the bastards who'd taken Shelby and pound them into the ground.

As he stepped down from the plane, a limousine rolled to a stop beside it. The chauffeur got out and opened the rear door. Patrick O'Hara got out and turned to help Kate to her feet. She crossed the tarmac and hugged Daniel. "Patrick and I have been beside ourselves since we heard."

"I can't believe it's happened again." Patrick ran a hand through his hair. "I can't imagine what Shelby's going through."

Daniel didn't want to imagine it, either. Though he'd tried to sleep on the plane, he'd been plagued with scenario after scenario, each worse than the last.

"Have you received any calls, ransom notes, anything?" he asked.

Kate nodded. "I got this today. It arrived in the mailbox."

Daniel turned the envelope over. No return address, no stamp and only *Kate Winston* printed in block letters. He pulled the slip of paper out of the envelope, unfolded it and read the words aloud, "'Publicly renounce your candidacy for president or your granddaughter dies.'"

"This sounds like Cartel tactics." Daniel glanced up.

"I had already toyed with the idea of backing out. My family has been through enough without bearing the additional threats and scrutiny of running for the highest office in the nation."

"And now?" Daniel asked.

"After all that's happened, and with Shelby missing again, I'm positive the position of president is not for me. I was encouraged to run to keep Richard Nelson from being elected. My sources tell me he's heavily connected to the Cartel. So your statement that this is mafia tactics might not be too far from the truth. The last thing this nation needs is a Cartel-owned government." She shook her head. "It doesn't matter whether or not I'm running or why. What does matter is that we get Shelby back."

"What are you going to do?" Daniel asked.

She slipped an arm around Patrick's waist and he hugged her close.

Daniel could see the love in Patrick's eyes for the former vice president. Apparently that love hadn't waned over the forty years since they'd last seen each other. What would it feel like to love someone so much you couldn't see yourself with anyone else?

An image of Shelby popped into Daniel's head. Shelby walking along the land bridge. Shelby's face shining in the glow of the fire, her smile when she ran to get on the WaveRunner, hot-dogging out on the water. He could still feel the softness of her hand in his and smell the fragrance of her hair.

"I have a press conference scheduled for tomorrow morning. I'm planning to make the announcement and hope she's released. If anything happens to my grand-daughter because of me, I could never forgive myself."

Daniel nodded. "We're going to get her back."

"Damn right we are," Patrick agreed. "She means the world to me."

Kate smiled sadly. "I want to know her. She's all I have left of the daughter I never met." Kate's voice caught.

Patrick's arm tightened around her. "Let's get back to the house. Kate's boys are gathering there. If we all put our heads together, we'll come up with a plan to bring Shelby back."

The three of them climbed into the limousine and the driver took them to the Winston Estate.

Thad, Trey, and Samuel Winston waited in the con-ference room, sitting in the leather chairs around the large table. They all stood as Kate breezed in and took the seat at the head, Patrick at her side. She nodded to Daniel. "Please, fill them in."

Daniel remained standing. He told them how they'd been sideswiped by a vehicle in Bar Harbor and how a boat had almost run them over on the WaveRunner. When he spoke of how he'd been knocked out only to awaken and find Shelby missing, the three brothers leaned forward, their jaws tight, fists clenched.

Daniel held up the note demanding that Kate for-mally announce that she had no intention of running for president. "This is just one clue as to who might be at the bottom of this."

"Mom's potential opponent for the party nomination, Richard Nelson, has been linked to a group that likes to call itself the Cartel," Sam said. " This is just the kind of dirty dealing they like to do. Rather than let the public decide, they've gone so far as to kill off candidates to ensure their nominee wins."

Thad sat forward. "I can ask around. We might have an undercover operative from the police force working with the Cartel."

"Check on it." Daniel glanced around at all the people in the room. "The whole purpose of me taking Shelby to my parents' house in Maine was to get her as far away from potential kidnappers as possible and hide her. Since she was kidnapped anyway, we know someone leaked her location to the Cartel."

The brothers all frowned at once and started to rise.

"Are you accusing us of ratting out our own niece?" Thad asked.

"He's doing no such thing." Kate stood and gave her sons a stern look. "Sit. Daniel has a point. Let him speak."

"Thank you." Now that he was on the ground, Daniel's head was clear and he'd had time to think about the entire situation. A couple of things stood out in his mind. "Over the past few months, members of the Winston family have been the targets of attempted murder on a number of occasions."

Trey piped up, "The shooting at the fund-raiser. The one that landed Mother and you in the hospital."

Daniel nodded, the injuries still fresh in his mind and still causing him some pain. He glanced across the conference table at Kate. She'd been in physical therapy almost as long as he had.

Sam added, "Then there was the brainwashing of soldiers to work as assassins, including my army buddy who tried to shoot Mother at Trey and Debra's wedding."

"And when Sam pulled a gun on Trey." Thad shook his head.

"It leads me to think the Cartel has some connections in pretty high places." Daniel paced to the end of the table and turned to face the Winstons and Patrick. "Places that have the means and position to capture or incarcerate U.S. soldiers and manipulate their minds to do their bidding. So far, their attempts have been aimed at the Winston family. And then there was D'Angelis."

"A Secret Service agent—" Thad started.

"One of your organization," Sam interjected.

"And a mole in our mother's security team," Trey finished.

"Murdered in a seemingly secure facility," Patrick said.

In between stabbing pain and semiconsciousness, Daniel's mind had played over all the scenarios. "The way I see it, everything culminates with the attacks on Shelby and the demand for Kate to back out of running for president. Someone has been targeting Kate and her family to keep her from running."

"Seems like a whole lot of trouble to get her to quit," Thad observed. "Why not use the usual tactics of mudslinging?"

"Whoever is behind all the attempts is connected with the Cartel and in a position of power within our own government. Capable of brainwashing and using

U.S. soldiers as assassins to do his dirty work. And he had to have known I was taking Shelby to Maine."

Trey raised his hand. "None of us would want our mother dead, and we wouldn't hurt Shelby. Hell, we didn't know she existed until Patrick came knocking on the door."

"And none of us are in a high position of power," Sam said.

Patrick gripped Kate's hand. "I don't think any of the people in this room could have leaked the information about Shelby's whereabouts. But there was one other person who knew, who was there when we discussed the plan."

Kate's face hardened. "Jed Kincannon."

Daniel's jaw tightened and a knot formed in his gut. "I don't like the idea of accusing my own boss of kidnapping, attempted murder or anything else, but it's the only scenario that makes sense. I called him from Maine to inform him of the attack on the truck I was driving and the boat incident. I knew then we'd been compromised, but he told me to stay put a little longer."

"So that his men could get in place and steal the girl," Thad said.

The muscles in Daniel's jaw tightened. "The more I thought about it, the more it began to make sense. Why else would the director of the Secret Service spend so much time with Kate? He's a director—he should be running the organization at the highest level, not working in the trenches."

"Jed was there the day I mentioned running for president." Kate sighed. "I thought it was a good idea. But after holding the office of vice president, I have no real desire to be the president. I'd rather spend time with my grandchildren, getting to know them." Her eyes filled. "I want to get to know Shelby and be there any time she might need my help. I didn't get to know my daughter. I'll be damned if I miss out on my granddaughter."

Patrick kissed her forehead. "You'll get that chance."

Daniel nodded. "So here's the deal. We need information on Jed Kincannon."

Thad stood. "I can run some checks, but I'm betting his record is clean. He wouldn't hold the office of director if he had any blemishes on his record. I'll notify the FBI and have them set up surveillance here in the house to monitor the phones. If the kidnappers make contact, they might be able to trace the call."

"My campaign managers are good at digging up dirt." Trey rose to stand beside Thad. "I can check old photographs of political events. Maybe something will turn up showing a connection between Kincannon and Nelson and any known members of the Cartel."

"An old friend of mine has contacts at the television station," Trey said. "Perhaps I can find video footage of Kincannon, Nelson and Cartel members."

Daniel's chest swelled. When the going got tough, the Winston family pulled together in a united front. "And I'll follow Kincannon and see if his movements shed light on his activities and possibly the location where they're keeping Shelby."

"What about us?" Patrick asked.

"You two have to be here with the FBI, or whoever sets up the communications surveillance, in case the kidnappers call." Daniel glanced around the room. "Keep in contact. If you find anything, even the most seemingly insignificant clue, let me know."

"It goes both ways," Thad reminded him.

Daniel nodded. "Everyone has their jobs to do. Let's get to it. I'm going now to report in to my boss."

Kate stared across at Daniel. "What are you going to say?"

"Just the facts, nothing about our suspicions. For now, I'd like to keep my return as under the radar as possible." He glanced around the room. "No one is to know I'm back. Please make that clear to the limousine driver and Maddie, the housekeeper. And it would be best if we all pretend this meeting never happened. I suggest you call Kincannon and let him know you got a note and want to know the status of your granddaughter. Act as if it's the first time you've heard the news when he informs you she's been kidnapped."

"I will." Kate laid a hand on his arm. "Be careful, Daniel. If it really is Kincannon orchestrating all this violence, he's proved that he's dangerous."

"I know. But someone has to get close enough to him to follow him. Who better than his direct report?"

Chapter 18

The car carrying Shelby drove for an hour or more before it stopped and the two goons who'd attacked her got out, slamming the doors.

In the pitch-black interior of the trunk, she had no clue where she was or what they would do with her. Having been kidnapped before made her numb to fear for herself. She was more concerned about Daniel. What had they done to him in order to get to her? Had they killed him or left him injured and bleeding somewhere?

Shelby prayed Daniel's family found him in time to save him.

This time, she had a glimmer of hope. If Daniel was able to, he'd come after her. He'd found her once; surely he could find her again.

Lying in the dark, all she had were the images in her mind of growing up with her grandfather and, more recently, the days and nights she'd shared with Daniel both in North Carolina and in Maine. To keep from going insane, she replayed those images in her mind like video recordings, examining every scene, noting the details as if she was admiring beautiful flowers. When she felt a panic attack sneaking up on her, she remembered how great it felt to be in Daniel's arms.

She'd told herself she was satisfied with whatever time she could have with him. But she'd been lying to herself. Maybe she was greedy and selfish, but she wanted to spend a lifetime with Daniel Henderson. He made her come alive in his arms, and to not have him in her life would be like not being able to breathe.

The trunk popped open and the two men who'd kidnapped her leaned in and grabbed her beneath the arms and legs and hauled her out of the car, standing her on her feet.

They wore ski masks over their faces, so Shelby couldn't tell who they were. One of them tossed a dark pillowcase over her head and duct taped it around her neck. What little light was available was snuffed out by the dark fabric.

The larger of the two thugs tossed Shelby over his shoulder and carried her away from the car.

Her belly bounced against his shoulder and blood rushed to her head, making her dizzy.

Unable to see, Shelby concentrated on the sounds around her. An engine started up. Not like a car engine, more like that of a small aircraft. Then the ape was carrying her up steps and ducking as if to enter a small space.

At last, the man dropped her onto what she assumed was a floor.

The engine sound increased and whatever they were in started moving, the entire craft rumbling across the ground, the speed picking up, faster and faster, then the rumbling stopped and the vehicle floated.

She was in an airplane, bound for where, she didn't know. Fear found its way back into her psyche, knowing she was getting farther and farther away from Daniel.

In a country as vast as the United States, they could be taking her anywhere and no one would ever find her. For all she knew, they could be taking her anywhere in the world.

By the time Daniel showered and shaved, the sun had risen. Dressed and ready for the day, he placed a call to Jed Kincannon using a phone Thad had loaned him that would display "Blocked Sender" in the caller ID on the other end of the call.

When the director picked up, Daniel said, "Director Kincannon, Daniel Henderson here. I'm glad you picked up. My phone is dead and I'm using one I purchased until I can get mine replaced. Did I catch you at home?"

"I was just about to head out to the office. What's happening?" Kincannon asked.

If this man was truly behind all the attempts on the Winston family, he knew damn well what was happening. Daniel sucked in a deep breath to calm his anger. "They got past me. The O'Hara woman was kidnapped."

His boss cursed. "Did you see who took her? Can you identify her attackers?"

"No, they knocked me out before I could get a look at them."

"I'll notify Mrs. Winston as soon as possible and send agents to your parent's home to help in the investigation."

"I'd appreciate that. I know how heartbroken she will be and I… Well, I just can't face her. I've failed to do my job and protect the former vice president's granddaughter."

"We'll discuss your performance when you return. When will you be heading back?"

"I got hit pretty hard. The docs here want me to take it easy, not go far in case of concussion."

"Let me know when you get back to Raleigh. I'll find you a new assignment."

"Thank you, sir. Please tell Mrs. Winston how sorry I am."

"Got a call coming in now from her. I'll tell her."

Daniel hung up and hurried downstairs, wearing a gray hoodie and sunglasses. Staying in the shadows, he walked out the front gate and down the road where Samuel Winston had arranged to leave a nondescript rental car for him.

Climbing in, Daniel grinned. On the seat beside him sat a pair of binoculars and a listening device like those used by private detectives. Where Sam had come up with the device, Daniel didn't know and really didn't care. Armed with it, he'd have a better chance of staying out of sight while listening in on Kincannon's conversations.

Daniel drove to Director Kincannon's home and parked a couple houses away along the side of the road. He slumped down in the seat, the listening device switched on.

He didn't hear any conversations and presumed either Kincannon was in the shower or had already left for the office.

Twenty minutes later, he heard the man saying goodbye to what sounded like his wife, then the garage door opened and Kincannon left his house in a sleek and sporty Lexus.

He drove in the expected direction, toward the building in which the agency had rented offices, parked in his reserved parking space and carried a briefcase inside.

Daniel aimed the listening device at Kincannon's office window on the second floor and waited for the man to slip up and reveal information on Shelby's whereabouts.

Twice people came into his office talking about mundane papers that needed signing, and Kincannon answered the phone on his desk three times. None of the conversations sounded like coordination with kidnappers or the Cartel. The longer Daniel sat in the car, the more frustrated he became. Shelby was out there somewhere, possibly being tortured or mistreated by her captors. He had to find her soon. And if she had seen or recognized the people who were behind her abduction, even if Mrs. Winston backed out of the presidential race, Shelby could be murdered to keep her silence. Time was not on their side.

Kate was due to give her speech at eleven o'clock that morning in front of the Raleigh courthouse. She'd called a press conference and had Debra notify reporters across the nation of the speech Kate would make.

Daniel hoped the public announcement would keep Shelby alive long enough for them to find and release her.

The lump at the back of his head ached, and he needed sleep, but he couldn't let himself drift off. Not when Shelby's life was at stake.

As lunchtime approached, the cell phone in the car's cup holder rang.

Daniel hit the talk button and fumbled with the phone to get it to his ear, knocking his head on the back of the seat in the process.

"Henderson, it's Trey."

"Whatcha got?"

"My campaign manager is a miracle worker. If you ever want to run a dirty campaign, he's your man."

"What did he find?"

"Several images of Kincannon walking and talking with Richard Nelson. There's another shot of him playing golf with Nelson at a club in Bethesda, Maryland."

"So he meets with Nelson. What else?" Daniel asked, impatiently.

Someone had entered Kincannon's office and they were talking in lowered voices.

"There are also clips of Richard Nelson talking with Frank Chambliss at a charity ball, and of them arriving at a D.C. gala in the same limo."

"Frank Chambliss." Daniel rolled the name over in his mind. "Hasn't he been rumored to be in bed with the Cartel?"

"Not only in bed, but he might just be the lead. Nothing verified. But then no one gets inside the Cartel easily, and once in, they don't get out. Those who've attempted to get out or share information about the Cartel end up in the Potomac River."

"Nice. Sounds like Richard is living up to the rumors."

The conversation in Kincannon's office was getting a little heated, the voices almost loud enough Daniel could hear them.

"Look, Trey, this is good information. Good job. I have to go now."

"Are you following Kincannon?"

"I am."

"Just remember, we don't need more heroes. Call us if you need backup. I'm going to text you the photos."

"Thanks."

Daniel hit the end button and turned up the volume on the listening device.

"Shh. She's about to go on now."

Kincannon's office grew quiet and then the sound of a news reporter came across the device, announcing Kate Winston.

Kate's voice came through some static as she spoke to the crowd in front of the Wake County Courthouse.

Daniel turned on his radio and turned the dial until he found a local station with Kate's voice crisp and clear.

"I want to thank all the people of Raleigh and of the country for their support while I was vice president of the United States and for their continuing support as I navigated my responsibilities after my term expired.

"Now I'd like to discuss the race for president of the United States."

A roaring cheer rose from the crowd and Mrs. Winston had to wait until the din subsided before continuing.

"Much as I enjoy serving the country that I love with all my heart, I want to quell all the rumors with the following statement. I am no longer considering running for president of the United States. If my party leaders ask, I will politely decline.

"I've already done my civic duty. It's time for someone else to step up to the plate. I think it's a great honor and a privilege. However, I want to spend time with my family.

"Again, thank you for all of your support. It means a great deal to me and I wish you happiness and peace in the future. Thank you."

The news reporter went on with a recap of the speech and Daniel switched off the radio, his heart swelling with the emotion he felt for Kate Winston. She was one classy lady. And if anyone deserved to be president, it was her. She had her head on straight and she wasn't afraid to stand up to either side of the political fence. The country needed more leaders like Kate.

"You think she meant it?" the man in Kincannon's office asked.

"Sure she meant it. If there's one thing I've learned about Kate Winston, she doesn't lie." Kincannon paused. "Should I make that call?"

"No. I want you to take care of it in person. We won't want to leave any witnesses."

"Got it," Kincannon said.

A door clicked closed in the office and the room was silent. Then the sound of a second door closing was the last thing Daniel heard.

Daniel sat forward, his heart racing. What did the

men mean when they said they didn't want to leave any witnesses?

Not once had they mentioned Shelby or a woman being held hostage. What else could they be talking about?

If they were talking about Shelby, would they kill her even though they'd gotten what they'd demanded?

Daniel started the engine and waited for Kincannon to leave the building.

Several minutes passed, and he didn't come out the front door. A vehicle exited from the back parking area.

Daniel lifted the binoculars to his eyes and focused on the dark gray four-door sedan. He caught a glimpse of the driver. It wasn't Kincannon. He shifted his gaze to the passenger.

Kincannon.

The vehicle turned onto the road and sped away in the opposite direction.

Daniel floored the accelerator and yanked the steering wheel hard to the left, pulling a U-turn in the middle of the busy road. Tires squealed as other drivers hit their brakes, screeching to a stop, just short of crashing into Daniel.

Unfazed by the commotion he'd caused but thankful no one was hurt, Daniel kept his eye on the gray sedan as he broke speed limits to catch up. He stayed back far enough he wouldn't be noticed, but close enough that he'd see when they turned.

His cell phone buzzed, indicating an incoming text. He ignored it, keeping his gaze fixed on the vehicle that could possibly lead to Shelby. It *had* to lead to

Shelby. He didn't have any other clues, and his gut said this was it.

They turned off the main road and wove through some smaller roads, heading into a rundown residential neighborhood where men walked the streets and small children ran around with no adult supervision in unkempt yards. The deeper they went, the more rundown the houses became, some of them boarded up, others with roofs caving in.

It became impossible to follow close behind the sedan and not be noticed. Daniel had to wait at corners and drive past turns to keep the driver from noticing his vehicle trailing them. He thought he'd lost them once when he had to parallel their path one block over.

His heart pounded against his ribs as he sped to the end of the street and turned back in the direction he'd last seen them.

Then he saw them at a stop sign, turning his direction.

Keeping his cool when his insides were quaking, Daniel drove past and kept going, watching in his rearview mirror as they turned into an abandoned schoolyard, the chain-link fence falling down and the windows busted out in the classrooms. It appeared to be an old high school that had long since sunk into disrepair.

Kincannon's vehicle pulled around the back of the building.

Daniel drove past the next house until he was certain his car was out of sight. He pulled up in the driveway of a vacant house, the for-sale sign trampled in the knee-high grass. Shifting into Park, he jumped out and ran back the way he'd come, dodging between trees, bushes and derelict buildings.

He had to get to Shelby before Jed and his thugs did something terrible.

As he neared the old school, he paused in the shadows of the vacant house across the street. There were no bushes or anything to conceal him as he crossed the road. He'd be risking his life if Kincannon had guards positioned in or around the building, watching for intruders.

He pulled the pistol out of his shoulder holster tucked beneath his jacket, released the clip, checked to see that it was full and slapped it back into the grip. Then he stared down at his phone. The image that had been texted to him was of the man he'd seen driving Kincannon away from the office building. The caption attached to the picture read "Nelson and Chambliss." Damn. He'd suspected the man who'd been talking to Kincannon was bad, but now he was beginning to think he was worse than he'd originally thought. Frank Chambliss was possibly the head honcho of the most powerful and notorious Mafia group in the country.

If Chambliss was who they thought he was, he would be ruthless. If he meant leave no witnesses, he was there to kill Shelby.

Daniel keyed his location into the phone and hit Send, returning the text to Trey with the message, Send backup, ASAP.

Trouble was, he couldn't wait for backup. Shelby might not be alive long enough for the cavalry to arrive.

He pulled the hoodie up over his head and ducked his chin to keep his face in the shadows, then he stepped away from the building, his gun in his pocket, hand on the grip, finger ready to pull the trigger.

He strolled across the street as if he didn't care where he was going. If someone looked out the window, they'd see a young man walking along, kicking pebbles.

He passed the school and walked on to a gap in the broken chain-link fence. Bushes almost covered the gap. At the very least, no one would see him from the school when he slipped through the hole in the fence. Once through, he had to cross an old parking lot to get to the side entrance of the two-story building.

He paused in the leaves of the bush and stared up at the building. A shadow moved in one of the broken upper windows. The metal tip of a rifle poked out, a man wearing dark clothes positioned behind it. His gun was pointed toward the front, main entrance.

When Daniel was as sure as he could be, he hurried across the open space, trying to move as quietly as he could. Just as he reached the wall, his foot dislodged a small rock and sent it skittering across the broken pavement.

He plastered himself to the wall of the building, praying the shooter in the window above couldn't see over the edge of the broken glass without sticking his head through the jagged edges.

Daniel froze and carefully looked up. The nose of the rifle pointed toward the location where the rock had rolled, three feet away from where he stood. After several long, agonizing moments, the rifle turned toward the front entrance again.

Letting the air out of his lungs, Daniel waited a fraction of a second longer and then eased his way around to the side of the building and peered through the dirty window in the door. The hallway was empty and the chain around the door had been cut, the door hanging drunkenly on its hinges.

Daniel passed it and checked the back of the building. The gray sedan was parked between two rundown portable buildings, completely hidden to the casual observer. Nothing else stirred behind the building.

Daniel retraced his steps to the side door and eased it open enough he could slide through. He listened before stepping inside.

Voices and footsteps in the hallway made him pause, his back to the wall. He waited for the voices to fade before he slid through the gap and ducked into the first classroom. The once-polished tiles were yellow with age, and a stack of old student desks was bunched in the middle of the room, most of them broken.

With his gun out in front of him, Daniel moved low and fast down the hallway, checking every room for Shelby. When he reached the halfway point, he noticed a doorway marked Staff Only leading into a stairwell that only went down.

Voices echoed off the walls of the basement below.

"You'd be better off taking her to where you want to dispose of her," Kincannon was saying.

"We won't find a more perfect place than here." Chambliss said. "It's abandoned. No one will come near here for weeks."

The sound of someone moaning made rage bubble up inside Daniel. He fought the urge to charge down the stairs, shooting every one of the men holding Shelby hostage and talking about killing her as if she didn't count for anything.

She was everything. Bright, beautiful, independent and fun to be with, and just beginning her life as an adult. She deserved to live longer, have children of her own and be happy, damn it.

"Go ahead, Jed," Chambliss said. "This has been your project from the start. Finish it."

"Have one of your men do it. I didn't sign on to bloody my hands," Kincannon claimed.

Daniel eased down the metal stairs, carefully placing one foot after the other. When the stairs began to angle to the left, he could see the basement stretched out in front of him, Kincannon and Chambliss at the center, Shelby bound and gagged with duct tape, lying on her side on the floor. She was the only one facing him. Everyone else, including the three thugs with AR15s slung over their shoulders, were gazing down at her.

Daniel could tell the moment when she spotted him. Her eyes widened and she jerked her head as if to say no.

He lifted his finger to his lips.

Chambliss shoved a gun into Kincannon's hands. "Do it now, or I'll kill her. And then I'll kill you."

Kincannon pushed the gun toward the man. "Don't threaten me. You and Nelson need me to see him elected into office. You kill me and you lose your government connection."

"Seems you already ruined that when your assassins were caught. And now that the Winston woman isn't running for office, we really don't require your services anymore." Chambliss took the pistol Kincannon had pointed at him. Instead of aiming it at Shelby, he aimed it at Kincannon's head.

"What the hell are you doing?"

"What does it take to get through to you that we don't need you anymore? I told you I was getting rid of all the witnesses. Since we don't need you, you're nothing but a witness."

No matter how much Daniel hated Kincannon for his betrayal, he couldn't stand by and let Chambliss kill him. He aimed at Chambliss's arm and pulled the trigger.

Chambliss yelped and the gun flew from his hand and skidded across the floor.

The three men who'd had their rifles slung over their shoulder tilted them upward, all aiming at him.

Daniel leaped over the railing as they opened fire, landed on the concrete floor, rolled and dived behind a short wall of concrete blocks.

Once on the ground, he picked off the thugs one by one until all three lay writhing or dead on the ground.

"Don't move and I might spare your lives," Daniel called out. From where he huddled behind the concrete wall, he could see Kincannon standing, but he couldn't see where Shelby lay on the ground.

Chambliss threw himself down, reaching for his fallen gun. Daniel fired again, hitting Chambliss in the head, killing him instantly.

When he shifted his attention back to Kincannon, the man had disappeared.

Daniel rolled out from behind the concrete wall, pointing his gun at the spot where Shelby had been.

Kincannon yanked her to her feet by her hair and pointed a pistol at her temple. "One more step and I pull the trigger."

"It's over, Kincannon. It's only a matter of time

before the police arrive, and you won't have any way of escaping."

"You know as well as I do that hostages make great shields. Miss O'Hara is my ticket out of here. Kate won't let any harm come to her."

"You won't get far."

Kincannon sneered. "Oh, I think I will. I prepared for this. I have a backup plan."

"You won't get out of here."

Footsteps pounded down the hallway toward them.

Daniel knew it was too soon for the police or SWAT team, but Kincannon didn't know that.

"They're coming. Put the gun down or they'll shoot," Daniel said, praying Kincannon would do as he said before the shooter from the third floor burst into the basement.

"No way. I'm not giving up my—"

Shelby pitched sideways, slammed her head into Kincannon's. She pivoted and brought her knee up into his groin, and then dropped to the ground, landing on her side.

As Kincannon aimed his weapon at Shelby, the shooter from the third floor stormed down the staircase.

Daniel had to choose whether to shoot Kincannon or the man coming down the stairs.

Daniel pulled the trigger, aiming for Kincannon, and then threw himself to the floor, rolled to his feet and fired at the man on the stairs.

Kincannon jerked backward and fell flat on his back.

The shooter on the stairs jumped to the concrete floor and raised his rifle, getting off one round as Daniel pulled the trigger again, hitting the man square in the chest.

The shooter's bullet hit Daniel in the shoulder less than a second later, slamming him backward to land hard, the goose-egg–size bump on his head bouncing off the concrete.

Daniel's vision blurred and he struggled to stay conscious. Sirens blared in the distance as he pushed to his hands and knees.

Shelby sat up, tears streaming from her eyes.

Behind her, Kincannon lurched up, holding his gun.

"Get down!" Daniel yelled.

Chapter 19

Shelby dropped back flat on the ground as a shot blasted out behind her. She glanced back at Kincannon, who had fired his gun. She spun back toward Daniel, her heart banging against her chest. Apparently, the shot had gone wide, giving Daniel enough time to raise his uninjured arm and nail the bastard who'd become a traitor to his own country.

"Henderson! Shelby!" A voice echoed through the hallway above them.

"Down here!" Daniel called, hurrying over to Shelby, his arm hanging down by his side. He carefully peeled the tape off her mouth, the adhesive ripping at her skin. "Are you okay?"

She coughed, cleared her throat and breathed in through her mouth, then answered. "I'm okay, but you're bleeding. Get me out of this so I can help."

With her hands still bound in front of her, she could only nod at his shoulder.

"Just a flesh wound." He tried to raise the arm, winced and left it hanging at his side as he tore one-handed through the tape on her wrists.

She raised the tape to her teeth and tried to bite her way through the thick tape. She had to get loose and help him. "Daniel, forget about me. Do something to stop the bleeding."

"I'm fine, I tell you." He smiled and pulled her against him with his good arm. "I'm just happy that I got here in time."

She laughed. "You and me both."

"I didn't realize just how much I'd miss you until you were gone." He bent to kiss her gently on her raw lips. "You scared me more than I've ever been scared in my life."

She leaned her cheek against his. "I knew you'd find me."

"I don't see how. At first, I didn't have a clue who'd taken you. But damn it, I had to find you." He kissed her cheek and softly brushed her lips with his again. "I'd move heaven and earth for you."

She smiled. "I know."

Footsteps clanked down the metal stairs into the basement. Men in black uniforms and bulletproof vests with scary guns stormed into the basement.

"You're too late." Shelby chuckled. "Daniel took care of it all."

"I had help from one amazing, determined woman." He kissed her nose as a paramedic eased him to the side and ripped the shirt away from his shoulder wound.

Another paramedic cut the tape away from Shelby's

wrists and peeled it off her skin. When she was free, she went to Daniel and held his good hand while the paramedic applied a pressure bandage to his shoulder.

"We'll have to take him to the hospital. He's lost a lot of blood and there's no exit wound. The doc's gonna have to go fishing for that bullet."

"Great." Daniel smiled and winced as they pressed the bandage to his shoulder. "I don't care. Shelby's alive, we've found the person behind all of the attacks and, if I'm not mistaken, Chambliss there is the leader of the Cartel. With the head pinched off the snake, there won't be much trouble coming from them for a while."

The medic leaned over him. "Sir, we're going to load you on the stretcher now."

"I can walk," Daniel insisted.

"Sir, let us do our jobs. Your job is done here."

Shelby laughed at the glare on Daniel's face. "Do it, you hardheaded man."

"I just found you again. I don't want to let you out of my sight. You have a habit of disappearing."

"I'm not going anywhere." Shelby turned to the paramedics. "Can I ride with him in the ambulance?"

"Are you a relative?" the medic asked.

Before Shelby could respond, Daniel said, "Yes."

"Then you may."

The medics eased a disgruntled Daniel onto a stretcher and carried him out of the basement.

Thad, Trey and Sam arrived as Shelby emerged from the old schoolhouse, and joined her as the medics loaded Daniel into the ambulance.

"He's going to be okay," Sam said.

Trey curled an arm around her shoulder. "We'll

bring your grandmother and grandfather to the hospital and sit with you while Daniel's in surgery. They'll want to be there for him as well as you."

Shelby smiled. "Thank you." Then, on impulse, she leaned up and kissed Trey's cheek. "I think I'll like having uncles looking out for me."

"Hey, where's mine?" Thad turned his cheek and bent for her to give him a kiss, and Sam did the same.

"Gotta go now." The paramedic helped her up into the back of the ambulance and they closed the door.

She held Daniel's hand all the way to the hospital, filling him in on what had happened from the time she'd been kidnapped to his finding her in the basement of the abandoned school.

She'd never been happier to see anyone.

When they arrived at the hospital, Kate was there with her grandfather. He had his arm around Kate's waist, and not like a friendly hug, but an intimate one.

Too worried about Daniel to think about the progression of a relationship between her grandmother and her grandfather, Shelby pushed it to the back of her mind and followed the stretcher carrying Daniel into the hospital.

Before they took him to surgery, Daniel said, "Wait."

The orderlies stopped and let Daniel address Shelby.

She lifted his hand and brought it to her sore lips.

"Will you be here when I get out of surgery?" he asked.

"You bet."

Daniel stared around her at Thad, Trey, Samuel, Kate and Patrick. "You heard her. I'm counting on you to make it happen."

"We'll keep an eye on her," Trey said.

Thad chuckled. "You singlehandedly took care of the threat. I don't know what you're worried about."

They rolled him away and Shelby turned back to her grandfather and Kate, tears welling in her eyes. "He's going to be okay, isn't he?"

Kate and her grandfather wrapped their arms around her.

"Daniel is a fighter," Kate said.

Lucy joined Thad, slipped her arm around him and addressed the folks gathered. "From what the paramedics said, he'll be okay. It's a fairly clean wound to his shoulder. Once they dig the bullet out, he'll be back to normal in no time."

The tears fell faster. And Shelby couldn't stop them.

"What's wrong, dear?" Kate brushed the hair from Shelby's wet cheeks.

Shelby sniffed and tried to get a grip. "Now that the threat is taken care of, Daniel will be reassigned."

"Oh, Shelby, that's what Secret Service agents do."

"I know," she sniffed. "It's just that I've gotten used to him being around. I don't want him to leave."

"Don't you worry, dear. Things always work out," Kate said.

"Sometimes it takes forty years, but they work out." Patrick cupped Kate's cheek and gazed into her eyes.

The ever-handy Debra pulled a tissue from her pocket. As she reached out, she doubled over slightly. "Ow."

"What is it, sweetheart?" Trey asked, his arm going around Debra, his brow wrinkled in concern.

Debra straightened and smiled. "Nothing. Just a really strong Braxton Hicks contraction. I'm okay. The baby's not due for another two weeks." She handed Shelby the tissue. "Got this from the nurses' desk. Thought you could use it."

Shelby accepted it gladly, patted her eyes and cheeks dry and looked around the room at the people who were now her family. They stood strong in support of Daniel and her. She only ever dreamed of being part of a big family…and now she was.

Her eyes welled again.

"What's wrong, Shelby Raye?" Her grandfather pulled her into his arms. "Lucy said Daniel's gonna be all right."

"It's just that it's nice to have so much support from…"

"From all of us?" Kate asked.

"No, from my family." Shelby smiled through her tears.

Kate's eyes filled and she pulled Shelby into her arms. "I'd give anything to have known your mother. But I'm very happy that you're now in my life so that I can get to know and love you."

Shelby's grandfather hugged her, as well. Soon, Thad, Sam and Trey, Lucy and Debra joined the hug and they ended up laughing and smiling.

When the doctor finally emerged from surgery, he gave them the good news that Daniel would make a full recovery and be able to return to duty soon.

Surrounded by her family, Shelby was happy for Daniel, knowing he loved his job as a Secret Service agent, but sad for herself. In the short time that they'd known each other, she'd learned that he was special. A man she could trust. A man she could love with all her heart.

And now he would be leaving.

Her heart already aching, Shelby wondered how long would it take for her to get over him.

Shelby glanced at her grandmother and grandfather. As far as she could tell, her grandfather had never loved anyone else for forty long years.

Would that be her? Would she refuse to love another after loving Daniel?

Daniel arrived back in Raleigh two weeks after his surgery. Shelby had been at the hospital the entire time he'd been there, fetching him water, fluffing his pillow and sitting with him when he thought he'd go nuts from boredom. And he'd only been in the hospital two nights.

As soon as he was released from the hospital, the new director of the Secret Service had called him to the main offices in D.C. where he'd spent the next week and a half debriefing a panel of agents and the director on Kincannon's role in the attempts on the lives of Kate Winston and her family.

When the hearing was over, the director had commended him for his selfless acts and had given him a citation for heroism. He and the panel had been so impressed with his efforts, the director had offered him any position within the agency Daniel wanted, including the highly coveted position of guarding the president of the United States.

Daniel had told the director he'd think about it.

And he had. Until he'd gotten a better offer.

Kate Winston had asked him back to Raleigh where she'd offered him the position of head of security for Adair Enterprises. She'd told him not to decide right away, but to come back for her official press conference where she had some announcements to make. At that time, she hoped he'd give her his answer.

Samuel Winston and his fiancée, Olivia, picked him up at the airport.

"Mother would have come with us to welcome you home, but things have been pretty crazy over the past couple weeks."

"Everyone is okay?" Daniel asked. He'd gotten close to the Winstons during his time as their bodyguard and had a lot of respect for Kate and her sons.

"If you're asking about Shelby," Olivia interjected, leaning over the back of the seat, "she's doing fine. She's fully recovered from her kidnapping ordeals and has gotten back on track with her studies. She's due to finish her coursework by the end of the semester."

Samuel grinned. "That woman is like a bulldog. When she wants something she goes after it. It's still hard to believe I'm an uncle twice over."

Daniel's brows drew together. "Twice?"

Samuel turned from the steering wheel. "You haven't heard?" He laughed. "Debra went into labor the day after you went to D.C. She had a baby boy. She and Trey named him Adair Winston. After the press conference, we're headed to the church for his christening."

"I guess I have been out of the picture. That's great news. What's the press conference about?"

"You'll see. Let Mother tell you all about it." Samuel glanced across at Daniel. "Have you thought about Mother's offer?"

Daniel had, but he hadn't made a decision. "Some."

"Well, if it helps, I was a career soldier. I was so

focused on being a soldier, I lost sight of what I was fighting for. I forgot to live my life. Being that focused is great to help keep you alive, but doesn't necessarily allow you to live. When I came back from Afghanistan, I didn't know what to do with my life." He shot a smile over his shoulder at Olivia. "I know now. You need to really think about what you want out of life. Leaving the Secret Service isn't a betrayal to your country. It's a choice to allow yourself to live life to its fullest." Samuel shrugged. "Think about it."

Daniel already had.

Samuel pulled into the parking lot of the church the Winstons attended and parked in a reserved spot. The lot was full of vehicles and news vans. Reporters gathered around the steps of the church.

"Mother decided to make her announcement here, since the christening is to take place immediately following."

Daniel climbed out of the vehicle, his arm still in a sling. He searched the crowd for one face. The face that had haunted his dreams for the past two weeks.

The double doors to the church opened and Kate Winston emerged with Patrick O'Hara at her side. She was followed by her other two sons, along with Debra and Lucy.

"Come on, the party is about to begin." Samuel held Olivia's hand and led the way through the throng.

Daniel followed, unsure of his role in this press conference as he hadn't given Kate his response yet.

"Thank you all for coming this fine day," Kate began, smiling brightly. "I have a few announcements to make, and then you all should go enjoy this incredible sunshine.

"I'd like to begin by sharing my joy at welcoming my grandson Adair Winston into the world. I, my son Trey and my personal assistant who happens to be his wife, Debra, are over the moon with the addition to our family."

Trey held the baby in his arms, smiling for the cameras as they flashed.

Kate went on. "I'd also like to announce that I have another grandchild." She paused, her eyes misting. "When I was a young woman, not even out of my teens, I gave birth to a baby girl. Carrie." Kate reached for Patrick's hand. "I was very much in love with the baby's father, but due to complications of a breech birth, I was anesthetized. When I awoke, I was told the baby had died. My father kept the entire matter from the public and I mourned my baby's death in private.

"Not until forty years later did I learn my baby girl had not died in childbirth. She'd lived and had been raised by her father and went on to have a baby girl of her own. Sadly, my daughter died in an automobile accident."

Kate blinked back tears, biting down on her lip to keep it from trembling. When she had herself together again, she continued.

"I'd like to present my first grandchild, Shelby O'Hara. A very special young woman I hope to get to know and love as much as I love her grandfather."

Kate drew Shelby forward to the sound of applause and shouted words of congratulations.

Shelby blushed and her gaze found Daniel's, her eyes widening. The corners of her lips lifted into a dazzling smile.

Daniel's heart swelled to the point he thought he

might bust the buttons off the suit jacket he wore. He couldn't wait for the press conference to be over so that he could go to Shelby and hold her in his arms.

Beaming, Kate held up a hand. "I'd also like to announce my upcoming marriage to Shelby's grandfather, my first love, Patrick O'Hara." She laughed at her sons' surprised expressions. "That was a surprise to my sons. You all are the first to know. As you can see, I won't have the time to run for any further political offices as my hands will be quite full while we plan the wedding. Thank you for coming."

Cameras flashed and news reporters spoke in front of their cameras. Eventually the crowd of media dispersed.

Trey, Samuel and Thad crowded around to hug their mother and shake Patrick's hand.

Kate laughed. "I was afraid you all would be upset to see your mother remarry."

"Are you kidding?" Trey asked. "We're happy to see you so happy and in love."

"You deserve all the happiness in the world." Sam smiled at Patrick. "Congratulations. You must be special for Mother to choose you."

"I'm feeling pretty lucky right now. I've never stopped loving her." Patrick slipped his arm around Kate and held her close.

"Since we're all making announcements," Thad started, "I have news to share." He grinned like a kid with a new toy. "Lucy and I are moving our wedding date up."

Kate's brows rose. "To when?"

"Sometime in the next eight months." Thad hugged

Lucy so tight she yelped. "Our six-year-old is going to be a big sister."

The family converged on Lucy and Thad and the congratulations began anew.

Daniel took the opportunity to sidle up to Shelby. "Hi."

She smiled shyly at him. "Hi, yourself."

"I missed you."

Tears welled in her eyes. "I missed you, too. How did things go in D.C.?"

"I was offered any position I wanted in the Secret Service."

She gulped and looked down at where he held her hand. "Congratulations. Does that mean you'll be leaving?"

"That depends."

She glanced up, her eyes narrowing. "On what?"

"On you." He pulled her into his arms. "Is there any way a society debutante like you can be interested in a banged up ex-agent like me?"

Her brow puckered. "I'm not a society debutante—" Her breath caught as if his words sank in. "Ex-agent?"

He nodded. "I handed in my resignation."

"But you love your job." Shelby gripped his hand, shaking her head. "What will you do?"

"I'm accepting another job, with Adair Enterprises," he said loud enough Kate could hear.

"Daniel!" Kate exclaimed. "That's fabulous news!"

"So what's your answer?" Daniel smiled down into Shelby's eyes. "Would you be interested in a banged-up ex-agent like me?"

"Yes! Yes, of course!" She flung her arms around his neck and hugged him tightly for a moment, but then pushed him to arm's length. "But why give up being in the Secret Service?"

He lifted her chin and brushed his lips across hers. "I'd rather be in North Carolina working for the family I hope to marry into someday. So what do you say? Wanna date me and see if we can get along enough to tie the knot?" Daniel held his breath, waiting for her response. When her eyes lit up, his heart took flight.

"You bet I do," Shelby said. "I thought you'd never ask."

Daniel kissed her, holding her close and loving every minute of it.

"Hey, if you two are finished sucking face, we have a christening to go to," Trey said, bouncing baby Adair in his arms. "Hear that, Adair? Before you know it, you'll have a dozen cousins to run around with. And if you want to be in the Secret Service, the army or even a fry cook in restaurant, I'm okay with that. You can choose whatever path your heart desires."

Kate laughed. "That's right. It's our legacy."

Shelby slipped her arm around Daniel's waist and followed her family into the church. "Our children will grow up in a family that loves them, and they'll always be encouraged to follow their hearts."

Daniel kissed the tip of her nose. "That's right. Just like us."

* * * * *

REQUEST YOUR FREE BOOKS!
2 FREE NOVELS PLUS 2 FREE GIFTS!

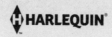

HARLEQUIN®
ROMANTIC suspense
Sparked by danger, fueled by passion

YES! Please send me 2 FREE Harlequin® Romantic Suspense novels and my 2 FREE gifts (gifts are worth about $10). After receiving them, if I don't wish to receive any more books, I can return the shipping statement marked "cancel." If I don't cancel, I will receive 4 brand-new novels every month and be billed just $4.74 per book in the U.S. or $5.24 per book in Canada. That's a savings of at least 14% off the cover price! It's quite a bargain! Shipping and handling is just 50¢ per book in the U.S. and 75¢ per book in Canada.* I understand that accepting the 2 free books and gifts places me under no obligation to buy anything. I can always return a shipment and cancel at any time. Even if I never buy another book, the two free books and gifts are mine to keep forever.

240/340 HDN F45N

Name	(PLEASE PRINT)

Address	Apt. #

City	State/Prov.	Zip/Postal Code

Signature (if under 18, a parent or guardian must sign)

Mail to the **Harlequin® Reader Service:**
IN U.S.A.: P.O. Box 1867, Buffalo, NY 14240-1867
IN CANADA: P.O. Box 609, Fort Erie, Ontario L2A 5X3

Want to try two free books from another line?
Call 1-800-873-8635 or visit www.ReaderService.com.

* Terms and prices subject to change without notice. Prices do not include applicable taxes. Sales tax applicable in N.Y. Canadian residents will be charged applicable taxes. Offer not valid in Quebec. This offer is limited to one order per household. Not valid for current subscribers to Harlequin Romantic Suspense books. All orders subject to credit approval. Credit or debit balances in a customer's account(s) may be offset by any other outstanding balance owed by or to the customer. Please allow 4 to 6 weeks for delivery. Offer available while quantities last.

Your Privacy—The Harlequin® Reader Service is committed to protecting your privacy. Our Privacy Policy is available online at www.ReaderService.com or upon request from the Harlequin Reader Service.

We make a portion of our mailing list available to reputable third parties that offer products we believe may interest you. If you prefer that we not exchange your name with third parties, or if you wish to clarify or modify your communication preferences, please visit us at www.ReaderService.com/consumerchoice or write to us at Harlequin Reader Service Preference Service, P.O. Box 9062, Buffalo, NY 14269. Include your complete name and address.

A Tibetan man and woman having a picnic meal